"Where do you [...] oud.

"You mean, w[...] ody?" Fanny corrected.

"Right there," Bob said, pointing to the blue water.

"Whoa!" Fanny shouted, and lurched back in her chair.

Ida screamed. Her necklace erupted, and white beads scattered and bounced across the table. Grady dropped his beer. The bottle fell with a thump, and sprayed a white geyser over my feet. A thin man in faded purple swim trunks, and probably not much taller than five-six, was staring at us through pale, unseeing eyes. His arms were extended out to the sides of his bloated, floating body, and his hair was feathered away from his head in soft gray fur.

"Otis Culpepper?" I asked.

"It *was*," Fanny said.

★

Previously published Worldwide Mystery title by
T. DAWN RICHARD

DEATH FOR DESSERT

digging

❧ *up* ❧

OTIS

T. Dawn Richard

WORLDWIDE.

TORONTO • NEW YORK • LONDON
AMSTERDAM • PARIS • SYDNEY • HAMBURG
STOCKHOLM • ATHENS • TOKYO • MILAN
MADRID • WARSAW • BUDAPEST • AUCKLAND

This book is dedicated to my father,
Dr. Mannon L. Wallace—a man of
incredible strength and character.
I love you, Dad.

DIGGING UP OTIS

A Worldwide Mystery/August 2007

First published by Martin Brown Publishers, LLC.

ISBN-13: 978-0-373-26610-4
ISBN-10:   0-373-26610-3

Acknowledgments

Thanks to the North Folk Oklahoma Writers, my critique group while I lived for two years in Altus: Your encouragement saw me through many rewrites. To Doris Jouett, a vibrant, beautiful woman who delighted in showcasing my books in her store, and to her husband, Donald, who kept me from falling asleep at my computer with his double-shot espresso drinks.

To my husband, Glenn, and my four children—Calin, Summer, Genny and Jesse—you're my reason for living. To Jennifer Hisel and Anita Romero, two of the best friends a gal could have—thanks for laughing with me. To Martha Jarred, the owner of the most awesome little bookstore in Haskell, Texas, I wish I could visit every day. And to my agents, editors and friends, Robert Brown and Sharene Martin, I owe a debt of gratitude, because you loved May Bell from the start.

And finally, to all the air force wives I've grown close to over the years. Your service to our country is often unsung. You are my heroes.

ONE

I SHOULD HAVE KNOWN I could never go back to a normal life after the first murder, not to my previous life of late morning naps, subdued quilting bees and ladies' teas. Staring death in the face will make you different. It did me. But don't misunderstand, it wasn't my own death I peered into on that dreadful day a year ago; it was the lifeless face of old Mrs. Berkowitz, her vacant milky blue eyes staring into mine after I tumbled over her tiny rigid feet and landed on top of her cooling corpse. Now *that* had redirected the course of my life. And maybe I'd been hasty keeping her body hidden from authorities for three days back then—didn't even report what I'd found. Thought me and my friends at the senior center might just be able to solve her murder.

And we did.

It's not that we didn't trust the local police department with the case at the time. It was simply a pragmatic decision to go it on our own. Ninety-year-old women turning up dead in a retirement home didn't often generate a lot of excitement for law enforcement. They'd just as soon write it off as a natural passing, but we knew better. It was anything but normal.

In retrospect, maybe I should have made that 9-1-1 call earlier, washed my hands of the whole affair. But then I would never have discovered my hidden talents.

My name is May Bell List. My knees are starting to groan like rusty hinges in the morning, I can't find my purse, and I'm a detective.

TWO

I SUPPOSE I SHOULD have believed Ted when he told me it wasn't such a good idea to take Trixie into the shower with me. But I'd seen a flea, she needed scrubbing, and besides, what did he know about cats anyway? And, I must add, although he is a doctor treating all manners of female problems, what did he *really* know about women? He might be the brainy one, but I'm aces in the domestic department. I'd show him.

It all started so well. Trixie was curled in a fluffy ball on top of my bedspread, my toes were curled inside fluffy pink slippers, and I'd already had two cups of coffee—you know, the best part of wakin' up. But mornings never truly get moving until after the shower.

And there she was, my little darling. So precious, with wet nose and yawning mouth, and the most adoring yellow eyes one could ever imagine gazing into mine. I scooped her up. I cuddled her securely under my sagging chin, dropped my robe to the bathroom floor, and stepped into the shower. I put the setting on pulse massage, and let 'er rip.

Oh my Lord.

Trixie wailed like I was dismembering her limb by limb. Certain my neighbors would be alarmed at the commotion, I slapped my hand down on Trixie's screaming mouth, whereupon she punctured the fleshy part of my palm with her needle-like teeth. I joined her in a full-throated soprano chorus, the likes you probably haven't heard since watching *The Texas Chainsaw Massacre*.

It was a reflex, I swear, an uncontrollable reaction that caused me to hurl the furry beast hard against the glass wall of the shower stall. It sounded pretty bad, but I didn't have time to regret the fling because, immediately afterwards, Trixie was up and doing frantic laps around the inside of the shower stall, getting higher and higher on the wall with every turn around my dimpled thighs.

The shower door flew open. Ted to the rescue.

Trixie clawed her way up my hams, used my belly rolls as a ladder, and scraped her way to my head. That was when I finally got a good hold of her. Ted and I juggled her back and forth a good five passes before the wet ball of fur shot over my husband's shoulder and disappeared.

Stupid cat. She'll pay for that later.

"Wipe that grin off your face," I said.

"Hey, why don't you wait a second and I'll throw in the hair dryer? Looks like you could use something to perk up your day." Ted snickered. "On second thought," he said, looking back over his shoulder, "why don't you just hop in the tub? I'll see if I can find our toaster, and then we'll play catch. Now where did I put that extension cord?"

Ted wandered off whistling *Surrey With a Fringe on Top,* while I assessed my war wounds. It was hard to tell where the claw marks began and the varicose veins intersected. Who said life begins at fifty? If that were true and my addition was right, then I was just sixteen, tight and lithe, with a drawer full of colorful bras. I grabbed a towel and encased my pendulums. Not by a long shot, babe. Not even close.

"Okay, the cat thing was a bad idea," I said as I walked into the bedroom swaddled in my king-sized towel. Ted was sitting on the edge of the bed pushing his feet into a pair of large black boots. Probably getting ready to sweep the walk before the neighbors stirred. His hair was full of dust bunnies, which meant he'd rescued Trixie from under the bed or armoire. She was on the window seat licking her chest, pretending to ignore me, but I knew she was planning a sneak attack for later in the day.

Before Ted could give me the "I told you so" look, the phone rang. Startled, I lost my grip on the towel, and it slipped to the floor. And there I stood in all my glory.

Ted took this as an invitation and lifted his eyebrows.

"I'm free," he said, kicking his boots into the air. I ducked in time to miss one as it sailed past my ear.

The phone rang a second time.

"Not now," I said, irritated and self-conscious. Not because of the exposure, but because I'd lost the antiseptic ointment and had resorted to covering my scrapes and scratches with Ted's jock itch cream. I was a human graffiti wall of white grease paint from sternum to saddlebags.

The phone rang a third time. "Can you get that please?" I nodded toward the phone and attempted a delicate squat for my towel. My knees cracked like twin gunshots.

Ted looked rejected. I felt kind of bad about that, but if I could swallow my pride, he could darn well show a little self-control.

"Um hm, uh huh, ummm, uh huh," Ted talked into the phone. Probably an emergency mole removal.

"Is it the hospital?" I whispered loudly.

"Um hmmm. I see." Dr. Ted nodded at the phone. Must be serious.

"It's for you," Ted said, and handed me the phone.

"Me?" I said, the towel sliding as I clamped down hard with my armpits. "Who is it?"

"Don't know. She didn't say."

"What *did* she say?" I gave up the fight and released the towel. It took most of the cream with it anyway, so I looked better. Trixie squinted her cat eyes at me from the window seat, no doubt appraising her handiwork, planning her next strike. *So much flesh, so little time.*

"I just heard a lot of wheezing," Ted answered.

I took the phone. "Maybe it's one of your patients, Ted, maybe someone's in distress!"

"Not unless she's leaking air from a very unusual place," Ted said. He grabbed his boots and left, singing, "Borrrrn freeeee."

I cringed and quickly dismissed the implication. I would need to get used to Ted's new practice. Being a G.P. was good;

specializing in gynecology was better—at least on the paycheck. Maybe this year he would finally retire. I could only hope.

"Hello?"

Wheeze. Wheeze.

"If this is one of those obscene phone calls, I want you to know I have caller I.D." I caught my reflection in the dresser mirror. I looked really forceful. "And I know how to use it." I wagged my head. Really powerful.

"Oh, May! Oh, May!"

I thought the wheezing sounded familiar. The voice was unmistakable.

"Ida?"

"Oh, May! You've *got* to come back. There's been another murder!" The wheezing was getting louder, gaining strength. I imagined bronchi popping all over the place.

"Ida, are you alone?" I looked in the mirror and put my free hand on my hip.

"No, no, I don't think so," Ida said. *Wheeze, wheeze.*

I turned sideways and sucked in. Nothing happened.

"Is Grady there?" I leaned in toward the mirror and bared my teeth. Still pretty good. I rubbed over them with a finger.

"Yes. He's here," Ida said. She was revving up for a full blow, and if she didn't get it together soon she'd be planting *her* teeth into the nearest piece of furniture. Since Ida was one of my only friends who still had her own pearly whites, I was concerned.

"Ida, go bag yourself and give the phone to Grady."

I heard rustling.

"May, Fanny here."

"Fanny? What's going on? Where's Grady?"

"Oh, he's back in the kitchen lookin' for the paper bags," Fanny said. "Maybe he should put a plastic one over Ida's head. That'd stop the wheezing," Fanny chuckled wickedly.

"Fanny!" I admonished. "What's Ida saying about another murder?"

"I told her not to call you, but does she listen to me? Nooooooo. Let's call May, get her on a plane, get her down here, she says."

I faced the mirror, put the phone between my cheek and shoulder and pressed my palms together. I pulsed. Should have elicited a little reaction from the pectorals. Nothing.

"Fanny, what happened?" I urged.

"Okay. Here's what's going down." Fanny was all business. "One of our own's gone missing. The senior center is a hot-bed of evidence, but the coppers don't want to take the case. Say it's an old man's right to travel."

It sounded like Fanny was cupping her hand around the receiver. I imagined her tiny wrinkled body crouched low as she ran through the details. Her white hair would be askew on her little round head, probably still sporting a pink cushy curler wrapped up at the base of her scalp.

"But you don't think he took a trip to Vegas." I was getting into it. I balled my hands into fists and raised my arms in a flex. There. A tiny movement in the biceps. Then they relaxed and dropped down into pooches of skin under my arms. Darn.

"And we don't think he just disappeared," Fanny said. "We think he was murdered!" She sounded excited about all of this, and I was catching the buzz in a hurry.

Another mystery. Another murder. How utterly alluring.

"What makes you think that?" I took the phone in my hand again and swiveled around while keeping an eye on the mirror. I pinched my buns together. No tone there. So much for the butt-buster. That was a waste of money.

"I'd better not say any more until I get a secure line," Fanny said in a rush. "Over and out. Roger, Wilco."

The phone went dead.

"Who was that?" Ted ambled into the bedroom again. He had a piece of celery coated in peanut butter sticking out of the side of his mouth.

"Ted, for breakfast?" I rummaged through my dresser for some underwear.

"I just wanted a bite, but now it's stuck. See?" Ted opened his mouth wide. The celery stalk remained attached to his upper molars.

"Oh, for Pete's sake." I yanked the celery from his mouth. Ted's head rocked back.

"Thanks," he said.

The celery went into the trash. "That was Ida, and Fanny, and Grady. But I didn't talk to Grady, he was bagging his wife."

Ted's eyebrows went up again.

I cut his smile off at the pass. "They said there's been another murder at the senior center, and I think they want me to come down there to help solve it. Isn't that incredible?" I slid a toe through one panty leg hole.

"What about Bob? Is he still hanging around with your friends?"

"I don't think he was there." I stuck my other foot through the second panty hole.

"And they all want you to come back to California to help." Ted watched me shimmy into my panties.

"Yup, what do you think?" I snapped the elastic waistband in place and smiled without giving him a chance to answer. I really didn't want to hear his list of reasons why I shouldn't go back to California.

"Would you look at this, Ted?" I pulled at the saggy cotton hanging in a fold around my abdomen. "I think I've lost a few pounds." I felt an uncomfortable creeping from the back, though, and plucked.

"Still, these things never do cover very well in the back." I tugged but couldn't get the cloth to stretch far enough.

"For what it's worth, May, I don't think you should go nosing around at any more dead bodies. That's my department. That's why I'm heavily insured. And…" Ted poked my tummy. "I think you should check the tag in your panties."

Ted left me. Soon he was braying in the shower, and I was rotating my underwear.

THREE

OF COURSE, I ignored my husband's opinion. *Another murder.* In my thoughts it came out in a low, slow whisper. The gang was calling me back.

"So, who's dead?" Ted walked through a wall of steam into the bedroom. He tossed his soggy towel on the bed.

"Do you mind?" I quickly grabbed up the towel before it soaked through to the mattress.

"No, not at all. You do what you gotta do." Ted found the dresser mirror and admired himself as he rapidly twisted left and right. There was a sound like babies clapping coming from below his waist. Ted grinned like a fool. "I still got it, Maybe Baby."

I rolled my eyes. "Put some clothes on."

"Not before my stretches." Ted laced his fingers and raised his arms overhead. Then he bent down over his long legs and groaned. When he came up for air his face was crimson. I had to admit, he did look good. No extra pounds or excessive wrinkles on this guy. He was blessed with a lean, tall frame and a metabolism that challenged any man half his age. Even his hair had refused to take the high road. It was still thick, graying only slightly at the temples.

"I don't know who's dead. Fanny didn't say." I tossed the towel into the laundry bin. "In fact, this guy—whoever he is—disappeared, but the gang's sure he's been murdered. That's all I know."

Ted put his hands on his hips and stretched forward, then back. I moved past him and stood in front of my open closet. Would it be the red sweat suit today or the gray? Decisions, decisions. Out of the corner of my eye I could see Trixie slinking along, spying on me. Ted was saying something like, "Woo, woo!"

He continued his inspection in the mirror.

"You really don't think I should go down there?" I asked, pretending like I didn't care one way or the other. Definitely the gray sweats.

"You aren't just a little curious?" Ted stroked the hairs on his chest. "I know you're dying to see what they've done with the Berkowitz proceeds."

"Not so loud, Ted. Trixie will hear. I think she's got it in for me. I wouldn't be surprised if she had a surveillance wire under all that fur."

"Served the old lady right you kept some of that money," Ted said. He took my hairbrush off of the dresser and ran it through the hair under his arms. "She was stealing from everyone."

"True, true. And we did give everyone their money back after Mrs. Berkowitz was murdered, didn't we? At least, to the ones we could track down." I looked at Ted for reassurance, while thinking it was high time I bought a new hairbrush.

"You did the honorable thing. Like I said. It was only right the gang put the leftovers to good use."

Leftovers. Ted made it sound like we'd come away with a spare meatloaf or something, instead of the millions we'd shoved into our own benevolent fund for wayward seniors.

"Yeah. And all that community service nearly got us killed. No, when you're right, you're right. I'll call Ida and tell her they're just going to have to solve this little mystery without me." Not a hint of interest. Nope. After all, I had a Saturday night Bunko game to consider.

"So are you going to fly down, or take the Camaro again?" Ted plucked some strays from the brush.

I smiled broadly. "Oh, I knew you'd understand. I'm dying of boredom here, Ted. I'll only be gone a few days. A week tops." I felt giddy. Back with the old gang. So delicious. I was struck with a thought. "Hey, Ted. Why don't you come with me? It would be nice for you to get to know my friends better, and you could take a little vacation while we sort through the evidence."

"Evidence. Now there's a word for you." Ted left the brush on the dresser and examined a pair of silk, paisley boxers. I tossed my gray sweats onto the bed and batted my eyelashes. Usually I was loath to stand naked in the light of day, but Ted would need some persuading. So I gathered all the feminine charm I could muster, pushed my panties down around my ankles and sidled slowly toward him.

"Come on, Ted, go with me. Pleeeeease." I pouted my lips and moved closer. I swung my voluminous hips in exaggerated arcs. "It would be fuuuun." I edged closer, baby steps now because the panties clung like leg-irons.

I shamelessly drew on my womanly powers of persuasion. It would be impossible for him to resist. *Work it, May, work it.* I put my hands against my ribs and thrust my chest out. Then I bent slightly and wiggled my shoulders. I gyrated. Ted's eyes began to glaze over and his lower jaw drooped slightly.

It was happening.

I was provocative.

A siren.

It was then I noticed our bedroom curtains were open. Mr. Fitz, our neighbor across the street, was staring at our window, his hands around a garden hose. The water was pouring out into the street, and he was smiling.

I squatted low and fast to get below the window ledge and out of sight.

Ted apparently thought I'd learned a new maneuver. I think he liked it.

I was clear of prying eyes. And I was stuck.

"Uh, Ted, I think I threw my back out." Oh darn. I watched Ted's excitement wither and along with it, any hope I had of convincing him to go with me to California.

"No problem," Ted said. He blinked. Back to reality. He raced around behind me, grabbed my shoulders and thrust a knee into my lower back.

"There!" he said, pushing and pulling at the same time. "All better?"

"All better."

I felt a slight tingle in my lower extremities. Either he'd put me back together, or he'd pinched off my spinal cord. I wiggled my toes. "Good as new." I duck-walked over to the window and dropped the blinds.

"Great. Now you'd better check the flight schedules if you're going to get out of here today."

"Today?" I crawled up onto the bed and sat gingerly on the edge while I hauled up my drawers. Then I felt around for my sweats. Somehow I'd have to face Mr. Fitz in the future.

Darn Ted.

"Yeah, you're right. Probably won't get anything before tomorrow. Is that soon enough?"

"I can't believe you're taking this so well. It almost sounds like you're trying to get rid of me." I laughed, but I was worried. Was there a new nurse working in his clinic?

You just go, May. There's plenty here to keep me busy. I'll just be going over my briefs with Jodi. What? Didn't I tell you I just hired a new temp? I've heard she takes great shorthand. Of course, in my case, I prefer long hand. Ho ho!

I shook my head. Knock it off, May.

"I know you miss your friends," Ted was saying, "and I think you're right. I could use a little time off. It will take me a day to finish up with Mrs. Higgenbotham, and then I'll catch a flight out on Sunday. How's that?"

"Oh, Ted," I squealed. "That's perfect. I'll start packing."

AFTER MAKING RESERVATIONS for the following morning, I called Grady with the news. Ida banged pots and pans in the background while I recited my flight schedule. When I left them a year ago, Ida was shrugging off Grady's advances. Now they were married. Grady was never the sort to give up easily.

"All right, May Bell!" Grady hooted into the phone. "Can't wait to see you. I'll tell the others, and we'll meet you at the airport."

I heard what sounded like a refrigerator door opening and slamming, then opening and slamming again. Grady must have covered the phone, because his muffled voice said, "Yes, Sweetheart, the light goes off every time." Then he was back on the line.

"There's a little waiting area right outside security. We'll be there."

"Grady, that's not necessary. I can take a taxi."

"Nothing doing, little lady, nothing doing. Wouldn't want to leave you standing unguarded while some young buck puts the moves on ya, right?"

I imagined Grady drawing down the corner of his mouth while winking at the phone. I knew it was useless to argue.

"I hope you don't mind, but I invited Ted. He has some work to do at the hospital, and then he'll fly down on Sunday."

"Great! The more the merrier!"

I heard the sound of a kitchen oven timer buzzing on Grady's end. Then Ida's voice sang out, "I'll get it."

"No, Honey, not the door. Not the door! Oh, never mind." Grady lowered his voice. "I'll give you all the details when you get here. All I can tell you is that a guy named Otis Culpepper has gone missing, and we suspect foul play in the worst sense, if you get my drift. Best not to go into it all now—too risky."

"Okay, Grady." I smiled. Ida's voice was closer to the phone now.

"It was a hit and run," she told Grady. The timer continued to buzz.

PACKING WAS A BREEZE. Ted went to the hospital to tie up loose ends. I jammed shorts, skirts, hose and shirts into a duffel bag, and ran a load of laundry for Ted.

And then there was Trixie. She would have to be crated, then hauled over to the Poochie Hooch, a no-star grooming and boarding facility I'd found in the yellow pages, and one I'd never have considered if this weren't an emergency. I showed Trixie the ad that said, "Yes! We do cats, too!" But that did little to allay her belief that I was really out to knock her off. The shower thing hadn't helped.

Demon cat.

I stood in the kitchen and quietly dialed the number for the Hooch. Trixie was sunning herself on the back of the living room couch. I watched her nervously through the portico.

"Is this the Poochie Hooch?"

Trixie raised her head and slowly turned to look at me.

"I'd like to make a reservation."

Cat eyes narrowed to mere slits.

"Yes. I can bring her in right away."

"Name of pet?" Trixie curled her upper lip. One fang hung out. I cupped a hand around my mouth. "Trixie," I whispered.

I SHOULD HAVE KNOWN Trixie wouldn't go in her crate without a good fight. Still, it shouldn't have taken me an hour to get my hands on her, and, for as much as we paid for our furniture, it shouldn't have disintegrated like it did. Granted, the ottoman wasn't built to withstand a flying frontal dive by a full-figured woman, and it wasn't very smart for me to hip-slide across the dining room table, but certainly the toilet lid shouldn't have ripped off in my hands just because I was trying to grab some leverage.

With a lot of screaming, cursing and tussling, I eventually tackled Trixie after she slid down the laundry chute. I saw that one coming. I wrestled Trixie into her crate and carried her up the stairs from the basement.

The front doorbell rang.

Breathlessly, I answered the door. "Yes?"

Two uniformed police officers stood on my porch, shiny badges and all. One of the city's finest was short and stocky, and busily curled his nightstick while studying my face. His partner was tall with one eye slightly lower than the other. A considerably off-center bulbous nose stuck out of his face. He'd drawn his gun and held it by his bony hip. A patrol car was parked cockeyed in front of our house with its bubble lights twirling.

"Everything okay, ma'am?" Shorty asked. "The neighbors called 9-1-1. Said they heard screaming."

"I'm so sorry." I pushed the hair out of my face. "Everything is fine." I glared across the street at Mr. Fitz. Busybody.

The tall officer looked around me and into the house, then glanced at his partner. "Maybe we'd just better take a look."

The first officer brushed past me and walked into my living room. "Holy moley," he said, and whistled long and low through his teeth. "What happened here?" He fingered my shredded drapes.

"Looks like a domestic." The taller one nodded knowingly, corners of his mouth pulled down into a look of seriousness. He raised his revolver and cupped his free hand under his gun fist. He tilted his head to the side, closed one eye and looked as if he were taking a bead. On what, I had no idea. Shorty pulled his gun and went down on one knee, waving his weapon left and right.

"Cat," I said, embarrassed.

"Oh. Well, that explains it," Shorty said, getting to his feet. The officers relaxed and holstered their guns. "We get at least three of these a month. My advice? Get something you can manage a little better. Like a pit bull or a Doberman." The policemen left, laughing hysterically.

"That does it, Trixie. I gave you away once, and I can do it again."

FOUR

THE NEXT MORNING I stood in line at the airport luggage check and kissed Ted good-bye. Although my lips made the expected smacking noises, my mind wasn't in the gesture. Was it possible? Another murder? Maybe my friends were jumping to conclusions.

At the security X-ray machine I dutifully handed over my shoes, my tweezers, my fingernail file, my bobby pins, and my itty-bitty book light. Couldn't imagine why that would be a threat. On my way to retrieve my shoes, I saw one of the guards drop my light into his pocket.

"Happy birthday," I said curtly as I brushed past him in my stocking feet. Oh my, now where did that come from? I was usually so polite. Something just came over me when I was on a case. I became daring and fearless. I laughed in the face of danger.

"Oh, pardon me!" I said, noticing I'd grabbed the sensible shoes of an angry nun. I blushed purple. Maybe not so daring and fearless. The feelings come and go.

I boarded the plane and did a difficult aerobic grapevine maneuver down the aisle until I found my seat number. Keeping my eye on the little letters overhead, I scooted in.

"Excuse me, ma'am, I think you've made a mistake." An executive-type held up his ticket. "This is my seat."

"No, I think it's you who's made the mistake. I would advise you to check again." I looked over toward the window. Fearless. I didn't travel alone very much and tried to disguise my trepidation, being wise to the ways of trickery. I waited for the man to move on, but he just stood there. I twisted around and gave him the once-over.

The man looked perplexed, then doubtful. He looked at his ticket. "No, I'm sure this is my seat." He glanced around uncomfortably. I could almost hear his thoughts. It wasn't going to be pretty, this guy wrestling an elderly woman for a measly plane seat.

I suspected he might be right, but I wasn't about to be intimidated. A flush worked its way up my neck. *Be strong, May Bell.*

"Okay, ma'am, we'll just trade. No problem."

"No, I'll be happy to move," I said, standing abruptly, thumping my head on the overhead compartment. I blinked back tears of pain. "There was probably a mix-up at the counter."

The man danced around me and took his seat. I was once again in the aisle. A flight attendant smiled like she was doing a toothpaste commercial and gently guided me to the appropriate cushion. My tough demeanor was quickly falling away. How in the heck was I going to be a good detective if I couldn't be authoritative?

I distracted myself by running through my airline checklist. Pillow? Check. Vomit bag? Check. Magazines? Emergency Exits? Oxygen masks? Check. Everything seemed to be in order. I folded my hands over the canvas travel bag in my lap. While I watched the other passengers settle in, I did some thinking.

The gang was sure there had been a murder, but, without a corpse, how could they be so sure? I was hungry for more information, but neither Fanny nor Grady were giving it up. "Too risky," Grady had said, so I just had to go on faith. It was all so exciting!

Once we were airborne, I pulled out my cross-stitch and started poking. I was amazed I'd gotten my sewing stuff through security, but I suppose the guy at the machine wasn't in the market for a tea towel. I admired The Last Supper scene beautifully stitched on white cloth. It was difficult for me to keep my mind on task with the news of another murder and all, and, after stabbing my finger three times, I finally gave up, got my notebook and pen, and wrote:

DATA
1) Dead man's name: Otis Culpepper
2) Cause of death: Unknown
3) Body: Not found
4) Reason to believe he's been murdered: Unknown

I looked over my list. Sheesh. Not much to go on here, maybe I should have stuck with my cross-stitch. A young woman in the seat next to mine sneak-eyed my list while pretending to read her paperback.

"I'm a writer," I said, feeling the need to explain. I always feel the need to explain things when I should have just given her a cold glare and reminded her to mind her own gosh darn business. Being a writer wasn't much of a lie; there were notebooks filled with plots, outlines and character sketches piled high in my den.

"How exciting," she brightened, not even apologizing for spying. "Writing a mystery?"

"Exactly. A story about an elderly woman who kills off pretty young career women with her needlepoint accessories." Let her squirm.

The sweet face paled. Serves her right, Miss Nosey. Of course, then I felt bad. I saw my church choir clucking their tongues and wagging their fingers, so I bought the woman a drink. By the time we landed, we were chatting away about nonsense. She was an intelligent, patient woman, and when I flipped through the wallet pictures of my daughter and son-in-law, she knew better than to ask the, "When is she going to make you a grandma?" question. Immunization work in Belize was hard enough without that added pressure. I could wait. Besides, I was pretty sure missionaries weren't even allowed to have sex while on the job. It's what I told my daughter anyway.

After we landed, the nice girl even gave me her card before unbuckling. *Janet Scott, Attorney at Law.* I stuck it in my purse. Never know when you're gonna need a good lawyer.

Or where you'll find one.

EVERYONE ON THE PLANE struggled with the overhead baggage. It was like some sort of signal for me to start getting all dewy and excited about seeing my old friends again. It felt like there were little tadpoles flipping around in my stomach. Maybe it was the tuna fish I'd had for lunch. Whatever it was, it felt pretty good.

Security wouldn't allow anyone to meet me after I got off the plane, which was just as well. I always did hate that craning, searching, lost-look embarrassment after deboarding, so I followed the masses down to baggage claim, with my chin up, striding with confidence. I couldn't wait to see my friends, but by the time I got down to that little spinny luggage wheel thingy, I was a quivering mass of nervous anticipation.

"May Bell!" A scream went up, loud enough to startle a skycap and upset his overloaded dolly. Hope there wasn't anything breakable in those bags.

Here they came. Grady, Ida, Fanny and Bob, a confusion of gray heads, liver spots and crepe-skinned grappling arms. The gang shoved through the crowd, tripping over one another to get in their hugs. Bob, best described as a meaty guy, swept me up in a full-bellied squeeze and my lungs nearly collapsed. He hadn't lost a pound since I'd last seen him, or an ounce of strength, even though he was nearing his seventy-fifth birthday. Fanny, a withered little wisp of a gal pushing eighty-plus if I had to guess, and the oldest of the group, had new teeth; she was proudly showing them off, turning this way and that with a smile so wide I noticed the thin line of demarcation at the top of her gums. She was gripping her aluminum walker, and when Grady cut her off to give me a kiss on the cheek, she rammed it into his calves.

"Darn it, Fanny, why did you bring that thing anyway? You know it's just a prop." Grady's hair was still thick and white; his eyebrows were dark caterpillars over twinkling eyes.

"Who made you king?" Fanny shoved. "Move out so I can get in there."

"Fanny! It's so good to see you." As I started to lean over her walker, she threw it aside. It clattered and skidded over the slick floor. Then she grabbed the sides of my face with her little knobby fingers. She pulled me down close enough to smell her denture cleaner. Her glasses had grown another half inch in thickness since I'd last seen her, and her eyes were gigantic behind the magnifying lenses.

"It's happened again," she said. Her lips barely moved.

I felt the need to glance around for hidden cameras.

"Keep your eyes on me," she said, gripping my cheeks tightly. "Keep smiling, May, you never know who's watching. And whatever you do, don't say B-O-M-B. They'll give you some of them steel bracelets to wear on your way to the pokey." Fanny released me and slapped her skinny wrists for effect.

"Why would I say that, Fanny?" I laughed.

Fanny snorted. "Just don't say it."

Ida, her plump cheeks blazing with glee, was nearby, bouncing and clapping her hands in front of her bodice. "It's so very good to see you again, May. We've missed you so much!"

"That's not all she's missing," Fanny said under her breath. She stepped aside, scooped up her walker and moved toward the luggage carousel.

Ida was beaming. "Oh, I get confused now and then," she said, and then she frowned deeply. "Did I already say that?"

AFTER WE COVERED all the pleasantries, Bob hefted my overnight bag and canvas tote and led the procession toward the parking lot. I offered to help with the luggage, but he shook his head.

"Best shape of my life," he said. "We've got twenty-five now in tap and just under that in ballet and jazz."

"You're still teaching then," I said. "I wasn't really expecting that, I suppose."

"I can still play the lunatic when it serves me," Bob said, as he turned to a family of three, dropped my bags and yelled, "What? What?" The father hustled his young daughter and wife toward the safety of their car.

"I see," I said.

"Things have changed a lot since you lived here," Grady said, walking along the parking lot with his arm around Ida. "Don't you think my new bride is the sexiest filly you've ever seen?" He gave Ida a peck on the cheek, and she blushed happily.

"Ugh," Fanny said.

WE LEFT THE airport grounds and rolled along a familiar high-way toward the small town where I'd lived briefly the year before. We rode comfortably in Grady's Suburban, a newer model, steel gray with all the amenities. While Grady proudly ran through its specs, I felt excited energy tickling my stomach again—mostly because I was in the company of my best friends in the world, but also because I was going back to a place where my life had changed forever. I was still curious about why they had summoned me, but no one was talking yet. Fanny had a pair of binoculars in her hands, scanning the horizon from her window as her sparse white hair whipped around her head like a cyclone.

After about thirty minutes, at the request of hungry Bob, Grady pulled into Denny's, and we piled out of the car for a cool glass of tea. Summer was officially over, but no one had bothered to mention this to the weatherman.

"We've got a conundrum," Bob said after we settled into a booth.

"It's a little snare," Fanny said while putting on lipstick. The mirror in her hand tilted this way and that. She was checking out the periphery.

Ida perked up. "I had a snare drum once, tried to play it for my high school band. Awful thing," she said. Bless her heart.

"You said there'd been another murder." I wrapped my hands around the sweating glass of tea and leaned my elbows on the table. That little excited feeling in my stomach was buzzing.

"Who's this Otis guy?" The name wasn't familiar. I had a little notebook in my purse, and I was aching to lick the tip of a pencil and start collecting data. But I knew that would upset Fanny, so I'd just have to wait and pay attention.

"Whoa Nellie, we'll get to that," Bob said. He'd ordered fries, baptized them in catsup and slurped them up in twos. It was hard to tell where the fries ended and his fingers began. The mound was going down fast.

"I see you've updated your wardrobe," I said. I'd seen Bob in many things, but the white shorts and plaid shirt were a first.

"Oh, not really. He's still got his tutus. I made him a whole new set of leotards, all colors, different fabrics, they're lovely." Ida looked proud.

"We've all made a few adjustments," Grady said. He ran his hands through his white hair. It was a bit thicker than I remembered. Transplants? I didn't think so, but looking around the table the crew was holding up amazingly well for a group in their declining years. Grady's black eyebrows seemed thinner. Bushy still, but more streamlined. Was he plucking? Or maybe electrolysis? Probably waxing.

I returned to the subject at hand. "Can you at least give me a hint about Otis?" I spoke quietly, remembering Grady's cautionary statement about the risk involved in our covert investigation. I really wanted a clue. Despite the fact that I had been on an airplane most of the day, I wasn't in the least bit tired. I'd passed over into that buzzing, disconnected feeling one gets after navigating two state lines. Besides, coffee in coach is free. I'd made good use of that little button over my head.

Grady placed his hand flat on top of a napkin and slid it over to me. Had I dribbled? Instinctively I brushed my chin for droplets.

"Take the napkin," Ida whispered.

"I think I'm okay," I said, "I have one here in my lap."

"Just take the napkin," Bob mumbled around a mouth full of fries.

Just because I was ten years younger than most of them didn't mean they had to treat me like such a baby. I mean really, I can wipe my own chin. I grabbed a corner of the napkin to keep the peace just the same and a newspaper clipping slid out from under it and went airborne. There was a commotion as eight hands clawed for the paper.

"Oh, for heaven's sake," Fanny said. The clipping had escaped over the edge of the table. She ducked down by our shoes and came up triumphantly.

"Be a little more careful, Butterfingers."

I started to apologize, but didn't. After all, there had been no warning. It had been a long time since I'd had to think covertly. This would take a little getting used to.

Fanny was agitated now and had her makeup mirror pointing this way and that.

I smoothed the clipping out on my lap but could barely make out the headline in the shadows. Then as the type came into focus, I frowned.

"It says that Mrs. Culpepper reported her husband missing Friday morning. Says he didn't come to bed after playing pool at the Sunken Balls pool parlor the night before. Witnesses reported seeing him leave the Sunken Balls around midnight. The police found his Hyundai in the carport, no sign of foul play, but neighbors say they heard what sounded like a heated argument between a man and woman outside of Culpepper's apartment shortly after midnight. Police are investigating."

Fanny scoffed. "Investigating, my asteroid. If wandering around asking a few questions is called an investigation, then I'm the next contestant on *The Price is Right!*"

"Come on down!" Ida squealed.

I looked around at the faces. They were in deep concentration, all except for Ida's, which was lit up like a Chinese lantern. "So, he did come home, right?" I asked. "His car was in the carport. So what happened after that? And why did his wife wait until the next morning to get concerned?"

"Thing is," Bob said, "the cops think this will clear up in a few days. Marital spat, the guy gets ticked off and takes a cab to the airport. Hops a flight for Tahiti just to make the wife suffer." Bob sucked on his front teeth. "Probably took his girlfriend just to make things interesting."

"He had a girlfriend?" I was shocked. I heard Ted's voice pass through my mind.

Come on, May, you can't expect a man with a healthy appetite to be satisfied dining at the same restaurant every day can you? A man needs diversity! A man needs variety! There's a whole menu out there, and I want to try every dish!

"What is it, May?" Ida said. "Are you thinking about the Sunken Balls?"

"In a way," I grumbled, as I struggled my mind back on track. "So the police are thinking Otis just skipped town."

"Ah, yes. The article says he's disappeared, but we know better," Bob said. "He was murdered, sure as I sit here." Bob jabbed the table with a meaty forefinger. "We've just got to convince the police."

Two young women at the breakfast bar turned to stare at us then hunkered down giggling over their muffins.

Immediately I felt darned self-conscious and wanted to leave. We were getting a bit too rowdy, which could have led to some loud loose lips in our otherwise cautious discussion. Fanny must have thought so, too. The compact in her hand snapped shut. She raised her arm into the air and waved wildly for the check.

It was time to go.

FANNY WAS OUT the door ahead of us, her walker going *ka-chunk, kachunk, kachunk,* followed by her tiny feet all-ascuffle moving in a blur over the sidewalk. She reached the Suburban and was giving it a sweep when we got there. "She's free of bugs," she said, emerging red-faced. "Get in and we'll talk."

Back on the highway, the conversation grew animated. Everyone chattered at once, and my neck was aching, trying to keep track. One lesson I'd learned well in the thirty-six years as a doctor's wife was how to be a good listener, so I pasted on my "I'm interested" face and gave eye contact where warranted.

Then I came to my senses. I wasn't the same old May Bell. She had gone the way of my sculptured nails and pretentious catered dinners.

"Hold it!" I voiced from the diaphragm. "Everyone, quiet!"

I'd never seen so many pinched faces since the prune juice tasting jamboree at the Grange, not to mention the residual puckering going on for days after.

"I'm really sorry I had to do that, but I can't understand anything you're saying. And besides, we're here."

"Why yes, I suppose we are!" Ida brightened. She sat up tall and kept checking my reaction out of the sides of her eyes.

"Wow!" It was all I could say. After all, the Active Senior Living Complex I had left was no more.

Grady maneuvered the burly Suburban through the stone gate entrance. On the white rocks was a handsome brass plaque. It read *Waning Years Estates*.

"Nice," I said.

"My idea," Ida beamed.

"Just look at this place!" I cried. We had just entered something that resembled a little slice of Heaven. We were on a nicely paved road, slender and elegant curving along, accented by shade trees and flowering bushes. I could smell the blooming lavender.

"What happened to my complex?" In place of the line of four-apartment jobbies where I had lived was an expansive grassy field. In the middle of the field was a massive white gazebo. In the gazebo, sitting on a wooden bench swing, were a pair of grandmotherly types. They watched as we drove past and waved energetically.

"Hi, Betty! Hi, Jill!" Ida shouted. She obviously hadn't lost her propensity for making friends. I wondered if she was still handing out homemade baked goods to the newcomers. Since the parking lot in front of the Waning Years Infirmary was relatively empty, I supposed not.

"Your old place? Burned to the ground," Fanny said, pulling out her binoculars. She answered my previous question while perusing the horizon. Her clunky glasses hung from around her neck on a sparkling gold chain.

"Mr. Ramirez?" I asked. Heads nodded.

"Another invention gone awry," Grady said. "No casualties that we know of."

"That's good," I said. The sound of my apartment landing coming down in a splintering explosion was still fresh in my memory. "Do they still live here? The Ramirezes?"

My question went unanswered because our attention was diverted when we passed some tennis courts. A gentleman swatted his racquet at a yellow ball and spanked it past the knee of his opponent. The victor raised his shriveled arms and started for the net. It took a long time before the man got to the net, although he was churning well just before he leaped like a gazelle and caught the top of the swinging hurdle with his toe. I wondered what it sounded like when his face hit the hard surface on the other side. I turned my attention to the front of the Suburban. I was brought up proper, after all, and didn't want to add to his humiliation. When I glanced back he was still in the prone position, unmoving, and his teammate was prodding him with the handle of his racquet.

"Over there are the stables." Grady directed with a thumb.

A cedar post corral was charming in its rugged construction. Inside, several well-appointed riders trotted along, their sharp elbows cutting the air.

"I enjoyed riding when I was still wearing my Depends," Ida said wistfully.

"After the corrective bladder surgery, though, it was just too chafing." She wrinkled her nose.

"I had to rub her down with aloe gel every night," Grady said. A faraway look came over his face. Good memories and obviously more information than I wanted.

"What's that?" I interrupted Grady's reverie as we crested a slight rise in the road. A pink Quonset hut that looked like a giant pig napping in a bed of petunias sat at the end of a short turnoff, and there were several cars resting in its lot.

"That would be our gift shop," Bob said. "Ida's got her own line of dancewear in there, and they sell as fast as we can get 'em in."

"Oh, there's other charming little things in there, too, like Hummels and Beanie Babies, crystal figurines, diving equipment, stuff like that," Ida said. She would be quick to take the attention away from herself. Gift shop? Designer dance wear? And diving equipment?

"Why the diving equipment?" I noticed the wooden sign out in front of the pig. It said Ramirez Rose. Could it be?

"You wondered about them Ramirezes. It's their shop,"

Fanny said. "If Mr. R. can keep from burning it down or blowing it up, they'll be on easy street soon enough. Charges too darn much for the most part, if you ask me." Fanny was fussing with her seat belt. She kept pulling it out, snapping it back, pulling it out, and snapping it. How annoying. I wanted to snap her a good one.

"Diving equipment?" I asked again.

"You'll see in just a sec," Grady said.

We rolled to a stop in front of a long, sleek, industrial-style building.

"This I've gotta see," said Ida, as if she had never seen it before. She was squirming, and I couldn't wait to learn what else the gang had done with the old Active Senior Living Complex while I was away. So far, the transformation was nothing short of amazing.

FIVE

WE PUSHED THROUGH the double glass-paneled doors of the large building.

"This is our athletic complex." Grady played tour guide.

The place wasn't at all similar to the dusty old hardwood aerobics room with its torturous exercise classes and wildly screeching drill sergeant. I stared all agape at the shiny marble counter top where a trio of blonde vacuous-looking young girls handed out towels. Grady gave them a smart salute, and they giggled.

"Hi, Grade!" they said in chorus.

Grady winked.

Ida smiled. "He's so popular."

I forced a pleasant look on my face. How sweet.

A menagerie of sporty sounds came from everywhere, mingled with piped in verve music. I recognized the music of Fleetwood Mac pounding out Tusk, undoubtedly to heighten the diminished adrenaline of my senior peers. I could almost hear flaccid muscles expanding and contracting with the beat, reaching toward a greater degree of tone. In the distance, I heard the metallic clanging of weight machines, and then a long, low scream pierced the air. One of the blondies grabbed the phone and punched a button with a French manicured nail. She caught my look of concern, smiled brightly and explained.

"9-1-1. Speed dial."

"Oh," I said.

A couple of medics burst from a room behind the counter and ran past us with a gurney, but Grady didn't seem the least bit flummoxed. He took my elbow and hustled me out of the foyer and down a long hall. The rest of the gang followed, and eventually we came to some foggy glass doors. We passed through the doors and into an expansive swimming area. The place reeked of chlorine, and the air was muggy, making my hair puff out, but the wonder of it all relieved my apprehension of looking too discombobulated.

"You've got to be kidding!" I gasped.

I followed the hollow echoes of my voice around the tile floors to the far end of the Olympic-sized pool where an imposing high-dive board jutted out over the deep end.

"Nice, huh? Check out the hot tubs over there." Grady pointed to the far wall where steam was rising in clouds. "Five in all, of varying temperatures. We made some adjustments after three of the residents conked out last month," he said. "The guard thought they were sleeping. By the time we brought them around, they'd sweated off about ten pounds apiece."

"They should've left Mrs. Flabbersham in there a little longer," Fanny said. She moved past me with her walker going, *kachunk, kachunk, kachunk.*

"Fanny!" Ida scolded.

"Don't you tell me those thighs of hers aren't a good fifty pounds apiece. Quickest chunk of fat she's ever lost." Fanny moved off ahead, scowling. "Now shake your own fat legs. New Detectives is in an hour."

"New Detectives?" I whispered to Grady.

"She's taking computer classes in Criminal Profiling. Watches all the forensic shows."

I nodded, remembering Fanny's intrigue with the investigative world.

"Look over there, May. Scuba classes are just starting." Bob pointed at the line of people emerging from the locker rooms. They were outfitted in diving gear with brilliantly colored fins on their feet. Masks and snorkels hung from their necks. Grandmas and grandpas splashed out toward the deep end, slapping their fins like awkward seals. That explained the diving equipment.

"You should see them getting those tanks on," Bob snickered. He crossed his arms over his chest and waited. Fanny stood nearby tapping her foot impatiently.

I watched transfixed as a bronzed Adonis in scanty, conforming trunks assisted, directed, and shouted instructions. He stood near a row of silver air tanks, which were attached to vest-like buoyancy compensators. He motioned for the first volunteer to accept her prize. She timidly slapped forward.

"Hey! That's Wanda Page!" Ida said with great excitement. "She does the most beautiful calligraphy I've ever seen. Hey, Wanda!"

Ida's voice echoed and bounced off of the walls like a hollow rubber ball. Wanda paused to search out the source of the call just as Mr. Adonis plunked a heavy aluminum canister over her shoulders. One flippered leg abruptly kicked into the air. Wanda swung her arms in tiny circles to gain balance. The old gal fought with vigor, I'll give her that. She pumped her arms but, having lost all control, goose-stepped sideways on her way toward the edge of the pool.

"There she goes!" Bob said. His hands came together in thunderous applause.

"Just couldn't keep your big trap shut, could ya?" Fanny glared at Ida.

Wanda did one last graceful high kick and let out a terrifying shriek before crashing into the water. A tidal wave lapped up over the edge of the pool, and Wanda was gone.

"Right this way, then," Grady said, and grabbed Ida's arm before Mr. Adonis could stare us down with his beady little eyes.

As we made our way down another hall, I heard an annoying cracking sound in irregular tempo. The noise got louder as we neared a small wooden door.

"Racquetball courts," Grady announced as he held the door open for us all. On my right were carpeted risers and on my left was a long row of Plexiglas rooms.

"Take a load off. My corns is killin' me, and we need to sit," Fanny said. Without waiting for the rest of us to agree, she dismissed her walker and found a place on the steps. We watched

two men in the first court pass a little blue ball back and forth
via short tennis racquets. Grady said, "That's Phillip and Albert. They've got a running battle going. Last count, I believe
Albert was up by ten games."

I tried to keep up with the hectic pace of the game, but it
was something of a blur with the blue ball bouncing chaoti-
cally against the walls, the ceiling, back against the glass wall,
and it took a few times for me not to duck when that happened.
The two men were obviously in it to the death. Their faces were
bright red and pouring sweat. I looked around discreetly for a
crash cart.

"It looks like this is it!" Grady said when Albert stepped up
to serve what I assumed to be the winning point.

Phillip didn't look like the type to give up without a fight.
After Albert smashed the ball, he bent over awaiting its return.
Phillip apparently had had enough. He took a bead.

I saw it coming and cringed.

That ball must have been going ninety miles per hour when
it struck the left cheek of Albert's gym shorts. The howl that
followed lasted a good two minutes, but by the time the other
courts began to empty out in response to the agonizing cry, we
were on our way.

Upon Fanny's insistence, we hurried through the rest of the
tour. She was determined to see her detective program, and so
the massage parlor, the ladies' lounge, the breast feeding room,
the bowling alley and theater flew by in a blur. I completely
lost all sense of space and direction. Small card tables lined
one of the halls where men played serious dominoes. When it
seemed like we had walked a mile, Grady finally slowed and
turned to me. He wore the look of someone who'd done a
heroic deed.

"Last stop. You're gonna love this," Grady said. He pointed
to a carpeted flight of stairs flanked by a wide wheel-chair ramp.
We took the stairs down, pushed through a door and entered a
dimly lit room. It took a minute for my eyes to adjust. The
sporty noises were gone; the smell of old tennis shoes, sweat
socks and heating gels disappeared. Violin music played softly.

"It's the Waning Years Lounge. Took almost the entire year to build," Bob said. "Let's get a table. I'll buy the first round." He caught the bartender's attention and twirled his finger over his head. The bartender smiled broadly when he saw Bob, reached under the bar and came up with five bottles of beer. Just like the good old days.

"They're not real," Fanny said. "We don't have our liquor license yet, so all we have is pretend beer and fruit drinks. Just as well, Bob had a couple of real brews last week and slept through two of his classes."

I assessed the cozy room. Candlelight lanterns glowed atop round tables. A gray burbur carpet covered the floor, and in one corner was a raised platform where expensive-looking stereo equipment sat behind a short wall of glass. Below and in front of the D.J. booth was a polished wood dance floor. The floor, however, was empty, and there was no D.J. at his post. I looked toward the bartender who carefully arranged the bottles on a tray. Behind him were shelves of sparkling glasses and a long mirror.

Very classy and elegant.

"Where is everybody?" I asked.

"It's early yet," Fanny said.

"Let's get our regular table. There's something else you have to see, May Bell. It's quite extraordinary!" Ida was so excited she was vibrating. She walked quickly across the floor and plopped her wide bottom on a tall chair.

The rest of us followed, and, as Grady held out a chair for me, the south wall suddenly came alive with brilliant color. I was momentarily blinded.

"Right on time," Grady said, checking his watch.

"It's the-the pool!" I sputtered.

"Night swim. Isn't it magnificent?" Ida beamed.

The entire wall was an underground view of the swimming pool. Pruny, blue-veined legs kicked bubbles around in watery tornadoes. A soundless splash preceded a rotund woman who quickly sank to the bottom of the pool. She did a quick turn in the water and opened her eyes. I don't think she could have seen us in the dark room, but she gave a wave just the same before kicking off of the pool floor, shooting for the surface.

"That was Pam Winlett! She speaks three languages!" Ida said.

"I don't know about this pool idea of yours, Grady," Fanny said. She scooted in beside Ida. "First of all," she said, "I'm not too keen on looking at the bottoms of people while I eat my pretzels. And third, what if that wall should give way? And, I might add, let's not forget what happened when Carl lost his shorts last week on that half-gainer."

"I think it's beautiful," I said, and although I was a little nervous about that much water straining against the thin sheet of glass, it was quite spectacular.

FORTUNATELY, we remained alone with the exception of the bartender who began watching a small TV behind the counter after he delivered our faux beers and pretzels.

It was time to talk.

I studied the faces of my friends around the table. It appeared as if they all wanted to say something, but we politely waited for Grady to begin. It was just the way we'd deigned the order of things. Bob took his casual position, leaning back in his chair to give comfort to his protruding rounded belly, and rested the base of his beer on the general area of his navel. His jowls were full, and he was frowning down into his collar, squishing his neck.

Ida's lipstick had worn away and her hair had fallen a bit, but she was unperturbed by any of that and leaned against Grady, occasionally gazing at him with doting eyes. She wore a pretty yellow dress with a string of beads around her neck, which she twisted gingerly.

Grady looked at his bride and then cleared his throat. He finger-combed his thick, white hair. It seemed a bit longer in the back than I remembered, and his eyes twinkled under dark bushy eyebrows. He smiled at me, showing a charming gap between his front teeth.

"For Pete's sake. I'm going to miss Detective! Speak, already!" Fanny threw a pretzel at Grady and rapped her arthritic knuckles on the table. "This case gets colder by the minute!"

"All right, Fanny. Pipe down." Grady pushed the pretzel toward the center of the table. "This is what we've got. Otis has disappeared. Last seen Thursday night playing pool, last heard arguing with a woman in front of his apartment. At least that's what the neighbors think they heard. His wife reports him missing, but waits all night before she calls the police. Strange? Maybe, but according to her, she doesn't notice he's gone until she wakes up and finds his side of the bed isn't rumpled. His car's still in the carport, and he hasn't taken anything from the home."

"What about the girlfriend?" I urged.

"It's news to Mrs. Otis, who finds out about the woman when the cops ask if Otis might have camped out at her apartment."

"Ouch," I said.

"The girlfriend doesn't know anything," Fanny said. Then in answer to our inquisitive stares she rolled her eyes. "I lifted the police report, all right?"

I gasped.

"Oh don't rupture a spleen, May Bell," Fanny said. "I got it back before the coppers even knew it was gone." She sat up tall in her chair and then leaned over the table. "He was definitely murdered," she said. She was talking behind her hand again, probably because one of the towel cuties had come in to flirt with the bartender and was now leaning over the counter, obviously unashamed that her shirt's top button was missing. Like a good investigator, I'd noticed that little detail when she passed us. I'll bet Grady had noticed that bit of evidence, too, but I'm pretty sure it wasn't because he was gathering case data.

"What makes you think he was murdered?" I directed my question to Fanny. Sure, she was aces when it came to forensics and lifting police reports, but as far as I knew there were no solid leads ending in support of murder. I wanted her to be right—I really did—otherwise, no high drama.

Grady explained. "I had lunch with him the day before he

disappeared. He never mentioned going anywhere. In fact, he said he was meeting up with Fanny to play eighteen holes the next morning."

"We were going for a foursome," Fanny said. "I still run the course here, and nobody walks away from a foursome."

That was true enough. Fanny took her golf game very seriously.

Activity in the pool was building up. Atrophied calves and pale hams were churning away. Three old gals were having a pantomime tea party at the bottom of the pool. Cute. A man swam by on his back. One hand held goggles against his face, the other hand pinched his nose. A woman above him was treading water. The man circled, apparently, looking for a good under-the-bleachers shot.

"Otis just disappeared without a trace," Ida said. She looked honestly pained.

"And you know what?" Grady leaned in.

The rest of us leaned in.

"They found a tackle box just outside of his front door. It looked like he was planning a little fishing trip that his wife didn't know about."

"Hmmm," I said.

Bob sighed loudly. "Hey. We're out of pretzels. Hold on, I saw a bag behind the bar." Bob got up, but paused to gaze at the giant fish bowl.

"Where do you think Otis went?" I wondered aloud.

"You mean where did someone dump his body?" Fanny corrected.

"Why would they take him?" Ida peeped.

"Where could they put a man like Otis?" Grady asked.

"Right there," Bob said, pointing to the blue water.

"Whoa!" Fanny shouted and lurched back in her chair.

Ida screamed. Her necklace erupted and white beads scattered and bounced across the table. Grady dropped his beer. The bottle fell with a thump and sprayed a white geyser over my feet. A thin man in faded purple swim trunks, and probably not much taller than five six, was staring at us through pale, unseeing eyes. His arms were extended out to the sides of his bloated, floating body and his hair was feathered away from his head in soft gray fur.

Suddenly, there was pandemonium in the pool. Legs acted as battering rams in a frantic attempt to keep the body away. Feet kicked out and bathing suits were ripped apart by thick thorny toenails. The swim party looked like one of the panic scenes right out of the movie Jaws.

"Otis Culpepper?" I asked.

"It *was*," Fanny said.

The boiling water lifted Otis on a current and propelled him toward our protective wall. The vision was captivating. Like a gentle bird in flight he advanced until his forehead met the glass. *Thud.* He swooped back and then surged forward again. *Thud.*

Ida began to wheeze. Grady covered her eyes, dragged her to her feet, and pulled her toward the exit. Bob walked up to the glass, put his hands against the pane, and tapped a message back to poor Otie.

"This one's for you, buddy," he said, and lifted his beer bottle.

"Come on, May Bell! We've got to get up top before those fools destroy the evidence." Fanny was on the move. Her walker forgotten, she trotted along on her toes making good time. I was right on her tiny heels and behind me I could hear Bob clattering along, having had the foresight to grab Fanny's walker as he flew past.

While we were high-stepping up the staircase, I got an urge to shout out a triumphant, "Whoopee!" Once again the gang had a case to solve.

Just like old times.

SIX

THE POOL WAS EMPTY of soggy human raisins when Fanny, Bob and I entered the bedlam, with the exception of Otis, who drifted near a pool ladder amid his purple swim trunks. Grady herded everyone toward a far corner, while Fanny fished around in the water with a long pole. She could just reach the floating Otis, for all the good that did, because it only pushed him farther down into the illuminated body bath.

"Oh farmer!" she said in exasperation, while swinging the pole away in an exaggerated arc that pelted us all with water dripping from the net.

"She's goin' in," Bob said, taking another swig of beer.

"No, Fanny!" I shouted. "Wait for the lifeguards!"

Fanny scowled but straightened up as two white-suited medics rushed toward us, stretcher between them. "Better call the morgue, boys, this guy's too late for a liplock."

"Where are the lifeguards?" I asked. The dripping, huddled mass of evacuated swimmers rubbernecked and elbowed in closer to get a better look at the tragic end of Otis Culpepper. The lifeguard chairs were strangely vacant. The *Life Guard On Duty* sign hung in place, swinging ever so slightly, as if it had been given a nudge by some invisible hand.

"It don't matter about lifeguards," Fanny said, flipping her fingers back and forth across her bifocals like mini windshield wipers. "Otis was dead before he hit the water."

"How does she know that?" I asked Bob, who didn't seem to care one way or the other. He scratched an armpit and let his hand stay, while appearing to be amused at Grady's predicament. Ida sprawled, wheezing, in a lounge chair with a hand over her forehead. The mob was getting restless, and Grady was quickly losing control. Meanwhile, guys with the stretcher were on hands and knees conferring intensely.

"When you drown, you float on top," Fanny explained. "After a while you sink down to the bottom. That's a sinker if I ever saw one." Fanny held the sides of her glasses and squatted at the side of the pool to get a better look.

The guys with the stretcher tossed a coin. The loser groaned loudly and began taking off his shoes. Then he paused, more conversation, and they began pounding their palms in a determined scissors-rock-paper game.

"Give me a break," Fanny proclaimed. She raised her hands high overhead, stood on her toes, and cartwheeled over the pool's edge. A white-haired old lady frogging it down and down into the depths.

"Fanny!" I cried out in dismay and grabbed Bob's arm. "She did it!" I shouted at him. "She went to Otis!"

"Is that Fanny down there?" Grady appeared beside me, having given up on the crowd control duty.

"Go, Fanny, go!" rose from the passionate throng. The white suits were in suspended animation. The one with the paper hand was about to defeat the rock hand, but it just didn't seem to matter anymore, because up came Fanny with her arm crooked around the neck of poor Otis.

"Get your lazy buns over here and give a help, would ya?" Fanny panted. It was amazing. She still had her glasses on her nose. Otis's head lolled back and forth on Fanny's shoulder. His eyes were open in a pleasant, dreamy look. Water trickled from his gaping mouth.

"We're comin' for ya, Fanny, just hang in there, girl!" Joyce, a rotund woman I'd met briefly while a resident at the old complex, pinched her nose, closed her eyes and grabbed her knees before slamming into the water.

"She's been working on that maneuver for a good two years," Bob said.

That was all it took. Timidity was overshadowed by unity of purpose, and the quaking old folks grew bold. Otis was one of their own, after all. One after the other they dove, jumped, flipped and fell into the pool, coming to Fanny's aid. The guys in the white suits just looked at each other, visibly happy to leave the chore to someone else.

Dozens of helping hands retrieved Otis and dragged him out onto the tiles. The white suits decided they'd better get involved and got to work on the body. There wasn't much to see after that, so Grady told everyone to go home. We found Ida off to the side, hidden by a lot of steam. She was sitting with her back to us on the edge of one of the hot tubs, feet dangling in the bubbles, humming *Three Coins in a Fountain*. Ida wasn't good in stressful situations. Grady helped her to her feet. It was unfortunate she hadn't thought to take her shoes off before her night wade.

"They'll have to drain and refill the pool," Bob said. "But at least we know where Otis is."

"On his way to the morgue," Fanny said while wringing out her skirt. Her hair was flattened against her head. "And I'm here to tell you, he didn't drown in this pool. Nope, he was dead long before hitting the surf."

"The floating thing." I remembered Fanny's explanation. *Otie no floatie.*

"Oh there's more to it than that." Fanny took her glasses off and shook them. Water flew. "I need a dry change, then I say we meet up at Grady and Ida's at 1900 hours. I can probably get the tail end of Detective. After that, I'll tell you what I found at the bottom of the pool."

SEVEN

I WAVED GOOD-BYE to the Suburban as it pulled away from the front of my guest Cabana. What a change from the carpet-stained digs of my former apartment. For the more advanced in financial stature, a smattering of Spanish Style haciendas rested in a courtyard, replete with fountains, walkways and benches. There was a profundity of plant life, tastefully situated to make the most of their fronds and foliage.

I walked through my temporary home, warming in the wide windows and retreating sunlight. Ceiling fans circulated the perfumed air, bringing calm and security to the unfamiliar place.

My bedroom was spacious. A tall bed was covered in a country-style patchwork quilt with more pillows than I could use heaped at its head. Sheer curtains fluttered alongside patio doors left open to permit fresh air. I wandered out through the patio doors and onto the terra cotta tiles. I crossed my arms over my chest in a selfish hug but kept in mind that I was there on business and that I shouldn't consider this a vacation.

We had a murder to solve.

The pink of the sky and a look at my watch said it would soon be getting dark, and I had yet to call Ted. Reluctantly I moved inside, latched the porch doors, and sat on the edge of my bed, pushing phone buttons while nudging off my shoes.

"May, honey! I was getting worried. How was the flight?" Ted sounded a bit out of breath like he did when there was something troubling him. I took guilty satisfaction in the knowledge he had been concerned about me.

"Fine, fine. The pilots were so awesome, Ted, you know

when the wheels don't come down on a plane, they have to land it on its belly? Good thing those guys in the cockpit knew what they were doing. But the slide down that plastic shoot ripped up my panty hose, and I think the explosion blew off an earring."

I heard Ted gasp. "Not really, May!"

"No, not really. But it sounds good, doesn't it?" I smiled broadly and leaned back into the sea of pillows.

"The place is empty without you, Bella May and the cat keeps glaring at me."

The cat? "Ted, I took Trixie to the Poochie Hooch yesterday."

"Oh. Who's this then?" Ted's voice trailed off. "Anyway, I miss you."

This was good. How many years had I wandered around an empty house wishing he'd come home? I reminded myself that things were different now. Lately, I was nearly smothered with all of the attention and care Ted showed me. A girl could get used to it.

I HAD AN HOUR to get ready to meet Grady and Fanny and Ida and Bob. I wandered into the bathroom for a quick shower, but the huge bathtub was more than I could resist. I dropped a handful of little jellyfish bath oil beads into the water and settled in.

As I relaxed in the tub I thought of Otis, a man who had disappeared, and then had reappeared in an unlikely place. It just didn't make sense. How would he have been placed in the pool without anyone seeing? There were people everywhere from the front door to the saggy swimmers cavorting like school children, and certainly, although most were probably farsighted without their glasses, it would have been impossible for them to miss a corpse sliding over the pool's edge.

But they had.

Fanny said there was something she wanted to tell us after her body recovery, but knowing Fanny, she would be careful about talking where unscrupulous ears might hear. This was a murder, after all, pure and simple. Maybe not so simple, and one can hardly say a murder is pure, but it was exciting to think I might be able to contribute in some way to finding the perpetrator of the mysterious activities happening around the Estates.

Suddenly, I sat straight up in the tub. Oh darn! I had lost track of time. I'd have to rush to get dressed, and then it hit me like a helicopter blade—I didn't have the slightest idea how to get to Grady and Ida's condo.

EIGHT

I GRABBED A FLASHLIGHT from under the sink and headed out with my purse over my shoulder. There was hardly any need for the light after all, since the walkways were aglow under tall amber lanterns, but in places the bushes made shadows, so I felt a bit more secure with the torch in hand. My hair was still wet, but I'd taken time for lipstick so I was half presentable. The air had cooled to a perfect seventy degrees, absent of any city noises like car horns or sirens. Even the sound of a jet flying overhead added to the tranquil personality of the evening.

I was concentrating on a row of condominiums in the distance, so I didn't pay attention to the sounds behind me until they were close. Maybe, I thought, the footsteps were echoes of my own. It was hard to tell in the jumbled collection of white statues, trees, and hodgepodge of leafy plants along the path, and besides that, I had found myself walking alongside a murmuring brook carved neatly into the landscape. It popped and gurgled and bubbled along, having a joyful, private conversation off to my left. In the daylight it must be beautiful, but now it confused distance and direction of other sounds. I slowed my steps while listening carefully. The footsteps behind me slowed, too. I stopped and turned. The footsteps stopped with mine, and I was feeling foolish. Just an echo, as I had thought before.

"Otis was murdered. Murdered, I tell you! Murdered!" I could hear Fanny whispering in my ear. I hurried along faster now, glancing repeatedly over my shoulder, but all I could see were black splotches along the walk. Someone, or something, was following me. I was sure of it. I stepped up my pace, but

my fear grew when a dense grotto swallowed me up. Vines hung overhead. Cicadas screamed their warning in deafening crescendo. I looked back again. My breath caught in my throat as something moved under the branches.

What was that?

The lights in the condos were closer now, but not close enough. The footsteps again, behind me, came fast. I started to run, well, lumber really, with my purse banging against my side. Vines slapped my face and snatched at my hair. I didn't want to look back again, for fear of what I might see. The thing behind me was running now, matching my strides two for one. Twenty yards traveled and my lungs were heaving. I knew it was pointless to waste my energy on a foot race.

I turned and lunged.

The poor old man didn't have a chance. I swung my purse wide and caught him behind the knees. He tumbled head over heels onto the damp lawn. I dove and straddled him. As I thrust the beam of my flashlight toward his face, I saw the running shorts and the Walkman tied to his waist. He raised his sweat-banded wrists in defense, blinking against the light. I'd knocked his headphones right off of his head and they hung around his neck, tethered there by a thin electrical cord.

"What do you want?" he croaked.

My fear was probably nothing compared to his, and I started to apologize, feeling my face burn. But then, thinking quickly, I stood up. Keeping the light in his face, I disguised my voice.

"You live here?" I asked gruffly.

The old man made a motion as if to get to his feet while adjusting his cockeyed headset.

"Don't touch that."

He stopped, his hands raised. "Why are you doing this?"

"Security," I said. I snapped my purse open, then closed for effect. "Don't you know there's a two-man jogging policy now?"

"No," he said, fear warbling his voice, "I always jog alone."

The man kept his hands in the air until I motioned them down with my light. He was a tall spindly man, and then on closer inspection I discovered that I knew him. It was a guy I'd named Lanky in my other life. I wanted to chuckle, but held it back.

"Not after tonight you don't, and thank your lucky stars I don't slap you with a big infraction. You'd better get out of here before I change my mind and file a report."

"Uh, yes sir, ma'am, yes, officer."

"But before you go. Where do Ida and Grady Knox live? I have something to discuss with them as well."

"First condo you come to. See over there?" Lanky pointed.

"Keep your hands where I can see them, buddy. Right. Just checking to see if you really live here. Good. From now on, see that you have a partner. Move your buns, cowboy."

Lanky left a streak of shoe rubber on the sidewalk as he ran like the wind (and maybe a little streak in his shorts, I might add). I felt a little guilty, but at least my faux pas hadn't been a total wash. I wouldn't have to go checking mailboxes for my friends' names after all.

IDA MET ME at the door, the ever-congenial hostess placing a drink in my hand before I had a chance to find a place for my purse. She directed me to the dining room, where I found Fanny working over a crossword puzzle at the table.

Grady scolded me. He said I should have called, that he would have walked me over, but I made up some excuse about not wanting to bother him, when in actuality I hadn't even considered calling for an escort. I was accustomed to doing things on my own, but I was moved that he'd regarded my welfare.

"I saw Lanky out jogging this evening," I said while sipping on a glass of ice water. There was a lemon wedge dodging the cubes and a little collection of seeds at the bottom of the glass.

"Who's that?" Fanny asked. She peered up through her oversized glasses. No, her glasses weren't oversized; it was her eyes, huge behind the magnifying lenses. Her hair looked nice, but she'd missed another curler in the back, a pink sponge job hanging on to a white, wispy pinch of hair.

"I don't know his name, he's tall and thin. Legs like a gazelle."

"Oh. Bill. He's dying," Fanny said and returned to her puzzle.

"Dying?" I felt really bad to think I'd accosted a poor, ailing man. "He looked pretty fit and healthy," I said. "In fact, it looked like he could run a marathon."

"He's been dying for about thirty years. Just talk to him for ten minutes and you'll understand. Polyps, prostrate, stones, palpitations—you name it. Sometimes I just want to say get on with it already." Fanny waved her hand over her head in a dismissive manner.

I got it.

"What do you think of our little summer camp?" Bob came out of the kitchen wearing a pair of sweat pants and a T-shirt with the sleeves cut away. Little gray hairs poked through the white skin of his meaty shoulders.

I raved and offered sincere compliments about my cabana. "I told Ted all about it."

"Did you mention anything over the phone?" Fanny narrowed her enormous eyes.

"About the…" I knew what she was getting at. "No. Just what was in the paper." It didn't matter really, because I knew nothing more than what I'd read and what I'd seen in the complex pool, so I was pretty safe from having leaked any news.

"I guess you're wondering what Fanny found in the pool," Grady said.

"We'll get to that, Mr. Knox," Ida said, taking my hand. "First I want to give May a tour of the place."

BY THE TIME Ida had led me through her condo, which was immaculately furnished and decorated, I was burning with questions about the murder—if that's in fact what it was. I think Ida saw my impatience, so she topped off my glass and we all retired to a comfortable loft overlooking the living room.

It was decorated lodge-style with overstuffed couches in burgundies and hunter greens. A gas fireplace cast a warm glow along the walls and cathedral windows. I sat on one couch beside Fanny while Grady cuddled with Ida in a huge chair. Bob took the hearth.

Grady began. "Otis went missing. Now his body's been recovered."

"What did the police say about Otis?" I set my glass on a heavy wooden coffee table and put my elbows on my knees.

"Oh, he's dead," Ida quickly responded.

Fanny snorted and shot her bony leg out as if to kick Ida.

"Fanny," I said, placing a restraining hand on her knee.

"What did they say was the cause of death?" I asked.

"Accidental drowning," Bob said with a good dose of sarcasm. "I just got off the phone with one of the officers."

"What?" I was shocked. "They already did an autopsy?"

"Sure 'nuf," Grady said, then pursed his lips.

"But there *was* a question about his death, wasn't there? I mean—he was missing all night." It was hard to imagine the conclusion could be that simple.

"There was if you're thinking that way." Grady held his hands out palms up. "These cops have enough to worry about without adding another chore to their busy schedule. To them, it's just a matter of some old fart wandering into the poolroom at night without his glasses on, and whoops! Over the edge and bye-bye Otis. They did find some partially digested sleeping pills in his stomach. Not enough to kill him, but enough to make him drowsy."

"They probably figured that's why he drowned," Bob said. "He had swim trunks on, don't forget, so maybe he gets in the water for a few laps, but he's just too sleepy to make it out."

"Could it have happened that way?" I looked at Bob, then Fanny, Ida and Grady. I didn't want to ask how Grady had been privy to all of his autopsy information after Fanny's earlier confessions as a police report thief.

"Not in a million years." Fanny looked angry. "Otis was an excellent swimmer. Besides, think about it. They had scuba classes in there before night swim. Even if he'd been banging around in the bottom of the pool, someone would have seen him, up close and personal."

"But how did he get in there without anyone seeing?" I asked.

"And why would he get in the water without his swim cap?" Ida blinked. Grady patted her hand.

"I don't get it," I said. "If he wasn't there during scuba classes, he must have slipped in while everyone was playing in the pool."

"And before they turned on the underwater lights," Bob added. "Or we'd have been able to see something."

"Maybe. Probably," Grady said.

"Fanny," I said. "You told us you found something when you went in after Otis's body. What was it?"

She waited a minute before answering, looking like she wanted us to be amazed at a magic trick before tossing back the drape to show us the trap door.

"That I did. That I did," Fanny said finally. She smiled her new teeth.

"All right then, Miss Brittle Bones, let's have it!" Bob was getting irritated.

Fanny dug around in her skirt pockets. She frowned and went from the left pocket to the right. She frowned again. "I thought I put it right in here."

"Geez, Fanny." Bob rolled his eyes. "Did you lose it in your all-fire hurry to watch Detective?"

"Don't get your tightie-whities in a wad, Bob." Fanny dug again. Then she smiled and brought up a fist. "What do you think of this?"

NINE

FANNY OPENED HER HAND, one finger at a time, starting with the pinkie, and worked up to her index finger. She had the floor, and there wasn't a sound in the room except for the ticking of a wall clock.

"Nothing," Bob said and slapped his thigh. Then he tugged at the collar of his shirt like he was looking for something to do with his hands besides throttle Fanny for keeping us all poised on the edge of discovery.

"Fanny," I said, worried that she was convinced she actually held something. "There isn't anything there."

"Is that what you're telling us? You didn't find anything? Is that the clue?" Ida seemed to be struggling to give her friend an avenue of escape.

Grady looked pale and tired. I know things are slow and dull when you're biding your retirement years, but there we were, thinking we had a mystery to solve, and Fanny had left us disappointed. Maybe we were just a bunch of fools kidding ourselves into wanting a little high drama.

"You're a bunch of darn idiots." Fanny pinched her palm with the other hand and waved her fingers around in front of us. It was all getting a bit creepy, and I glanced at Grady, who usually was the most sensible in times like these. What would my husband do? Write a prescription?

"Look again," Fanny said.

"Well, I'll be," Ida said. "It's a string." Somehow Ida had gotten hold of Fanny's binoculars and was peering through them from across the room.

Bob got to his feet. I watched Bob, twisting his head this way and that to get a better look at Fanny's hand.

"Not just a string. It's fishing line. Steel Head line, if I'm not mistaken." He pinched Fanny's hand and came away with air.

In the dim light—I hadn't seen it before—a nearly invisible string hanging limply in Bob's hand. But there it was.

"It was wrapped around his ankle when I got to him. Otis was tethered to the ladder with that, not that you would have seen it from the top."

I was impressed. Good thing Fanny had gone in with her glasses.

"It got tangled in my hands, but came away quite easily when I gave a yank. I figure that was the plan all along. I did a little research after Detectives. Got the facts wrong. Seems after someone's dead for a while, then they float. Gas and bloating, stuff like that. Anyway, to keep him from bobbing, someone had to tie him down until he was kicked free. Then, whoever did this would just go back later and haul up the string. But I got there first."

"Great job, Fanny," Ida said, training the binoculars on Fanny's little white head. "But I don't think there are any fish in our swimming pool."

"It doesn't add up." Grady interrupted our happy moment. "He wasn't there during scuba classes, and it would have taken a while to tie him down."

We started brooding.

"There was time," I said firmly. "Between scuba and night swim. Not much time, but it could have been possible. But why?"

Grady frowned, lost in deep concentration. "Something has been bothering me about this since Fanny pulled Otis out of the pool," he said, "but for the life of me I can't put my finger on it." He shook his head.

"Besides the fact that he was dead meat? You don't see that every day." Fanny carefully wound the fishing line into a little ball.

"Cold cuts?" Ida reached for a platter on the coffee table. She passed it around.

"No, it's not that," Grady said. "He looked different. Something about him wasn't right. Oh, I don't know."

Bob took the tray and scooped up a slab of salami. "Darn

right he looked different. Buggy eyes, swollen lips—he looked like a blowfish."

"Sardines?" Ida let the binoculars fall around her neck. She reached for a second tray.

"Something else," I said. "Grady, didn't you say Otis had left his tackle box on his door step? Like he was going to go on a fishing trip?"

Fanny punched me in the shoulder. "I see where you're going, yeah. We need to get a look at that tackle box. Compare fishing lines." She reached around in the cloth bag she kept tethered to her walker. She flipped open a baggie and dropped the fishing line into it. "Got to protect the evidence," she said.

I rubbed my bruised shoulder. "I don't know how that will help."

"Clues, girl, clues!" Fanny hunkered down and scanned the room with her enormous eyes. Her hands were spread as if she were about to grab something.

"Sandwich?" Ida said.

I rubbed my temples. The day's events were finally catching up to me. I needed sleep to clear the cobwebs, and maybe tomorrow I could sort through it all with a new perspective.

THE GANG DECIDED to meet at Denny's for breakfast the next morning. I remembered Ted was flying in, and I wanted to be fresh and alert. With regret, I realized I was going to miss church. The choir would probably put me on their black list.

Grady and Bob walked me back to my cabana. Once they were satisfied that I had everything I needed, they said goodbye. The bed was as soft as a cloud. I didn't realize how tired I was until the alarm clock went off, and I noticed it was the beginning of another sunny day, another day closer to solving the murder of Otis Culpepper.

TEN

TIME FOR BREAKFAST. The gang settled into a booth at Denny's. The waitress was speedy with our orders and slid plates all around. Bob's platter overflowed with steamy eggs, sausage, bacon and pancakes. He attacked. I had fruit, toast and coffee. The others had slam jams or flim flams or whatever they were called.

"When's the funeral?" I asked.

"Tomorrow," Grady said. "I checked around. His wife wants it done right away, and she sure isn't wasting any time getting Otis in the ground."

Very curious.

Fanny rubbed her spoon with a napkin and started her surveillance. One eye squinted, while the other peered into the spoon.

"I'll bet poor Otis was cold in that water," Ida said. "That's probably how he died. If he'd have curled up like this he probably could have survived." Ida collapsed into a fetal position, which was quite an achievement, considering she was squeezed between Grady and the wall. Her hands looked like claws under her chin.

"Sit up, Ida!" Fanny hissed and rapped her plate with the spy spoon.

Bob laughed heartily and shoved in more eggs.

The waitress thought we needed attention and swiftly topped off our coffee mugs.

Grady seemed edgy. I'd never seen him like that before. Usually, Grady was laid back, the calm one in any storm, but now his eyebrows were doing a rumba, and I saw a vein pulsing along his neck.

"Grady, are you okay?" I was truly concerned.

"He didn't get his prescription this week." Ida put her elbows on the table and pursed her lips. Grady slumped.

"What?" It wouldn't have been good for Grady to go without his blood pressure medicine.

"His Viagra." Ida said it so quietly I only figured it out by reading her lips.

"Usually I get them in the mail," Grady said. He looked utterly despondent. "But this week they seem to be missing."

Ida nodded. "And so is Grady." She said it in a way that hinted like she was happy about the whole thing. Maybe she was. An old mare needs pasture time now and then, after all. I quickly shifted the conversation.

"Ida, I was thinking. Why don't we gals go get our hair done before Ted's plane comes in? What about a nice perm for all of us?"

"You buyin'?" Fanny perked up at this.

"I'll take care of the whole thing. What do you say?"

THE GUYS WENT OFF to play some tennis while I went with Ida and Fanny to the Waning Years Estates Beauty Shop, open seven days a week. A small old house left unattended on the grounds had been transformed in a beauty parlor. Caustic odors of unknown origin shot up my nostrils the minute we stepped through the doors. Everything was decorated in bright lavender, right down to the smocks hanging on the wall.

"Mrs. Blankenship!" Ida rushed a rotund woman in a wheelchair. Unfortunately for Mrs. Blankenship, the wheels weren't locked, and she rolled out of Ida's exuberant grasp backward into the sink room. A fast-acting young attendant whirled the chair around. She pressed the palm of her hand against Mrs. Blankenship's forehead and tipped the large woman's head back into a sink. She squirted water over the woman's face.

Mrs. Blankenship had a head full of suds before she could protest. "I was only here for a pedicure, but okay, if you think I need a wash, okay, you know best, okay."

"Good job," Fanny said to the embarrassed Ida. "Remind me not to ask for your help down the stairs."

."Ladies, what will it be today?" From the back room came someone I recognized.

"Joyce? You're working here now?"

"Since last month. I think I'm getting the hang of things. It's a really good change from the laundry. Who would have thought bleach could do so many things? Anyway, they thought it was best if I put my tinting talents to something more useful."

"They who?" I looked from Ida to Fanny.

"Job committee. It's a way for the seniors to get a little extra cashola. Makes them feel useful." Fanny was shrugging into a smock.

"So, you here for some coiffures?" Joyce smiled brightly.

Coiffures? Who says coiffures?

Joyce was so giddy she laughed a deep throaty guffaw, which worked its way out and virtually exploded from her lips. Spittle flew, and Fanny slammed her eyes shut.

"Hey Joyce, say it, don't spray it, okay?" Fanny made exaggerated wiping movements down her smock.

I didn't want to be rude, but this woman had been here a month tops, with no professional training that I could remember, and there was the question about what she'd done with that bleach. I was having significant second thoughts, but Ida and Fanny seemed not at all concerned, so I followed their lead.

"Can I take that for you?" Joyce pointed toward Fanny's walker but Fanny just waved her off and briskly folded her metal cage into a compact mass.

"Just stick it…" Fanny said.

Joyce blanched.

"…in the corner," Fanny finished. "It's such a pain."

"Still getting the best parking spots?" I asked Fanny.

"Works like nobody's business."

Fanny took a chair, crossed her legs and rummaged around in her walker bag. After Ida and I helped each other into smocks, we looked like bloated plums. We stood there wondering what to do. Fanny stuck out her toes and nudged my hips with her miniature white canvas tennis shoes. Guess that meant

I was to sit. Ida took the chair beside Fanny, and I timidly sat in the last. Surely Joyce wasn't the only one who did the perms around here.

I looked around anxiously. The perky attendant in the sink room was on the final rinse, and I didn't see anyone else of a professional nature. I could hear Mrs. Blankenship murmuring softly. The water must have been a little on the cool side.

"All I wanted was a pedicure," Mrs. Blankenship peeped.

Joyce had disappeared into a little back room. I could hear her back there giggling away. I looked around the beauty parlor, fretfully wringing my hands. Fanny dug deeper into her bag and then found what she'd been looking for—a crumpled pack of Marlboros. She pulled one out and lit up.

"Fanny, when did you start smoking?" I was shocked.

"Oh, since about last week. Takes the edge off." She blew out smoke and waved her hand through it.

"Takes the edge off what?"

"I accidentally got some of that Darjeeling tea and didn't sleep for six nights. Finished fifteen 3-D puzzles, learned Farsi and reupholstered my davenport. Now I'm tryin' to settle down, and these smooth out the jags."

"Good grief." I reached over and grabbed the cigarette out of her mouth. Her puckered lips made a little popping sound.

"Dagnabit, give that back," she said.

"You can't smoke in here anyway. Can't you smell the fumes? We'll all go up like Mr. Ramirez's paper shooter."

"Oh, all right. I guess you can have that one. But if you try that again, I'll brain ya, and don't think I won't."

Fanny shrunk down in her chair and scowled in her lavender smock. Her bony ankles stuck out from under her Capri pants. As I looked around for a place to snuff the butt, Joyce walked out carrying a tray of little bowls.

"May, tsk, tsk. I didn't know you'd started smoking. You'd better give that to me. You can't smoke in here—too many fumes." Joyce pinched the cigarette like it was a bug and handed me the tray.

While Joyce was looking for a place to deposit Fanny's

butt, I examined the collection of bowls. Man, did they smell bad. White goo, some other pearly colors, other stuff, too.

"I was thinking." Joyce was back. "Why don't we just touch up your color a bit while we do the perms? A total make-over!"

Her enthusiasm was catching. Maybe I could use a new do. Color the gray, add a curl or two. Ted would be so happy.

The young girl in the sink room was finished with Mrs. Blankenship and had the mumbling woman's head swaddled in a fat towel. "A few minutes under the dryer should do it," the girl said and wheeled the poor woman into a corner, ripped the towel off, pulled down something that looked like a clear salad bowl and flipped a switch. Once the dryer was humming, she turned to Joyce.

"Want me to do the washes?" The girl may have gotten some of that tea of Fanny's. She was busily pushing her sleeves up to the elbows.

"I think an assembly line thing is the way to approach this." Joyce took the tray from me, looked at Ida, Fanny, then me, and pointed to Fanny. "She's first." Then to me, "She's next." Ida was last. I tried to hide my worry. It wasn't possible to back out now since I'd promised to foot the bill. They didn't seem in the least nervous about all of this potential assault, so I was just probably overly concerned for no reason.

I swallowed hard and forced the corners of my mouth to curve upward. Maybe if I'd asked for a bikini wax they would have just given me a pedicure and left it at that, but I said nothing, and the make-overs began. Ida and I sat in the bullpen waiting for our turn at the sinks. Fanny followed the girl, after tossing her glasses into her cloth bag.

THE WANING YEARS Beauty Shop was a popular place. Betty and Jill stopped by to chat with Ida. I looked back toward the sinks to see Fanny wrestling with the young woman with the sprayer. Fanny had jerked the snaky hose from her hand and water flew. The girl grabbed and missed. "Good night, nurse!" Fanny hollered. "You're freezing my scalp."

Apologies, and the girl adjusted the knobs. Fanny settled down with her miniature head bent back into the sink, her eyes closed. I probably should have let her puff a couple of times on the cigarette.

"Do you remember May Bell List? She lived here about a year ago." Ida did the introductions.

"Don't you think the changes are marvelous?" Jill was short with a very pink face. Her hair was a dark bob; her full lips were slathered in shiny ruby lipstick. I detected a slight British accent. I didn't recognize her at all.

"Did you live here back then?" I worked really hard to place her. She wasn't someone I would have forgotten easily, but I hadn't lived here very long, so there were many people I hadn't met.

"Yes! Of course! I've been here since, oh, 1910. I don't blame you for not remembering, dear. Back then I was much taller. And I was oriental." Jill turned back to Ida.

I rubbed the back of my neck. Yikes. Next thing she would say is that she was a man named Jacque, and I just didn't have the stomach for that. Betty didn't say much, just plucked lint off of her sweater and looked around the shop. She was all bones and joints, put together like a collection of tinker toys, and wore three thin cotton dresses one on top of the other. The faded yellow sweater looked like an afterthought, dotted with enough lint balls to make a scarf and mittens. Pluck, pluck.

"Next!" Joyce had Fanny seated in front of a mirror, brush in hand and jerked her head toward the sink room. The girl was prepared for another tussle, but I sat back compliantly, and had my head soaked, my face washed and ears filled with water before my soggy smock and I were given the heave-ho. Ida passed me on my way to the curl and dye chair.

"Use the tight ones," Fanny barked. "I don't want my perm falling out in three weeks. Wrap it up good, Joyce, and don't worry that you'll hurt me. I've got a tough head."

Joyce took Fanny at her word and yanked away.

Time passed in a blur of water, combs, clips, gunk and funky smelling stuff, blasting dryers and comb-outs, and there

we were, three ladies with new do's. We were lined in front of
the wall mirrors for our assessment.

I nearly fell over.

"What's this color?" I found my voice. "Blue? Pink? Purple? What is it?" The curls were fine, all tight and puffed on
our heads, but I had no idea the objective for Joyce was to
match us with the lavender smocks, now stained and damp.

"What in the hell have you done to us?" Fanny was looking
at her aluminum crutch. I could see the headlines: *Beauty Shop
Employees Pummeled by Disgruntled Senior.* I looked at my
watch. Ted's plane was due in an hour, and there just wasn't
any time to remedy the situation. Besides, Joyce was crying
now, in hitching, contained spasms, and I hated to make her
feel bad.

"What a change!" I tried to sound happy about it all. "My
husband won't know what to do with me!" I could think of a
few things, like an annulment, but Joyce seemed temporarily
consoled. Ida wasn't in the least bit disconcerted, so I hustled
Fanny out. She was shouting something about a lawsuit as we
made our way to the Suburban. I tried to remember if I'd
thought to pack a scarf.

ELEVEN

AT THE AIRPORT Ted was nice, polite, and cordial, taking the hands of my friends in his. He didn't say a thing about my hair. Good old Ted. Always in control of his emotions. I was so proud of him, especially when the gals gave me the silent approval. Ted was handsome. I'd seen the way other women looked him over when he passed, tall and regal, and when he laced his fingers through mine, I'm ashamed to say, I felt a little snobbish satisfaction because he was my husband.

"I'm so glad you came." I stood on tiptoe to give him a kiss.

"I just hope Mrs. Franks doesn't get bent out of shape," he whispered in my ear. We were waiting to cross the street to the parking lot. Fanny was in a snit and held up her hand. A limousine slid to a halt, and we followed the walker.

"Mrs. Franks?"

"I left her on the exam table yesterday in one of those little yellow paper gowns."

"Oh, Ted," I chided, although I couldn't blame him. Mrs. Franks took every opportunity to make appointments with the charming, handsome Dr. List. Thyroid, goiter, rickets—you name it—she had it, at least until after the exam. Then she was feeling oh-so-much better. Never mind Ted was specializing in gynecology these days, her complaints didn't have a particular geographical preference.

"I handed her off to Dr. Ronk. Won't she be surprised?"

"Dr. halitosis, sinus condition, Ronk?"

"He agreed to work my weekend shift. I left instructions for him to be very thorough. I also said she was hard of hearing and that he'd have to get really close to explain the procedures."

"She'll be bent."

"Maybe." Ted kissed my hand. "What else could I do? I've never been able to resist the call of a pink-haired goddess before."

"You noticed." I wanted to go invisible. So humiliating.

"Noticed what?" Ted kissed my hand again. Good husband.

Ted oohed and awed at all the right times as we ushered him around the Waning Years Estates, but I could tell he was tired and being polite, so I begged off the full tour and Grady dropped us at the cabana with plans to get together at Ida and Grady's later that evening.

"So what's the scoop? You solve the murder yet?" Ted dropped to the floor by the bed and started doing push ups.

I opened drawers and unpacked Ted's things.

"No, but at least we have a body."

Ted strained. "Where did you put it?" He panted.

"It was in the pool. The white guys took it."

Ted collapsed. "A racial killing?"

"The guys in the white coats," I clarified.

"Oh. Psychiatric killing." Ted's mouth was in the carpet.

"No, no." I was getting impatient. "He's at the coroner's office, I guess. His funeral's tomorrow."

Ted twisted and sat up. "Then he's at the funeral home. Did they do an autopsy?"

"They said it was an accidental drowning."

"Great!" Ted brushed his hands together. "That tidies things up. Sorry you don't have a mystery to solve, though, May. I know how much you were looking forward to it."

"Oh, he was murdered, all right," I said. I was feeling smug. "When Fanny went down to pull him out, he was tied to the ladder with fishing line." Really smug.

"Well, that does change things, doesn't it? It was wrapped around his neck?"

"His foot."

"Hmm?" Ted stood.

"His ankle, actually, it was tied from his ankle to the ladder. And get this. He was planning a secret fishing trip just before he disappeared, and he had a girlfriend to boot."

"Why would he want to boot his girlfriend?"

I started to get really impatient with Ted, but I noticed he was teasing me.

"Really, Ted, it's creepy. He goes out to play billiards Thursday night. Then later, the neighbors hear some kind of argument outside his apartment. His wife doesn't report him missing until the next morning, but she says he didn't come home all night."

"Were the fighting voices male or female?"

"Both. Male and female. That's what I understand."

"Motive?"

"Not sure. But if he had a girlfriend, and he was fighting with his wife, it could be a crime of passion."

"Is his wife a big woman? Could she have forced him to the pool and held him under until he drowned? It would have taken some muscle. Could she have tied him to the ladder?"

Good one, Ted. "I don't know. I've never seen her. I just thought, well, it would have been an easy explanation."

"Maybe we should pay a visit to Mrs. Otis."

I got nervous thinking about this. If she killed once, she could kill again. We would have to be careful. Really slick.

"Oh! I almost forgot. Grady said something was strange about Otis. Something looked odd, or out of place, or unusual when he saw the body by the side of the pool, but he couldn't figure out what it was."

"Is it important?"

"It could be. Anything could be important. I just wish he could figure it out."

The creepy feelings were growing. Maybe we were being too obvious. Had the gang been asking questions around the estate? Were we making someone nervous?

The phone rang.

Ted wheeled around.

We looked at each other.

"You answer it," I whispered. Don't know why, but it seemed appropriate.

"No, you answer it."

"I don't want to. What if the place is bugged?" I looked over at the lamps. Now I was beginning to sound like Fanny, for Pete's sake. "I'll get it." I reached across the bed and lifted the phone. Ted nodded.

"Hello?" My voice was strained. There was no answer. "Hello? Hello?" I asked more forcefully.

Click.

Suddenly I didn't feel safe and secure in my homey little cabana. I tossed Ted a clean shirt.

"Let's get out of here, Ted."

I grabbed my purse and flashlight, and we were out the door when the phone started to ring again. "Don't answer it. Come on."

The sidewalk looked less cheerful. The lights were beginning to come on, the cicadas were screaming at us as we hurried toward Grady and Ida's condo. A shadow moved under the long, hanging vines and I gripped the flashlight tighter. "Hurry, Ted, please hurry."

We heard the footsteps behind us. It sounded like a mob, moving in a rush, fast, heavy footsteps. "Come on, Ted, we're almost there!"

The brook was deafening, tumbling over the rocks, lapping at the banks near our feet.

"Run, Ted!"

The footsteps overtook us, and I held the flashlight by my shoulder. Ted balled his fists and turned.

"Got a partner this time!" It was Mr. Lanky, ambling past us waving his sweatbands. Another man, equally tall and spindly, lifted his knees high and tried to smile, but he was obviously in some discomfort.

"Good, good, just keep it up!" I called after them and lowered my flashlight. They plodded along and left us quivering on the sidewalk.

Ted put his hands on his hips and looked at the sky. "I digress," he said.

"It happens." I resisted the urge to laugh. There were too many serious things to consider at the moment. "Let's get over to Grady's. We still have a few details to sort out."

TWELVE

IDA'S HAIR WAS wrapped in a black garbage bag when she opened the door. She must not have been expecting us so soon, and maybe that's why she was flustered. Not because of the unusual turban, she seemed not to be aware of that at all, but because she wasn't quite finished with her last batch of cookies. I looked at the evenly spaced piles of chocolate chips on the baking sheet and thought our interruption was for the best, but she fretted over them just the same.

"I'm sorry we didn't call first," I apologized. Grady appeared and relieved Ida. She seemed distracted and left the room in a hurry.

"She's trying something new with her hair," he explained. He upended the cookie sheet and poured the drops into a bowl. "Thought the color didn't quite go with her wardrobe. I didn't mind, really, but she insisted I pick up something from the drug store. I phoned you a minute or two ago, but I guess you were on your way. Now, what can I get you to drink?"

I'd nearly forgotten I was sporting a pinkish do and thought it would be a good idea to make a stop at the all-night druge-rama if I could coax Grady into letting us use his Suburban. I couldn't wait to see what Ida had done.

"So, you called us." Ted glanced at me and gave me a look that said, "See? There was nothing to worry about." But he'd been just as nervous as I, so it wasn't really much of a look.

Grady was reaching into the refrigerator when a scream erupted from the master bath. He slammed the door and raced past Ted. I found my wheels and followed. Ted was right behind me.

"Oh my gosh! Isn't it wondrous?" Ida squealed. She had the most vibrant, fiery head of hair I'd ever seen. Red as a ripe tomato.

Grady lurched to a stop, hands on either side of the doorframe. He was gasping but clearly relieved. "You nearly gave me a heart attack, woman!"

"Look at this color! Like a California sunset!" Ida turned to look at us, and we were obliged to agree. "I feel like a two-bit hooker!" she crooned.

"Just you wait right here while I get my coin purse." Grady turned and winked at Ted, then thrust a thumb in the air.

"Very, uh, elegant," Ted said to Ida.

"Wow," I said. "What brand was that?" I wanted to be sure I didn't make the mistake of picking up the wrong box.

"Oh, it's right here." Ida reached into the trashcan and pulled out a box. I put my hand over my mouth as I didn't want to blow her elation. She'd used fabric dye, but wasn't it a beautiful color?

"I think there's a little left over." Ida shook the box. A little cloud of powder flew into the air.

"Thanks, Ida, but I'm thinking about going blonde. We don't want to get the boys too worked up."

"What in the tarnation is going on in here? What's all the screaming about?" I heard the *kachunk, kachunk, kachunk,* of Fanny's walker moving along the hall floor. She appeared at the bathroom door and shoved us aside.

"I've been standing at your door for a good hour, Grade, heard the commotion and thought there had been another murder. For landscape, Ida, what have you done?"

"Like it?" Ida was turning this way and that.

"Looks like you've set yourself on fire," Fanny said. "Dagnabbit, we've got to get you back over to the beauty shop post haste."

Ida looked hurt and checked herself in the mirror. Her face sagged. "You don't like it."

"Like it? That was intentional?" Fanny wiped at her glasses. I nudged her and shook my head. She took the hint.

"Like it? Of course, I like it. Why wouldn't I like it?" She frowned at me like I'd forced her to eat worms, and left us all to restore Ida's confidence. It was hard, but we managed.

"I'll get the drinks," Grady said. "Why don't you all go upstairs and get comfortable."

WE WAITED IN THE LOFT while the minutes dragged along. Bob was due, and we didn't want to get anything started until he showed, but making small talk was difficult. My mind kept wandering.

Oh my. I remembered our close call the last time we discovered a murderer. Maybe I didn't want to gather any data. Maybe it would be better to leave all of this to the pros.

I was on my third glass of Twitch (*four times the caffeine and twice the sugar!*) when Bob showed his face at the top of the stairs.

"It's about time!" Fanny dug in her glass for an ice cube and threw it at Bob. He caught it in a fat fist and threw it back. Fanny took it on the chin. Bob took his place on the hearth.

"Yoga took longer than I anticipated," Bob explained.

"Bob, what are you wearing?" I asked. He had on a silky black robe with an orange dragon dancing across his left breast, which, when he sat, parted at the knees. His hairy legs were bare. He wore high tops on his feet. White sports socks with red stripes bagged around his ankles.

"I wanted to be comfortable," he explained.

"Well, pull it together, man, you're flashing us all." Fanny waved her little fingers at him. He pulled at the fabric, then stuck a toothpick in his mouth and sucked.

Grady had been poised on the arm of a large chair, waiting patiently. Now he patted Ida's hand and stood. He cleared his throat.

"Together again," he said. We all nodded and looked at each other. Ted leaned back on the couch with his arm around me. Fanny was on his left, Ida in the big chair near the fireplace.

Grady walked to the fireplace mantel and leaned against it. His face was in shadow, but the glow of the fire reflected off the windows and flickered in his eyes. He looked at us all in turn.

"I've spent all evening trying to figure out what it was that looked so out of place when I saw Otis's dead body. It took me a while to remember, but now I know what it was."

We held our collective breaths.

"Honey, remember that time when our power went out? We didn't have any hot water, and I had to shower at the athletic center?"

Ida shrugged. She sat in the large chair, her hands between her knees.

"Yes, I did. And so did Otis. His power was out, too. We showered together."

"Please, Grade," Bob closed his eyes and put his hands up. "Don't ask, don't tell."

"I mean, we were in the showers at the same time."

"I thought you told me Otis was married." Ida looked hurt.

"Gosh darn it, we didn't share the soap or anything, we just happened to be…never mind. The thing is, I saw him naked."

"Nothing to be ashamed of," Fanny said. "I've seen a lot of nakeds in my day."

Grady started to unbutton his shirt.

"Hold on, buckaroo," Bob said.

"Wait. Just wait." Grady continued to unbutton. He pointed to a bare spot on his chest. "Otis had a tattoo. Right here."

Ida craned around to look at her husband. "I don't see it," she said.

Fanny threw an ice cube at her. The ice sailed over Ida's head and rained droplets. Ida held her hand out and looked at the ceiling.

"Otis had a tattoo on his chest. It was a picture of the Mona Lisa. Pretty good one, too. When he lifted his arms her smile got big."

"Oh my gosh!" I gasped. "The guy, the Otis in the pool, didn't have a tattoo."

"Nope. Not a one."

"What are you telling us, Grade?" Bob said.

"I'm telling you, the guy Fanny pulled out of the pool wasn't Otis."

"But it looked just like Otis," Bob argued.

"Except for the over-inflated lips and general puffiness," Fanny said.

"Like a blowfish," Ida added.

"Those were Otis's swim trunks. I'd know them anywhere," Grady said. That got a few raised eyebrows. "Don't forget the job committee assigned him to towel duty. He was at the pool all the time."

I looked at Ted, who had been listening quietly throughout the entire exchange. Finally he chimed in, "He could have had it removed," he said casually.

That dampened our enthusiasm a bit.

"He could have had the tattoo surgically removed. Happens all the time."

The gang looked like a bunch of kids who'd just been informed recess was cancelled.

"But we don't know that," Fanny said, looking around the room, trying to get the energy going again.

"Yeah. We don't know that," Bob echoed.

"There is one way to find out," Ted said.

"How's that, honey?"

"Anyone up for a trip to the funeral home?"

That's when my head began to throb.

"Oh, that reminds me." Ida jumped to her feet. "I have a batch of pecan sandies downstairs. Just made them today. I'll get them." Ida hustled off down the stairs.

IT WAS DECIDED that Ted would go to the funeral home with Fanny. They would knock on the door and request a private viewing of the body. If no one answered the door, they would sneak in. Ted explained there would be scarring if Otis had his tattoo removed. But what if there was no scarring? I was having a hard time getting my mind around the meaning of that.

Ted would go because he had credentials. If they were discovered after the break in, he would explain he was Fanny's physician. Fanny was a relative who wanted to pay her last respects, and, because she had a heart condition, the funeral would be more than she could handle. Ted was there to revive her if she keeled over.

"I don't know, Ted. This is all so chancy," I said. I could feel my brow furrowing. That didn't help my headache.

"Chancy, schmansy. We've got to get in there! This case is getting colder by the day." Fanny paced.

"And so is Otis," Bob said. He pulled his toothpick out and examined it.

"We've only got one shot at this," Ted was saying. I looked at him in surprise. He was certainly getting into this.

"If they bury him tomorrow we've blown our opportunity. I say we go now. If it isn't Otis, then we go to the police."

I didn't like this at all. Not one bit. There was a killer out there, and we were taking huge risks. What if the killer was watching us? What if we were followed to the funeral home? Surely, there must be another way.

"Pecan Sandie?" Ida suddenly appeared by my elbow.

My heart jumped.

I took one of Ida's cookies, held it in my hand and wondered if rat poison could be absorbed through the skin. Ida still hadn't gotten new glasses, and her recipes tended to get a little jumbled. Bob didn't seem to mind, though. He waved her over and scraped a handful into the lap of his silk robe. Ida looked delighted. I deposited my sandie under the couch cushion.

"Umm. That was delicious, Ida." I wiped the back of my hand over my mouth.

"Now you just hold on while I get the tea," and the conversation resumed.

Fanny stroked her chin. "My neighbor has emphysema. Has one of them oxygen tanks with her all the time. I'll ask if I can borrow it, just for effect."

"I don't think that's such a good idea," I said. I envisioned Fanny yanking the plastic tubing out of the nose of her air-sucking friend. *For the mission, May Bell, for the mission.*

"No, that won't be necessary," Ted agreed, thank goodness. "But if you know anyone with a seeing-eye dog…"

"Ted!" This was all getting insane. My temples were pulsing.

Fanny glared at me. "You got any better ideas?"

I sighed and scratched my forehead. "I guess not."

They were right, of course; Ted needed to get a look at Otis's chest. If we waited, Otis, or whoever he was, would be buried, and any hope of learning the true identity of the corpse would be lost.

"You know what I'm wondering?" Bob sputtered crumbs. "If that ain't Otis, then who is it?"

"It sure looked like Otis," Grady said.

"Only one way to find out." Ted held out his hand. Fanny offered her elbow and my assertive husband hooked his arm through hers.

Oh, Lawdy.

Ida was on her way up the stairs with a silver tea set as we headed down. We nearly collided. It was so close that the tea set to rattle around on the tray. Grady took it from her and said, "Thanks dear, everything was so delicious."

Ida smiled. "I'm so glad you enjoyed everything. How was the tea?"

THIRTEEN

THE FUNERAL HOME was dark and foreboding. Grady pulled the Suburban to a stop by the front doors and we sat, looking at the building without saying a word. Finally, I broke the silence.

"What are we going to do now?" I whispered. "It's all locked up!"

"Good," Ted said. "We won't have to explain anything to the caretakers."

"But how are you going to get in?" My headache was building.

"Wait here," Fanny ordered, as she jumped out of the Suburban and scurried off around the side of the building. She crouched low in the shadows, hanging close to the hedges, looking left and right. A cool evening breeze scattered leaves and sent Fanny's skirt whipping around her thin legs.

"Now what?" Grady said. The street was quiet, but we didn't want to be seen idling in front of the funeral home. We needed to get Ted and Fanny inside the building and hide the Suburban.

"I'll take a look at the lock. Grady, do you have a crowbar?" Ted jumped out without waiting for an answer, all action. Since the interior lights were now blazing, anyone could have seen us if they'd driven by. I waved at Ted to get going. What did he want with a crowbar? Grady pointed over his shoulder and Ted pulled open the back doors. They creaked.

"Shhhh," Ida said.

"You can't break the door down," I said, my anxiety growing.

"This isn't for the door." Ted lifted the crowbar and ran his hand along the thick metal. He didn't explain, just slammed the doors closed and jogged up the steps to the front of the funeral home.

"Shhh," Ida said.

"We'd better move this tank," Bob said.

Grady nodded and pulled away from the curb, slowly. As we drove past the side of the building, I saw the shadowed image of Fanny hanging through an open window. Her feet rapidly scissored, and she was up and over the ledge. She was in.

"Spry old gal," Bob said.

"She can open the front door from the inside," Grady said. "We'll circle the block for ten minutes or so. That should be plenty of time. Any longer than that and someone might notice."

Ten minutes? It may as well have been ten hours. We drove around and around, and each time we went past the funeral home I wanted to stop and shout, "Get out of there!" But we didn't see a thing until thirty minutes—and a quarter tank of gas—later.

"There they are!"

Out of the shadows ran Fanny and Ted, tumbling into the Suburban and falling to the floor as Grady sped away.

"Did you find anything?" I tugged at the back of Ted's shirt collar. Fanny was sitting on his head. She came to her senses, disengaged, and maneuvered around to the front seat.

"It took some doing, but we found his casket."

"Good. And the tattoo?"

Ted looked crestfallen. "The casket was sealed," he said. "Should have known that. I got the crowbar under the lid, worked at it for a long time trying not to make any marks. I might have made some headway, but we were just spending too much time."

"So, you didn't get a look at the dead guy?"

"No. I'm sorry, no, but we really tried." Ted pulled himself up and into the seat beside me.

"That's okay, Ted. I know you would have gotten it open if you could have."

"I was afraid I was going to make a mess of the thing. So I quit." Ted tossed the crowbar into the back of the Suburban where it clattered among the other tools.

"Shhh," Ida said.

Fanny was pouting. "He refused to give me the crowbar."

"She threatened to smash her way through." Ted looked at Fanny.

My headache was banging.

"Why don't we just go to the police? Tell them what we suspect and let them take a look."

Now why did I go and say that? I was met with shocked silence from the gang. Angry, shocked silence. I'd just broken a cardinal rule. We were on the case. It was up to us to solve this thing. Otherwise, what was the reason for living? No police until after we'd gathered all of the incriminating evidence. Not until we could lay down the MO, the perp, the DNA, and the smoking tattoo. But we were a far cry from anything substantial. Sheesh. I hadn't even gathered data! My little notebook was as blank as the day I'd arrived.

"Okay. I take that back," I said to the staring party. "But let's do this sensibly. What do we know about this Otis guy? What was the motive? All we have is a missing Mona Lisa, a piece of fishing line, and second-hand testimony of a late-night lover's spat."

"She's right," Fanny said.

I couldn't believe it. She was defending me for the first time that I could recall, and she watched New Detective. She had at one time been married to an L.A. detective, and, as far as I knew, still dated a forensics guy. She was the expert. We depended on her wisdom.

"Thanks," I said.

"She's right about the police—after we go to the funeral. Maybe we can get a look at the corpse there." This brought a cheer from the gang, a lot of high-fives, and they started chattering away.

So much for stealthy detective work. My head was ready to explode.

GRADY DROPPED US at the entrance to my cabana. The funeral was scheduled for ten o'clock the next morning.

As Ted and I walked up the short walk to the front door, a train rumbled past moving along slowly in the distance. Why was it going so slowly? Was there someone watching us that very minute? Even the little brook seemed to have grown quieter, stealthier. The cicadas weren't talking at all.

My hands shook as I fumbled with the keys. I couldn't get them in the darned hole and poked a few more times before Ted gently took them and opened the door.

"I need an aspirin or something stronger," I said, rummaging through my purse. "Got any Percocet?"

"Percocet?"

"Valium, Percodan, Vicodin, Demerol, morphine?" I dumped my purse onto the bed. Nothing. Just junk—a comb, tissue, wallet, and an old roll of breath mints. "Oh, hell and damn. Damn it all to hell." I sat hard on the edge of the bed and sulked.

"May. You don't use those words." Ted lifted an eyebrow.

"Please don't tell the choir." I fell backward on top of my junk, arms wide.

"It'll be in the next church bulletin," Ted joked, "May List says Hell."

"I learned that from the preacher."

"Change that, May List gets Hell from the preacher."

"And all the people said?"

"Amen!" Ted smiled and I felt the tension slip, a little.

"Ted, do you think I'm backsliding?" I'd just used two words of profanity, and my moral standing was on shaky ground.

Ted slid a hand under my rear end and felt around. "Not much, but it is a little saggy."

I punched Ted right in the gut.

FOURTEEN

THE FOLLOWING MORNING Ted and I had breakfast in our kitchen. Conversation was polite and without much substance—an attempt to keep the mood light. The task ahead loomed dark and sinister. We would be meeting the rest of the gang for Otis's funeral in a few hours. How were we going to get a look at the body? The casket had been sealed, which meant we weren't going to have the privilege of a public viewing.

Last night I was happy to get Ted out of the funeral home unscathed, but now I lamented his failure to jimmy the casket lid. He'd pried and pushed, he said, but it was a good quality casket. Good and heavy, solid wood. It seemed Mrs. Culpepper had spared no expense.

That was strange.

"Ted, didn't Mrs. Culpepper have to identify the corpse?"

"Someone had to." Ted slathered a croissant with peanut butter.

"Then it must have been Otis." I felt sick. We were chasing windmills again. "Surely his own wife would have been able to tell if it wasn't."

"Good point." Ted bit down on his croissant. "Oh shucks," he lisped. "I've done it again." Ted opened his mouth. The croissant was stuck.

I reached across the table, poked at it with my fork, and the bread fell in his lap.

"Thanks."

Yes. Good point. I felt a surge of bravado. "All the more reason to get a look at his chest. If there is no scarring this makes things really interesting."

An abrupt knock sounded at the patio doors. Four shadowy images stood behind the curtains.

I threw the door open and waved everyone inside. I was excited to share my epiphany about Mrs. Culpepper.

Bob listened while taking inventory of the refrigerator. Fanny leaned on her walker. Ida clutched her bosom. Grady stood behind his bride and ran his hands up and down her arms.

"Good work, May, but we've been discussing that already this morning." It was just like Fanny to burst my bubble. She reached inside her bag and pulled out binoculars. She shuffled over to the windows and set up surveillance behind the curtains.

"Of course," I said, not wanting to appear disappointed that I hadn't been the first to think of the widow's identification mistake.

"We won't really know where this will take us until after the funeral," Grady said. Leave it to Grady to be practical. "Let's not jump to any conclusions until after that."

Jump to any conclusions? That's all we'd done!

"Look," I said, sounding really strong and powerful. "Everybody take a seat for a minute. We need to talk about Otis. We all made the mistake of thinking this guy in the pool was Otis. At first."

"Who wouldn't? He was a dead ringer," Bob said.

"And for all we know, it was Otis. We haven't gotten that straightened out yet. After all, Otis is still missing."

"Officially, he's dead," Fanny said. "Looked like Otis."

"So do you think maybe whoever killed him thought the same thing? Who would have wanted him dead, and why? Just throw everything out there, and I'll put it down."

I grabbed my purse. My notebook was there, empty except for the few notations I'd made on the plane. I flipped to a fresh sheet, put my pencil to my tongue and waited.

Before long I was scribbling away. Otis was somewhat of a scoundrel, after all. He spent a great deal of time at the Sunken Balls Pool Hall, hustling newcomers out of their wages. He couldn't resist a challenge and would bet on just about anything. Apparently, he owed a few people around town some hefty change, and he'd made a lot of enemies.

"He had his good days and his bad days," Grady explained. "He'd win big, and then just as quickly turn around and blow it. He wasn't always good about paying off his debts, but he managed to keep most of the guys at arm's length."

"He could have tangled with the wrong fella," Ted said. "Motive enough to snuff him."

Snuff him? Had Ted been talking to Fanny?

"Nah." Fanny emerged from behind the curtains. Her glasses hung around her neck by a gold chain. "They wouldn't want to snuff their cash cow. Break his knee caps, sure, rough him up, but they wouldn't want him dead." She shoved the binoculars in her bag. "You always look at the ones closest to the victim. Start with the family. Don't forget he had a girlfriend. I say take a good hard look at the little wifey."

"Motive?" I scribbled.

"She's pissed!" Fanny said.

"Let's not forget," Ted said, bringing us back on track. "That dead guy might not even be Otis. And if he's not, then where's Otis?"

"Maybe, just maybe, it was a message to Otis from the bad guys. You're next, the killers were saying, so Otis takes the hint and skips town."

"An Otis look-alike?" Ted asked and shook his head. "I don't know."

My scribbling stopped. We mulled this over silently.

"Anybody want an omelet?" Bob reached under the counter for a skillet.

"I have an idea." It was Ida.

She'd been so quiet that I'd almost forgotten she was there. I was preparing for something ludicrous.

"Why don't we just go to the morgue? The autopsy report would have a record of identifying marks on the body. We could just read the report and know if it was Otis or not."

It was brilliant. Brilliant!

We were all stunned.

Fanny grabbed the notebook from my hands and wrote in large block letters:

IDA HAS A LUCID MOMENT.

I frowned at her.

"I'll go." Ted quickly grabbed his lab coat from the closet and answered my confused look. "I brought it just in case."

"You go, I go." I grabbed my purse.

"We'll stay here and work on that motive thing." Bob was cracking eggs into the skillet. "Got any green peppers?"

Grady reached in his pocket for his keys and tossed them to Ted.

"Come on, May." Ted palmed the keys and headed for the parking lot.

NEITHER TED NOR I knew which direction to take. The morgue wasn't on my list of favorite tourist haunts, and it wasn't on the city map of must-see places, either. I caught sight of a Starbucks and lusted for a Frappuccino, but that went by without even a pause. Too bad. I could have used a shot of liquid courage.

"Which way?" Ted said, while navigating a small alley. The Suburban was practically leaving paint on the sides of two brick buildings, but he seemed to know what he was doing, so I let it go.

"Just keep driving. I'll look." I clutched the dashboard as we sped out onto the road, barely missing a teenager on a moped. He shook a fist. I mouthed an apology, as if it were my fault.

"Was Otis bloated when you brought him out of the pool?"

"Yes."

"Were his eyes open or closed?"

"Open."

"Was he gray or bluish?"

"Gray I think. Why?"

"Just making conversation."

Ted hammered the steering wheel and turned down another alley. We tapped a metal trashcan and scattered its contents. I ducked my head waiting for an angry civilian to write down our license plate number.

"Slow down, Ted. You're going way too fast." Starbucks again, we were going in circles.

"Where's the dadgum morgue?" Ted was flushed. His jaws pulsed. He looked left and right, but I didn't dare suggest we stop for directions. It would have been a breach of male ethics.

We shot down main street, got caught in a line of traffic going well below the speed limit. Ted groaned in frustration.

I perked up.

"Ted, we're in a funeral procession."

"What?" Ted was veering back and forth, looking for a way around the car in front of us.

"See? There's a police car up front stopping traffic. Don't you think the lead car looks a bit funny?"

"Well, I'll be. It's a hearse, all right. What are the odds?" Ted hit the steering wheel with an open palm and accidentally blasted the horn.

The people in the car in front of us stared at us with expressions of shocked surprise.

I waved.

My worry was mounting. Instead of looking disappointed, Ted acted as if he'd just found a pot of gold, or won the lottery, or matched all of his socks. Could it be?

"Otis," Ted said, answering my question.

"They must have changed the time! We're too late," I was clearly disappointed, or maybe I was relieved. "We'll need to turn around. Even if that report proves anything, Otis will be in the ground before we can show the police."

"Maybe not." Ted looked at me and smiled. Way too happy. He lifted his foot off the accelerator and fell in line.

"We're not going to his funeral like this, Ted? We've got to go to the morgue, don't we?"

"You did know him, didn't you?"

"No. I might have met him last year, but I can't remember."

"It wouldn't be odd for you to pay your last respects."

"I guess not." Oh, brother. What did Ted have going on in that brain of his?

We puttered past Jacob's Java, another up and coming coffee drive-through. I gave Ted a hopeful smile, but he bent over the steering wheel. "Not now, May Bell, don't want to lose my place in line."

"What exactly are you hoping to accomplish by going to Otis's funeral? You said the casket was sealed."

I was really getting nervous now. Maybe the killer would be at the funeral. Maybe that's what Ted was hoping for. I was possessed with boiling fear. I needed to make a point, to keep Ted from doing something he might regret later. I unhooked my seat belt and crawled to the back of the Suburban. I reached over into the back and came up with the crowbar.

"Are you going to smash through the casket?" I was practically screaming.

"Keep that down. Someone might see you."

"Gosh. Someone might see me. Wouldn't that be horrible?" I really wanted an espresso. I was getting punchy again, so little sleep, so many questions, and there hadn't even been enough time to enjoy night swim. Besides everything, I had ridiculous hair. What next? Irritable bowel?

"Please, May, come back up here. I won't do anything crazy, I promise."

I reluctantly dropped the crowbar, took my place back in the passenger seat, and hooked up again. I was pouting.

Ted grew somber. We were slowly pulling into a gravel parking area. Members of the Waning Years Estates were tumbling out of their cars. Some I recognized, some I'd never seen before.

"Well, here we are," I said, taking a deep cleansing breath. Ted turned the key and the Suburban ticked as it cooled.

A creeping sensation ran up my legs. I looked at Ted, feeling squirmy and nervous again.

Darn. I sure hoped Jacobs's Java was still open on the way back.

I TOOK TED'S ARM, and we joined the mourners. I certainly wasn't dressed for a funeral. The cheery gigantic flowers on my pink skirt attracted reproachful glares from my sister seniors. Ted's bare legs under his short white lab coat didn't get equal treatment. Apparently, if you were toned at the age of seventy-two, you were forgiven.

People were crowding around a big hole in the ground, heads bowed, hands folded in solemn reverence.

I spotted Joyce across the lawn, and she wiggled her fingers at me timidly. Probably expected me to shake my fist and point at my hair. Being brought up proper, I smiled and waved, and that seemed to brighten her day, although it didn't look like she needed much help in that area. The sunlight reflected by the green sequins and beads covering her dress almost blinded me—glitter, glitter, sparkle sparkle. Ouch. How in the world could she stand up with all that weight?

Ted bent down and took the hand of a withered, wrinkled man in a wheelchair. "So sorry about Otis," Ted said.

"Otis? Otis who?" The man looked bewildered. "Isn't this Patrick Monahan's funeral?" The man glanced around, and then noticing his blunder, cursed loudly enough to garner some gasps and a lot of tongue clucking. He clutched his wheels and rolled off, shouting expletives to everyone within earshot.

A young gentleman in a white collar and robes stepped up beside Ted. "He's been to every funeral this week, poor soul. Keeps looking for Patrick Monahan. As I recall, we buried him in '92." The man clutched his Bible and floated off.

"This is it." Ted pointed toward the hearse. "They're bringing him out now."

From the back of a long hearse came a coffin, sleek and shiny. Several members of the Waning Years Estates were positioned on either side. They looked grim.

"That casket looks awfully heavy," I said quietly, watching the guys heft the box up onto their shoulders.

"Maybe they should have found some younger guys to help with that thing," Ted whispered into my ear.

The men moved in lock step toward the hole.

"Ted, that guy's knees just buckled. Look how his legs are shaking," I said out of the corner of my mouth.

"Do you think I should go help?"

"You want a hernia?"

"It's for the mission, remember."

"I think that second guy just slipped a disk, Ted. He's all bent over grabbing at his back."

"The first guy's legs are really shaking now. Think I should help?"

"Wait," I said. "They've cleared the back of the hearse, just a few more steps and…oh boy, they're not moving very fast, are they?"

"The guy in back is really struggling. His face is turning purple. Think I should give a hand?" Ted took a step forward.

"Hang on." I clutched Ted's sleeve. "I think they've got it…oh, oh my, no, oh my God, Ted, have you ever seen that before?"

The guys in back had held up pretty well, but the two at the head of Otis's casket took some quick baby steps and then collapsed just short of the burial site. The head end of the coffin struck the ground, and its lid popped open. The guys in back were in a forward momentum. They were determined to push the rest of the way to the hole, but only hefted the back of the heavy box high into the air. The satin lining was slippery, and Otis was on the move.

"Dead man walkin'!" Ted proclaimed.

I NEVER HEARD SO MUCH screaming since the premier of *Carrie*. Gray hairs backpedaled and tumbled over one another. Legs tangled. Arms flailed. Even the young priest was crossing himself.

Joyce swooned. On her way to the ground the back of her dress caught on a tree branch. The ripping sound of fabric was slow and long, and lowered her down gently, glittering all the way.

"Move aside, folks." Ted took charge. "Nothing to worry about. You can put that down, now."

The men at the back of the casket seemed to quiver under its weight, not sure what to do. At Ted's order they looked relieved and dropped their end. Luckily the men in front had the foresight to roll away.

Otis hadn't made a total escape; he was still encased from the waist down. I'd seen the position before, I think it was called a backbend, or a bridge, some gymnastic term. I thought dead people were stiff after a while. Apparently, Otis had passed over into the pliable stage. He looked relaxed, smiling up at the clouds.

Ted bent over the arched Otis and palpated him swiftly. The crowd of mourners took tentative steps forward to stare, compelled I suppose, by macabre curiosity.

"What is he doing?" A chubby, squat woman turned to ask a man with the face of a hound dog—all jowls, waddles, and thick lips. He leaned over his cane and shrugged his shoulders.

"Just making sure he's dead," Ted explained. He thrust his hand under Otis's starched collar. This drew a whole host of shocked exclamations. Joyce had come around and sat on her shredded skirt and began sobbing loudly into a wad of tissues. I wished Fanny were there to give the woman a smack in the back of her head. After what she'd done to my hair, it would serve her right.

"Yup, he's dead." Ted stood and motioned for some helping hands to shove Otis back into his box.

WHEN THE CHORE was done, I handed out moist towelettes from my purse, and made it through the funeral, but my mind was elsewhere.

"May Bell?" Ted was nudging me. "It's time to go."

I allowed Ted to lead me back to the Suburban. "Well?" I asked, once I'd adjusted my seat belt.

"I found what I was looking for." Ted turned the key.

"What did you find, Ted?" I started digging for more moist towelettes.

"Just what I thought I'd find." Ted shoved the lever into reverse. "Exactly what I expected. And something else, something that told me Mrs. Culpepper could not have murdered her husband."

FIFTEEN

AFTER THE FUNERAL, Ted was once again driving like a mad man. We approached a railroad crossing as the arms came down. Red lights flashed a warning, and I could hear the long pull of the engine's whistle, but Ted didn't appear fazed. Instead, he punched the accelerator and rapidly serpentined through the barricades. I felt my pink hairs go white. His shoulders were up around his ears; his eyes stared intently through the windshield.

"What is it, Ted? What did you find?" I planted my feet on the dashboard and clung to the Suburban's panic loop up by my ear.

"Can't explain yet. Got to get to the morgue." Ted set his jaw, rolled down his window and pumped his fist at a slow-moving manure truck.

"Ted, we just passed that guy on the shoulder." I gripped my loop with both hands.

"So?" Ted growled. "He shouldn't be driving that stuff through town."

"Oh, there's Jacob's Java." I pulled my feet down, and looked longingly. Ted rolled his eyes, but he bent to my wishes and took a hard left. My feet flew up sideways, coming even with his jaw.

Ted steamed up to the window, and I screamed for a twenty-ounce Granita. I'd have made it a fifty-ouncer, but they didn't have those anymore, so I settled for what I could get.

Ted was so impatient waiting for me to get my coffee that the minute I had it in my hands, he was burning rubber. I had to throw the tip change at the window and heard a few coins hit pavement in the wake of our screeching tires.

"Why are you going so fast, Ted?"

"If my guess is right, we might have just enough time to grab that autopsy report before they file it away for good." Ted swerved around a school crossing guard. She took her flag in both hands and swung at the back of the Suburban. A solid hit.

"You're gonna pay for that," I reprimanded.

"See any cops around?" Ted pressed his foot on the gas.

"Slow down, Ted!" The front right tire bounced over a pot-hole. My teeth clacked together.

"See any cops?" Ted repeated. He pressed harder.

"No, but if we get stopped, don't worry, I'll just flash 'em. That should get us out of trouble." Ted was kind enough not to make note of the fact that I wasn't perky anymore. I had visions of Ted pulling over, the steel-toed cop approaching the driver's side, and me tossing off my shirt before leaning over to ask, "What's the matter, officer?" The guy most likely would shout, *"Lady! Egad, have you no shame? Have you no pity for this heterosexual, red-blooded man? What are you trying to do to me?"*

Ho-hum. I sure hoped we didn't get pulled over.

Ted bent farther over the wheel. I could see it coming. A green light in the distance, and we were doing about fifty-five in a thirty, but we had a clear path. Yellow light, now doing sixty. I braced, closed my eyes, and said a Hail Mary, (although I wasn't quite sure what that was, being a Baptist). We shot through the red doing about seventy. I'm guessing here, since my eyes were clamped shut, but by the sounds of the horns and the brake noises from the cars around us, it's what I figured.

"Made it!" Ted exclaimed.

"You're insane!"

"Not yet."

"What do you mean by that?" I opened my eyes. Ted hadn't moved from his take-the-hill position.

"Let's get everyone together. Then I'll explain." Ted reached for his waistband and pulled off his cell phone like he was drawing a gun. "Here. Quick. Call everyone." He threw the phone at me. I wasn't ready, so it shot out my window.

"Great. Now we're really going to need to hurry." Ted floored it. "Where the heck is the morgue?"

I closed my eyes again. I didn't even open them when we passed something on the right and rumbled over the little corrugated shoulder bumps.

THE GUYS AT the morgue were solicitous to the visiting Dr. List. They didn't even bat an eyelash when he requested a copy of the autopsy report. Afterward, we got everyone sequestered into the Waning Years Lounge without much trouble. Fanny was on the golf course when we summoned her, but seeing the Suburban parked over the eighth hole must have given her a clue that something was up. Still, she was pretty angry when she took her place at the round table.

Bob got some glasses, cheese fish crackers and the beers, Fanny fussed with her cloth bag, Grady yawned, and Ida's red hair glowed in the candlelight.

"Heard about your little incident with Otis today." Bob was back. "Sorry I missed the show." He read my surprise. "Joyce asked for a private yoga lesson. She needed some calming down."

"How did she do that? We got back here as fast as we could." Visions of the irate crossing guard were still fresh in my mind.

"Phone consult," Bob said.

I didn't have any idea what that meant, so I let it go and directed my attention to my husband while Bob poured the drinks.

Ted took some papers from his lab coat and opened them up. He laid them flat on the table. He still hadn't explained what he'd found at the funeral because he'd said he wanted to wait until we were all together. What he said confirmed our theory.

"This is Otis." Ted pointed to a pencil sketch of a nude body.

"Yep, looks like him," Grady said, in deep concentration. "All except for the tattoo."

"And this isn't Otis," Ted said.

"Right," Ida said, pointing at the paper with its penciled sketch. "Too small. Too flat."

"It says Otis Culpepper here on the form, but it's definitely not him. See? No tattoo, no mention of scarring, and I didn't find anything on him at the funeral."

"Okay, we've got that settled," Bob said. "Anyone want pretzels?"

"How does that prove his wife didn't kill this, this, whoever he is?" I asked.

"May," Ted said, "think back to the funeral. I know there was a lot of confusion, and everything, but think about the grieving widow. Was there anything unusual about her?"

I closed my eyes. I could see Joyce weeping into her tissue. I saw the priest with his ever-loving hands fingering his rosary, and I saw the men with their rifles. Otis had been a vet, got a military funeral and wasn't the flag so lovely? The 21-gun salute dropped a few of his post-traumatized vet buddies to their bellies, but I couldn't think of anything so strange about the wife. She had acted appropriately, had looked sad while she took the carefully folded flag as she sat there in her electric wheel chair...

"Well, she was in one of those motorized chair things," I said.

"Right. Any idea why?"

"Best parking places," Fanny said, hefting her walker.

"May, what kind of shoes was Mrs. Culpepper wearing?"

"Oh!" I gasped and covered my mouth with both hands.

"Exactly," Ted exclaimed.

"Exactly what?" Fanny insisted.

"She didn't have any legs," I peeped. "And that's why she couldn't have killed her husband, or the Otis impersonator. She couldn't have gotten him into the pool. That also means she must have known that the dead guy wasn't Otis, or she would have noticed the missing tattoo."

"If I have anything to say about it she's not going to get away with whatever she's doing," Fanny said.

"She doesn't have a leg to stand on," Bob muttered.

"Wonder what happened to the old gal," Grady mused.

"Maybe Otis lost her legs in the war?" Ida was trying to be helpful.

"Well, he definitely drowned." Ted lifted the autopsy report and held it near the candlelight. A little too close. Ted got three glasses of near-beer thrown on him before noticing the paper had caught fire. He calmly patted out the flames, and continued to explain. "They found water in his lungs, and the chem analysis is consistent with what's used in the pool."

Fanny banged on the table with the meat of her fists. "Doesn't nobody but me think it's strange that the real Otis hasn't shown his face? Does that make anyone a little curious? And what about the fishing line? What about that? We still need to get a look at that tackle box, and then I say we give the widow a full interrogation. A few hot lights and some glue guns, and I say she cracks in under five hours. Any takers?"

"Hold on, Fanny. We need to think this through." Grady reached across the table to take her hand. She slapped his away.

"Maybe Mrs. Culpepper thought that was Otis. I mean, it looks an awful lot like him, she might have been confused," I said.

"Sometimes it happens," Ida said.

"And pigs will fly out of my…"

"Fanny!"

"Do you get that, too?" Ida asked.

"Hey, Ted." I turned to my husband. "Did they take fingerprints? I mean, is that a common thing during an autopsy?"

"Probably not in this case since the body was identified. No real reason to take fingerprints." Just in case, Ted looked through the singed papers.

Nope.

"That would have been one way to prove who's in Otis's grave. If we've made a mistake and it really is Otis, there would be records since he was in the military. Too bad we can't check that way." I leaned back in my chair and chewed on some cheese fish.

"Wait a gosh darn minute." Bob swallowed hard. There was a gleam in his eye and I didn't like it. "It's just a coupla miles to the cemetery. The ground is still soft, and if we all pitch in…"

I can't explain the feeling I had then, but it was something like being hot and cold at the same time, all jiggly and rubbery around the mouth.

"Yes," Fanny said, leaning forward on her elbows. "Yes, yes, yes! But we should do it after dark. I've got some shovels, and it just so happens I've got some ink kits. Keep them around just in case."

"What are you saying?" I was horrified at the implication.

Fanny took the sides of my face in her knobby fingers. She pulled me close, and then touched her forehead to mine. "What we're saying my friend, is this—tonight we're digging up Otis!"

SIXTEEN

IT WAS SETTLED. We were going after the smelly corpse of a man buried under the name of Otis Culpepper. All for a set of fingerprints in order to set the record straight, and to possibly point out foul play. You just didn't get drama any higher than that.

But we had the day ahead of us. It wouldn't be dark for several hours and we still had a tackle box to inspect and leads to follow. Fanny wanted to spend the afternoon on the golf course and then have a chat with the girlfriend. The boys were going to check out the Sunken Balls. That left Ida and me to visit the grieving widow.

The boys took the Suburban.

Fanny drove away, a puff of blue hair, gnarly fingers and big eyes barely cresting the top of the steering wheel in her long, pink Cadillac.

I took Ida's arm, and we moved off in the direction of the Culpepper apartment. Ida had changed into a soft peach-colored dress, which didn't go very well with the red hair, but it was nice, and she carried a basket of fruit. I watched the cracks go by on the sidewalk thinking my choice of skirts was definitely a poor one.

We smiled and waved at passersby. Each apartment building had a nicely manicured lawn, hedges were flowering, and shade trees kept the sun off.

"What are we going to say when we get there?" Ida whispered to me.

"I really don't know," I admitted. My job was to get some of that fishing line, but that meant I would either have to go searching for the damnable tackle box or come right out and ask for it. That would raise some suspicions. I started getting moist in the pits then and gripped Ida's arm tighter.

"You just get her talking," I said to Ida. She was good at that, and I wasn't too worried about her doing anything to give me away. "I'll think of something."

We got to the Culpepper apartment soon enough. The sidewalk looked very long. We took slow steps forward. I could see Mrs. Culpepper's door at the end of the walk, but it felt like my feet were sinking in cement.

"Your feet are sinking in cement," Ida said from the lawn.

I looked down. Oh darn. A man was bent over by my feet. He had a trowel in his hand, smoothing out the last of his newly placed sidewalk, and I'd just walked through it. The man cried out and shook his fist at me.

"Missed a spot," I said curtly.

I walked stiffly on the grass the rest of the way to Mrs. Culpepper's door. She answered as if she'd been expecting us.

Her motorized chair filled the doorway. Mrs. Culpepper was slender, looked to be about seventy-five years old with close-cropped brown hair, steely blue eyes and enough face wrinkles to lose count. She had a sharp nose and no visible lips at all. Her knees, or what should have been her knees, were pointing at us like accusing sausages.

"Oh, dear." Ida jumped to her aid. "You must be cold. Let me help you." Ida pulled at a lap blanket and swiftly covered the woman's stumps.

Ooooeee. I thought. Thank you, Ida.

"What do you want?" barked Mrs. Culpepper.

Not what I expected from the grieving widow. This woman looked like she wanted to slam the door in our faces.

Ida held out her basket. "Fruit?"

Mrs. Culpepper eyed the basket in Ida's outstretched arms and fingered a banana. I gave Mrs. Culpepper the once-over. I was looking for a shift in the eyes, a tic or a glance over her shoulder. She did none of these. Solid as a rock.

"Got any papaya? I like them papaya fruits," she said.

Ida rummaged and came up with a kiwi. "Is this close enough?"

The guy behind me had his trowel going and mumbled along the sidewalk smoothing and smacking down the gray matter. I thought my own gray matter was taking its share of smacking with all of this detective business. Mrs. Culpepper hadn't cleared the way to her apartment yet, but the gang would be really disappointed if we didn't at least try to find a way in.

A voice from inside saved the day. "Ida? Is that you?" Jill came up behind Mrs. Culpepper and squealed her delight when she saw us there in the door. Mrs. Culpepper didn't flinch. She was turning the kiwi over in her hands.

Jill and Ida embraced awkwardly over the head of Mrs. Culpepper. Ida took a deliberately planted banana in the solar plexus and grunted.

"Puleeeaase," Mrs. Culpepper said. She struggled out from under the hugs and pushed a little stick by her right hand. The motorized chair did a one-eighty. "Come on in and join the festivities."

I started to follow the chair into the living room, looked at my soiled shoes and kicked them off onto the porch. Ida did the same, although her shoes were just fine.

When Ida and I entered the Culpepper condo, three women sat around the kitchen table sipping tea. It was the official Otis mourning party. Jill poured the tea for two more, Betty slumped in a chair plucking white lint balls from her sweater, and Joyce rested her elbows on the table with a cup of tea between her hands. She was in her work apron and an overflowing cosmetics basket sat on the floor beside her feet. She looked up as we entered. Her smile disappeared when she saw Ida's hair. First she paled, then she looked confused, and then she turned a shade of red just short of Ida's flaming locks.

"Did I do that?" She spoke into her cup of tea. "I can't remember. It could be a chemical reaction. What could have gone wrong?"

Mrs. Culpepper pointed to a chair, and I slid in beside Joyce.

I whispered to her, "Don't worry. It was self-inflicted." Joyce gave me a look of gratitude.

"Fruit?" Ida set the basket in the middle of the table and sat beside Jill. "That's a beautiful sweater, Betty, what is it, cashmere?"

"Siamese," Betty said. Pluck, pluck.

I nodded knowingly, wondering how Trixie would like a shave with a straight razor. I smiled at the thought.

The sound of Mrs. Culpepper's chair faded. She was on the move. Joyce watched her back, and then when the widow was out of earshot she clutched my arm. "The poor woman is beside herself. She is so distraught! So devastated!" Spittle flew.

"And who wouldn't be?" Ida sympathized. "You just can't get papayas this time of year."

Betty stopped her plucking. She lifted an eyebrow, scanned Ida's face for a split second, and then resumed her activities. There was a ball of lint on the table in front of her the size of a skein of yarn. Pretty soon she'd have enough for a second sweater.

I sipped my tea. Hot. I touched my bottom lip to see if the skin was sloughing off. No harm done this time, but just the same I let the tea cool before going for a full exfoliation.

Mrs. Culpepper's chair was humming away in the other room. What was she doing? Hiding evidence? That made me edgy. What if I just sat there while the old woman stashed or shredded or ingested critical clues? It certainly would not bode well for the case.

Standing quickly, I said, "Excuse me ladies. My lunch didn't sit well." I screwed up my face and clutched my abdomen. "No, don't get up. I'll just ask Mrs. Culpepper if I can borrow her bathroom." I made a dash toward the sound of the chair.

The widow's back was to me when I found her in the den. Her head was bent over something. She didn't hear me come in. Her elbows were out, skinny, pointy elbows jutting and moving. I couldn't see her hands, but the way those elbows were bobbing she was doing something—and she was in a hurry.

I crept forward. I was breathing fast, my heart was tripping along, and I had the words prepared.

"Okay, lady, the gig is up," I said in a low, stern voice.

"Huh?" Mrs. Culpepper wheeled around. In her lap she held a long orange and black afghan. The crochet needle was in her left hand; the little chair handle was in her right.

"Oh, that's beautiful." I stammered. "Did it take long?" I glanced around the room. Nothing suspicious, nothing out of order. On a nearby piano, I saw the face of Otis smiling at me from inside a picture frame. So sad.

"I've been so restless since Otis disappeared," Mrs. Culpepper said. "I just had to do something." She tucked the afghan around her thighs. There were tears in her eyes, and I wanted to kick myself. I would have let the widow do it for me, but well, never mind.

Since Otis disappeared. She didn't say since Otis died. Hmmm.

I came over to the woman and took her hands in mine. "We're here now, Mrs. Culpepper. You have a lot of friends. We'll help you through this."

Oh, what a horrible woman I was. Even as I consoled the distraught widow, I was sizing her up. Could she have been so confused as to think the man in the grave was her husband? No, she had said *since Otis disappeared.* Something was definitely all a-kilter.

"Please call me Grace. I'm afraid I'm not a very good hostess right now. I'm just not all here."

I really had to struggle to maintain my composure after that comment. I bit my scalded lip, stared at the ceiling, pinched my navel and thought of yelling, *"Sanctuary! Sanctuary!"* Horrible woman, I was.

"Well, you just rest and let us help you. You'll be back on your feet in no time." I wanted to shriek. What had I said?

Grace let the comment pass without batting a lash. "I'm not going to stay here, there are just too many memories. I'm moving away."

"Oh?" I tried to act impassive, but this did put a wrinkle in things. "Aren't you being a little hasty? Shouldn't you hold off a few days?" Wait 'til I told the gang our Gracey bird was getting ready to fly the coop. I hoped Grace didn't detect the sound of alarm in my questions.

"No, there's nothing left for me here. The packers are coming tomorrow."

Tomorrow! I had to gather data, and I had to gather it fast. The clock was ticking. Any evidence from this apartment would soon be on a moving truck and out of our reach.

"Yoo hoo!" Jill stuck her head through the door. "Grace, dear, Betty and I are going to take off. May Bell, it was good to see you again. Remember when we used to hunt squirrels together? Those were good days, weren't they?"

I pinched myself again. "Sure thing, Jill."

"Haiti is always nice this time of year. Well, Gracey, you just call us if you need some help with the packing tomorrow."

Grace lifted a limp hand. I shot a look at her arms. There was very little muscle tone under the gauzy skin, and it confirmed for me that she could not have hefted a man up and over the edge of a swimming pool.

Ida came up behind Jill, and they hugged each other before Jill left with Betty. "May, are you feeling better? Did you find a bathroom?" Ida's brow was creased.

"Down the hall. First door on your left," Grace gestured. She sounded tired. I played out the scenario and wandered down the hall, thinking, thinking.

Once in the bathroom, I made use of the toilet. As I sat there, I noticed an unusual smell, and this time I wasn't to blame. I finished my business, flushed, and stood there sniffing the air. What was it? I turned slowly in the bathroom, homing in on the strongest direction of the odor. The bathroom wasn't large, and it took no time for me to find the source. I pulled the shower curtain away from the bathtub and quickly put my hand over my mouth and nose. My eyes were watering. Whew!

Reminiscent of the Waning Years Sports Complex, swimming pool chemicals, chlorine and other things were drifting up into the air. I leaned over the edge of the tub and put my nose down by the drain. I reeled back. The tub was reeking of the chlorine smell.

Okay, not so unusual, I thought, a lot of people use bleach to clean out their tubs. That got my curiosity up, though, so I did something no proper lady should do. I went on a snoop. I opened the medicine cabinet and took inventory.

Muscle-Eze, hemorrhoid cream, headache pills, gas relief, vitamins, SleepNow, mascara, rouge, lipsticks of various shades, some prescription bottles with the names of Otis and Grace on the labels. Some expired. Nothing out of the ordinary. I quietly closed the mirrored door.

I knelt and pulled open the wooden cabinet doors under the sink. Super Scrubber, window cleaner, a vaporizer, heating pad, a water bottle, and a cardboard box. I pulled the box out.

"May Bell, you okay in there?" Ida was at the door. My head shot up. I'd been in the bathroom way too long after the flush.

"Oh, my stomach's not feeling too good," I sang out. I pulled the box flaps apart while making loud gagging sounds.

"Oooh, honey, we need to get you to bed!" Ida sounded close to the door.

Retch, retch. "I'm feeling better now!" I opened the box and peered inside.

"You need Pepto right away. I have some at my house." Ida sounded very worried.

"Much better!" *Gag, retch.*

Inside the box I found several white plastic jugs of various sizes. I pulled them out and read the labels. Yes! Chemicals, the industrial kinds used in swimming pools. Did it mean anything? Otis was, after all, in charge of keeping the Ph levels up to par in his duties as pool guy. Why store them in his apartment, though, and why did the bathtub reek of the stuff?

"Get it all up, honey, cleanse your system." Ida sounded like she was talking through the crack under the door.

"I'm just about finished, I think!" I closed the box up and put everything back where I'd found it.

I ran the water in the sink and remembered to flush the toilet a second time. I patted my pink hair while smiling into the mirror. At least I wouldn't go back to the gang with nothing to show for my efforts. At last I had some *data.*

When I opened the door, Ida was on her hands and knees with her cheek pasted to the floor.

"Ida, get up!" I hissed, and glanced around. Mrs. Culpepper was nowhere in sight. "Let's go. I've got something to tell you."

Grace was on the phone when we passed her in the kitchen. She was giving her address to the moving guys. We'd need to hurry.

Ida kissed Grace on one cheek, and I kissed her on the other. We said our good-byes and left quickly. With our shoes in hand, Ida and I raced back to her apartment. I didn't lick my lips until after a clean swipe with a towelette.

Once through the doors of Ida's condo, I pulled up short. Dang! I turned to my friend.

"Your stomach?" she asked, so worried.

"No! I forgot to find the tackle box. Oh, Ida, I've failed."

Ida smiled. "Is this what you wanted?" She reached into her purse and pulled out a spool of fishing line.

I gasped. "Ida?"

She blushed. "I accidentally walked into the front closet looking for the bathroom. The tackle box was right there on the floor."

I gave Ida a full squeeze. "You're incredible," I said. And I meant it.

SEVENTEEN

IDA AND I WERE alone in her condo. The men hadn't returned, and neither had Fanny. Since the guys had taken the Suburban, there wasn't much we could do until they got back.

I followed Ida out onto the back patio. My shoes were wasted, so I borrowed a pair of Ida's terry cloth slippers. A wooden privacy fence surrounded the back lawn, so we got comfortable rocking in her porch swing while mulling over my discovery.

"Ida, do you use bleach to clean your bathrooms?"

"I used to, but I kept ruining all of my good towels. Now I just use toothpaste."

"Exactly." Then I paused. Toothpaste? I shook my head. From the smell of Mrs. Culpepper's bathroom, she'd dumped a liberal amount of the pool chemicals in her tub, but I had a gut feeling they hadn't been used as cleaning agents.

I'd watched Grace carefully. She seemed bright enough, coherent, articulate, and fully in possession of all of her faculties. But she was nervous. She'd kept that chair moving, squirming under her afghan, and it was apparent she hadn't been too happy about the uninvited company. She had looked very uncomfortable. She definitely had something to hide.

I held the spool of fishing line in my hands, turning it this way and that. It didn't mean a thing to me. It had a brand name on the side, a price sticker, and some other things that didn't offer up any clues.

"Ida, there's no telling when the rest of the gang will show up. I just can't sit here doing nothing when Grace is preparing to move out tomorrow."

"Do you want to make potholders or something?" Ida asked.

"I have a better idea. Is there a sporting goods store around here? Some place where they sell this kind of stuff?" I held out the fishing line. "Maybe we could get an idea of what this was used for, what kind of fishing, and where Otis bought his gear. That might lead us to some other clues. You know, follow the trail. Sniff out his history, who he hung out with, where he went, that sort of thing."

Ida sat on the swing in her peach dress and beet-colored coiffure, smiling sweetly, listening intently. I tried to gauge if my words sparked a few neurons.

"May Bell, you don't have to bang around the bushes with me. I know what you're up to. We're not going to a fishing store to see who Otis hung out with." She sounded like a kindly aunt gently scolding her sister's daughter.

"We're not?"

What she said next nearly toppled me onto the porch floor.

Ida wrapped her velvet hands around mine and shook her head. "No, honey, it's okay. I should have thought of it myself. We're going to the store so we can buy an identical roll of fishing line. Only this one will be new and uncut. Then we're going to take it and plant it in the tackle box so's we can watch what Grace does when she sees it. We're going to shake the old gal up a little, aren't we?"

My mouth dropped. "Well, Ida, you've found me out. Yes, you're right. That was the plan all along."

Ida patted my cheek and stood. "You were always the clever one, May Bell, just wish I could think the way you do."

I took the credit without protest, only because it would have taken too long for me to explain she'd just come up with the most ingenious idea I'd heard to date, and because we didn't have that kind of time.

"Ida, do the city buses come through the estate somewhere?"

"No, but there's a shuttle service that stops in front of the laundry room. We can get a ride to the front gate and catch a bus from there. It's a wonderful service, really. It runs day and night, and it doesn't cost a thing."

ONCE WE FOUND SEATS on the shuttle, I had time to refine Ida's plan. Yes, yes, yes. We would get some fishing line, new and untouched, put it in the tackle box and find a way to draw Grace's attention to it. Then we would watch and see if she reacted. My guess was that she would be very concerned. I was quite certain she was involved in the murder, and, therefore, she knew something about the fishing line. Maybe she had even measured and cut it.

On the other hand, if it caused no reaction, then at least we could rule her out as an accomplice. Still, there was that niggling question. Who was in Otis's grave, and where the heck was Otis?

Ida thanked the shuttle driver and dug out a handmade potholder from her purse. He thanked her and said he'd put it with the others. Good old Ida.

We stood under the bus sign, watching the road. Soon the behemoth wheezed up in front of us, and its doors swung wide. Quickly the driver jumped down from his perch and offered a hand. Ida climbed the steps and then it was my turn.

When the bus driver took my hand, I was surprised to see a familiar face.

"Lance! I mean, Brad! When did you start driving a bus? Last I heard you were managing the apartments here." I motioned toward the estate.

Brad was his name, but to me, he would always be Lance. A name I'd given the young man for the skewers he still sported, although I had to admit after living in Spokane for a year, they almost looked commonplace. He still had the metal loops through his eyebrows, but had added a new one, silver and dangling. I reached up and with my middle finger gave it a thump.

"Hey, that hurts. Just got it last week, and it's still sore."

"Serves ya right. Didn't your mom ever tell you it's not natural?"

"Just you, Mrs. List. Hey, it's really great to see you. I quit my job here when I was no longer needed. The job committee nudged me out. Hey, are you here for a visit?"

"What's that?" I grabbed his jaw and pulled down. "I thought so. When did you get that thing in your tongue?"

Brad rolled his eyes. "Ah, come on Mrs. Lisht, I always had one. Thish one's just bigger."

"See? You can't even say my name now. It sounds like you said Lisht."

"It's a shtatement."

"A statement? What kind of a statement? I'm stupid? Or, see me destroy my gorgeous face, statement?"

"Come on. I don't have a gorgeous faysh." Brad blushed.

"You're adorable. You'd be better lookin', though, if you lost the hardware." I chucked him under the chin. His teeth clacked together.

"Ouch," he said again.

Brad helped me to my seat and adjusted the mirror before pulling the bus back onto the road. I think he was checking his face. Maybe I'd made an impression.

"Wasn't he going for his MBA?" I asked Ida. She was staring out the window.

"Oh, I don't think so, May. He's not tall enough to play basketball."

I sighed and watched the back of an oily old head in front of me.

IT DIDN'T TAKE LONG to get to the heart of the town. People got on, people got off, and I kept my eye on the storefronts. There must be a fishing gear store around here somewhere. We rolled past the Sunken Balls, and I nudged Ida. The Suburban was parked near the front, so the boys must be doing some good in there. Also, it was a lucky break for us. At the next stop, I spotted a building with the sign *Fishing Licenses* on its wall. If we hurried, we could probably catch a ride back with the guys.

"Come on, Ida, this is our stop." I pulled Ida by the elbow and moved toward the front, yelling for Brad to hold up.

I thanked Brad and was down the first step before he stopped me.

"Too bad about Otish, isn't it? I always liked the old fart, even if he owed me twenty bucks."

That stopped me. "He owed you money?"

"He owed everyone money." Brad shrugged. "No biggy, but it was a little creepy to know I probably gave him his lasht bus ride. Now he's on that big bush in the sky." Brad folded his hands and looked up at the clouds.

"You gave him a ride?" I backed up to the top step. "When was that, Brad?"

"The night he dishappeared. He got on at the edge of town, and I gave him a ride to the shuttle."

"What time was that?" I put my hand on Brad's shoulder. He flinched slightly, probably waiting for me to flick his eyebrow again.

"Eleven o'clock. I remember, because I was almost done with my shift. He was the only one on the bush, in fact, but he was acting a little bit shtrange. Quiet. Not like Otish. That guy was normally trying to con me out of every penny I had. That night, he just took a sheat at the back and didn't shay nothing. And another thing, he was carrying a duffel bag and a tackle box. One of those green plashtic things. Shtunk up the bus, too. The driver after me wouldn't even take it out until I hoshed it down."

"You didn't pick him up in front of the Sunken Balls?" My hands were getting sweaty.

"No, right at the edge of town."

"At eleven? You're sure?"

"Yeah, like I shaid. Last ride on my shift. Can't forget that shmell."

I leaned over and gave Brad a kiss on the forehead. "I think one of these days I'm going to adopt you Brad-Lance," I said.

I left Brad squirming and tripped the rest of the way down the stairs. This was just too perfect. The eyewitnesses at the pool hall had said unequivocally that Otis had left the place at twelve o'clock. The argument in front of the Culpepper condo had been shortly after that. Whoever Brad had carted over to the complex was not Otis.

Finally, something solid.

NOW, I'VE BEEN IN a lot of stores in my day. Linen stores, department stores, gift shops and antique markets, but never had I been in a place like that tackle shop.

Ida and I pushed through the glass door and immediately Ida clutched my sleeve. On a table to our right a plastic lobster sprang up, waved its claws and started singing *Rollin' On the River*. It gave us quite a scare.

We moved past it in a hurry on our way to find a clerk. Through the aisles we went, past hundreds of little bins containing all manner of things like rubber worms, and metal fish heads, hand-written signs that said spinners or cloggers or something like that, hairy flies, colorful fish eggs. We passed a glass display counter with all manners of handguns, stun guns, pepper spray, machetes and num chucks. Around a corner we fought our way through racks of neon orange vests, jackets, hats and camouflage everything. We shuffled down another aisle with rifles, fishing poles, inflated rafts and suspended tents. It all made my head dizzy. Somehow Ida had emerged with a hunting cap sitting sideways on her head, one fuzzy green earflap over her eyes. I brushed it away and kept moving.

I heard some shouting from the back followed by the banging sound of a cash register. We were getting close. I made the mistake of glancing up. High on the walls hung stuffed fish and other things like moose heads and antlers. Tough-looking customers were milling around. I could smell the testosterone.

We rounded a corner and came face to face with a grizzly bear. No, it was a grizzly man, unshaven and growling, with wild hair. It looked as if a badger was tossing around on his head and a porcupine was clinging to his chin. He had the smell of a skunk. He spat something brown into a soda can.

"You need somethin'?" he barked. Ida started to wheeze. I pushed her around behind me and stood up to my full height. All five feet, four inches. I set my jaw.

"We need to purchase a roll of this." I dug into my purse and held out my hand.

The man curled up his lip showing badly stained teeth. "Dental floss?"

I looked at my hand. Darn. He probably thought I was hinting at something. I rummaged again. "This!" I felt the perspiration building on my upper lip.

The man stared at me really hard like a man who'd been insulted.

"May, where did you get that pecan sandie?" Ida poked at my hand. The cookie disintegrated.

"Oh, for Pete's sake." I spun on my heel and walked over to a cluttered counter by the cash register. I turned my purse upside down and dumped it.

"This?" The man came up and pulled the roll of fishing line out from under my moist towelettes.

"Yes," I said. "Just like that." A thin sweat trickle was running down my back.

The man turned the spool over in his hand. He held it up to the light. Then he plunked it down on the counter.

"That's Steelhead line. Don't get much call for that around here," he said. He spat into the can again.

"Do you have some? Just like that?" My pits were moist.

"Not that brand. Hold on." The man placed his can by the register and reached under the counter. He pulled out a smudged, heavy book, cleared a spot and thumped it down on the counter. He flipped through it and tapped a page with his finger. "That brand's out of Portland, Oregon. You're gonna have to order it if you want that brand exactly, but I have something that might do just as good."

"No, we want this brand."

"Won't be here for about a week or two, but I can order it."

I narrowed my eyes. "So you're telling me you don't have this brand?"

The man leaned forward over the counter. "I can get it."

"But not today." I pushed my face toward his.

"A week tops." He pressed his lips together. A tiny brown bubble escaped.

"You get orders for this brand?" I put my hands on the counter.

"You're the first." The man put his hands on the counter.

"Fine."

"You want me to order it then?"

"Forget it." I huffed and scooped my stuff back into my purse. I was trying really hard to be firm and forceful. I didn't want to cry just yet. I walked calmly and purposely out of the store. I waited until we were out the door before I let the tears fall.

"May? What's wrong? It's okay, we'll think of something else. It's all right, May." Ida gently patted my back.

"It's not that."

Ida gently pulled the little spinner out of my hand. It wasn't fully imbedded and not too painful after the initial bleeding stopped. Must have leaned onto some strays by the cash register.

"Come on, Ida, let's catch the boys before they leave."

As we hurried toward the Sunken Balls, I questioned Ida. How long had Otis lived in California? Where had he come from? Did he ever leave town?

No, he never left town; he'd lived in California most of his life, and Ida didn't know where he came from or where his family lived.

The puzzle pieces were shifting into place.

EIGHTEEN

HAPPY HOUR AT the Sunken Balls. It smelled of stale beer, leather and flatulence. A long cloud of blue smoke hovered just about eye level. The only source of light came from the jaundiced bulbs hanging under glass lampshades with beer brand names painted on their grimy surfaces.

The place was crowded. The clack of ball on ball was steady but sporadic. Ida and I clung together as if we might lose each other, but that was hardly likely. We stuck out like Amish wives at a kegger.

I searched through the bodies for signs of Ted, Grady or Bob. Ida did the same, craning and weaving around me. Her dress had lost its crisp, neat appearance and sagged in the stuffy air. Her bosoms drooped like two loaves of bread, and the thin belt around her waist rode high, lost under the folds. I was wearing holes in the bottoms of Ida's slippers, and my pantyhose itched, the crotch slipping lower and lower with each step. I put my forearm on my waist and hitched.

Of course, there were the inevitable stares. At the first table, two wiry cowboys studied the green felt. They each had brown bottles in one hand and pool cues in the other. When we approached, they grinned, snickered, and then one handed me his bottle.

"Hold this for me, Grandma, will ya?"

I took the bottle on instinct. He whipped the stick around his back and took aim.

"Hey!" Ida stepped forward.

The man flinched and his pool stick glanced off the cue ball.

"She's not your grandma." Ida grabbed the bottle and

handed it back to the man. His partner jabbed the tip of his stick at the man's chest. It left little blue chalk circles on his white shirt.

"She's not your grandma, Joe." The man laughed and bent over the table.

We moved on.

At the next table, two couples were nearing the end of their game. There was one black ball on the table and the little white one. A girl with long blonde hair and eyelids at half-mast swayed atop a stool while a big man in a leather vest, white T-shirt and jeans walked around the table. Every now and then he would close one eye, bend over and hold his stick like a rifle. Then he'd shake his head and readjust his stance.

In the back a man yelled, "Rack 'em up!"

Ida and I watched—interested to see what Leather Vest would do. He scratched his chin. He scratched his crotch. He pulled his beard. Finally, he made his decision. He spread his legs and bent his knees slightly. He made a little "v" with his thumb and forefinger and rested the end of the stick on it. The blonde listed to the side of her stool. The man drew back.

"Rack 'em up!" Ida shouted out.

The man lurched and dug his stick into the green felt. There was a sickening, ripping sound, and the man froze. He slowly turned toward us, his face bright red, his jaw pulsing. There was smoke coming from his nostrils. The girl listed one more time, then toppled to the floor.

"Oooh, Ida," I whispered loudly. "You shouldn't have done that." I grabbed her belt and pulled her away and into a group of sweaty, tattooed men, the likes of which were more menacing than Leather Vest. Most of them wore T-shirts stretched over protruding bellies with Harley Davidson logos on their backs. This was getting worse by the minute, and there was no sign of the boys.

The bikers circled us. One had a cigar hanging between very bad teeth. "Ladies? Are you lost?"

My knees were failing me. I kept swooping, but not so much that anyone would notice. The little band of moisture on my top lip was forming into dewdrops. *Not now, May, show 'em who's boss.* I lifted my chin.

"Ida, give me the money," I said firmly.

"Huh?" Ida blinked.

"Oh, never mind." I unsnapped my purse, grabbed my wallet and lifted out a twenty. Then I walked up and slapped it on the ledge of the table. "Any takers?"

The bikers stepped back and looked at each other. They looked worried.

"Hey lady, we're not finished here." A girl with red spandex pants and spike heels chewed her gum at me.

"In that case, forget it. You had your chance." I reached down to grab my money.

I'd shown them.

A meaty hand clamped down over mine.

"Not so fast." Cigar ash fell onto the floor.

"Rack 'em up!" Ida shouted.

The man squinted his eyes and chewed his cigar for a minute, and then he released my hand and reached under the table for a little plastic triangle thingy. The other three in his party hastily pulled out the sunken balls and placed them on the table. Cigar Face gathered them into the triangle and sorted through them.

What now? I thought. My pantyhose crotch was down around my knees. Ida reached up and started massaging my shoulders. I rolled my head, shook my hands by my sides, and blew out through my teeth.

The man waited.

I cracked my knuckles, did some shallow knee bends, and jogged in place.

The man bit the end off of his cigar.

I lifted my arms and bent side to side.

The man swallowed the bite of cigar.

I got my purse out and slowly wiped my hands with moist towelettes, one finger at a time.

"Hey!" the man shouted impatiently. I halted him with a quickly raised hand, palm out.

"Hey? Are you saying hey?" I took a step toward the towering smoker and drew my eyebrows down into a serious frown. "You want to do this or not, fat boy?" I turned my face to the side and raised just one eyebrow this time. I flared my nostrils. *Show no fear.*

"Yeah, fat boy," Ida said. She was at my side busily rolling up my sleeves.

"Because," I said firmly, "I can just take my money and go home if that's how you want to play this game." I reached for the twenty.

"You break," Cigar Face said, moving to block my extended arm.

Break? Break what? I held up a finger and stepped back to confer with Ida.

"What does that mean, 'break'?" We had our heads together.

"I think it's obvious, May Bell, can't you smell it?" Ida waved her hands through the fetid air. "I'll do it, I've been holding back since all that fruit at Grace's anyway."

Ida stepped up to the table and screwed up her face. She was starting to bear down when I jumped in and stopped her before anything embarrassing happened.

"No, Ida, I've got it."

Good thing I was a fast learner and a good spy. I'd seen the girl at the table to our left smack the white ball into the gathering of colored ones. It had been like an explosion. *Good break.*

There were some pool sticks lined against the wall. I selected one carefully. Ida handed me the little blue chalk square. I chalked.

"Lady, I ain't got all day," Cigar Face said.

My hands were trembling as I set the white ball. I put my fingers in a *V* just like I'd seen before. I sawed the stick and gripped my tongue between my lips. I grunted forcefully and might have done something embarrassing when I punched my stick toward that little white ball, but I can't remember. The stick glanced off the top of the ball, but got it rolling.

Slowly—ever so slowly—the ball made its way down the

table. Ida screamed out, grabbed the sides of her hair, and then clapped wildly. My pantyhose dropped down around my calves.

The ball kissed its blue friend and then just stopped.

The crowd of Harley players erupted in stomps, hoots and roars. The girl on the floor lifted her head, smiled a toothless grin, and then fell back again.

"Lady, you don't play, do ya?" Cigar Face wiped tears from his eyes. His belly was quivering.

I blushed, then smiled. "You can't blame a girl for trying."

The man handed back my twenty. "Here. You go buy yourself an ice cream."

I waved him away. "You keep it. This has been ten times more fun than shooting craps in Vegas."

"You did that, too?" Ida frowned. "I never told anyone, but once after I ate a whole bunch of grapes—back when I was wearing my Depends…"

I clapped my hand over Ida's mouth.

Just then, over Ida's shoulder, I saw Ted emerge from a room at the back of the pool hall. He was in a hurry, and when he caught sight of me a brief look of surprise flitted across his face. He jerked his head toward the door. I caught his sense of urgency and grabbed Ida by the sleeve. She resisted, wanting to reward the Harley group with her homemade potholders.

I didn't give her a chance. I just reached into her purse, scooped up a bundle of the things and threw them toward the group.

"We've gotta go," I told the group quickly, and shoved Ida toward the exit. I took short, quick steps, mindful of my hose problem.

Ida looked crestfallen and glanced over her shoulder on the way out. "But I was going to share my sauce recipes with that spandex girl!"

"Later, Ida, later!"

Ted was out the door, and I was moving Ida along pretty quickly when I heard Cigar Face call out, "Hey, lady, you two come back any time!" I turned to see him waving my twenty in the air.

"Thank you, honey, we will," Ida sang out politely.

That got the biker group roaring again.

Five more steps and we were moving quickly past the cowboys. I noticed Ida was still clutching my pool stick. I grabbed it, thrust it in the hand of Mr. Rude and said, "Here. Hold this for me, will ya, Joe?"

Joe's friend snorted and shot beer from his nostrils.

Three more steps and we were within arms' length of the door. Through large, nicotine-stained windows I saw Ted on the sidewalk searching through a ring of keys. There was a look of agitation on his face. No, I thought, when I looked more carefully, he wasn't agitated. He was terrified. My protective instincts kicked in. Something had frightened my husband, and it was up to me to defend my man. Hand to nose, knee to groin, elbow to eyeball. Whatever it took.

I immediately regretted giving up my pool stick.

NINETEEN

IDA AND I BURST THROUGH the doors of the Sunken Balls. On the fly, I breathed clean air into my lungs and rapidly hauled up my hose. Ted stood at the open door of the Suburban, frantically motioning for us to hurry.

"Where's Grady and Bob?" I asked, hoping what I'd just seen was a figment of my active imagination. It wasn't.

"They're right behind me, and they're in trouble. Get in quick and I'll give you the lowdown."

"The lowdown, Ted?" I helped Ida into the Suburban while Ted dove behind the wheel and cranked the engine.

"Let's just say there's more talk around a poker table than around a pool table, if you get my drift."

"Oh, Ted. Don't tell me."

"Sorry, May, but it was for the mission."

I held out my hand. Ted absently gave me his checkbook and began tapping the steering wheel muttering, "Hurry up, boys, hurry up, now."

"Five hundred dollars? Five hundred dollars? Ted? How could you?"

"I'm sure it was for a good cause," Ida said.

"If you say one more thing about the mission, I'll scream." This was too much. I covered my eyes and groaned.

"I wouldn't worry too much about it because Grady's in there cleaning them out. By the way, we got a boatload of information about Otis. And it sure ain't pretty."

I was aghast. What had happened to my subdued, dignified husband? He even smelled of sin.

A loud banging on the side of the Suburban rattled my

teeth. "Get the door open, May!" Grady hollered, clutching fistfuls of money.

Grady and Bob tumbled in, and I slammed the door closed just as an angry trio of mobster-types tumbled out through the door and onto the street. One of them hurled a deck of playing cards at us. Aces and kings, deuces and hearts struck the windshield and splayed across the glass. A tall man who looked bent on disfiguring Grady, Bob, or both, tripped, sending a shiny motorcycle into another until the whole row dominoed in a thunderous crash.

The Harley boys came boiling out behind, just in time to see the last bike crash to the pavement. Cigar Face took one look at my face, grinned, and hooked his beefy arm around the neck of some guy on a direct line for our car. There were some pounces, some swinging fists, and a whole wad of raging leather.

Ted burned rubber before we could officially be considered witnesses. As we shot around the corner, I caught one last glimpse of the bikers and gamblers rumbling around on the sidewalk behind us and breathed a huge sigh of relief.

"That was close." Ted hunched over the steering wheel, using his whole body to jockey it through alleys and around utility poles. He struck some orange cones and sped over a protected manhole just as the man poked his head out. I believe the guy ducked in time, but I'm not sure on that point.

I knew better than to grill the boys on details until we'd reached a safe haven. Besides, Ted was veering so wildly, I was pinned to the inside wall of the Suburban wishing for one of those panic handles. I was hardly in any position to make conversation.

Ida wheezed like a punctured tire, poor thing, and no paper bags in sight.

Grady counted his money, catching air with every bounce. Bob jostle-grunted in the passenger seat.

"Pull in there," Bob yelled, pointing toward a Subway sandwich shop.

"What? Now?" I looked worriedly behind us. Nothing but a cloud of exhaust. It looked like we were in the clear.

"A man's gotta eat," Bob said.

When I hazarded a glance at my watch I was surprised. The day had gotten away from us. There had been so much excitement that it wasn't until I saw the sandwich sign that I noticed my stomach, all empty and complaining. To sweeten the deal, Starbucks was around the corner.

THE SUN WAS HIDING behind gray clouds, and it looked like it would rain, so we ate quickly. I sucked at a Frappucinno between mouthfuls, feeling the bliss.

Like pigs we ate, suckling, smacking, and slurping. Bob belched loudly.

"Excuuuuse me!" he said.

Ida dribbled relish down her chin, and Grady ticked it off with his napkin.

Ted two-fisted his hoagie.

"It's gonna rain," I said through a mouth full of seafood and crab.

"I just hope it holds off until after we're finished," Ted said, peeking out from under the umbrella.

By the way we were stuffing our faces, I thought we would be pretty safe, and would finish before any rain fell, but then I realized that's not what Ted was worried about. I'd almost forgotten, or maybe it was just denial. After all, this was the night we were goin' in.

Just hours away from digging up Otis.

I squeezed my eyes shut. No, strike that. We were digging up the fake Otis. The guy who looked like Otis without the tattoo. The whole purpose of desecrating the grave marked "Otis Culpepper" was to get fingerprints and prove this was an imposter. Maybe we all were just a little crazy. Maybe that's what Ted was alluding to when I asked him if he was insane, and he'd said, "Not yet." Perhaps we had reached that moment of senility.

Ted shoved his plate away. "I was surprised to see you two at the Sunken Balls. What were you thinking?"

"Well," Ida said, her eyes sparking, "May had this great

idea. We took the fishing line from Mrs. Culpepper's house and went to a little store in town. We wanted to get another new spool just like it so we could replace the one in her tackle box."

"Whatever for?" Grady asked.

"Because, if Grace—that's Mrs. Culpepper—knew about the fishing line, we figured we could see it in her reaction," I said, trying to make it all sound sensible.

"If she saw a new package in the box," Ida nodded, "she'd probably freak."

"I don't know about that, Ida, but she would do something. Oh! And guess what else? When I was in her bathroom, the place reeked of pool chemicals. I did some looking, and found a box of the stuff under her sink. And, the bathtub was full of the odor. Chlorine smell. It was coming up through the drain, and my guess is that someone poured a lot of those chemicals down the drain."

"Did you ask her why?" Bob said.

"No," Ida jumped in, "because she was ralfing in the toilet."

"The chemicals made you sick?" Ted looked concerned.

"No, I wasn't sick. I just pretended to be sick so I could look through the cabinets. I went through the medicine chest, but nothing really interesting in there."

"What did you see?" Ted urged me on.

I stared at the underside of the umbrella and searched my memory. I ticked off the inventory. When I was finished, Ted asked me to repeat myself. When I got to the SleepNow, he stopped me.

"Sleeping tablets?"

"Is that important?"

"Remember? In the autopsy report, Otis had sleeping pills in his system when he drowned. Same type of ingredients you'd find in SleepNow, if my memory serves me." Ted tugged an earlobe.

Grady ran his hands through his hair. "You know, if I were a cop, I'd come to the same conclusions they did. Here's a guy identified by his wife, he's got sleeping pills in his apartment like the ones in his system, he's in Otis's swim trunks, looks like Otis, floating in the Otie pool, and nobody has seen Otis since. Are we going in the wrong direction here? Are we really trying to convince ourselves there's someone else in Otis's grave based on the absence of a tattoo and some fishing line?"

"Well—" I leaned over the table "—listen to this. They only sell that kind of fishing line in Portland, Oregon. Otis hasn't been out of California in years, and this line," I dug through my purse and found it on the first try, "is pretty new. The label is hardly worn at all."

"So?" Grady said.

"Also, I talked to the bus driver. It was Brad, remember him? He said he'd picked up Otis on the outside of town and took him to the Waning Years Estates around eleven. I heard the police say Otis had been at the Sunken Balls until around twelve!"

"So? So? Maybe Brad got it wrong, or maybe he saw somebody else who looked like Otis."

"My point exactly!" I hit the table, caught the tines of a fork and flipped it through the air.

Bob shot out a hand and snagged it.

"The guy on the bus was probably the guy Mrs. Culpepper said was her husband. They looked the same. So close, in fact, that Brad told me it was Otis." I stopped because I had to catch my breath.

"It jives with what they told us at the Sunken Balls." Ted nodded.

Bob nodded.

Grady nodded.

"You guys were actually doing something besides losing your shirts?" I seared Ted with my eyes. He caught the sarcasm.

"You're not the only one who can gather data," Ted shot back.

I gasped, hurt. So insensitive! My eyes started to pool. He knew how important this was to me, how could he have said something so heinous?

My friends were drawing away from the heat. They looked from me, to Ted, and then back to me. My lower lip trembled. I was losing it.

Ted chuckled and took hold of me. He wrapped me in his arms and held me tightly to his chest. I struggled for a while, but finally gave up.

"You always were a feisty one," he said. "That's what I love about you."

"Really?" I sniffed loudly.

Grady winked at Ida, lifted his thumb into the air and nodded.

"You're just tired. After we explain what happened, I think you'll get a better appreciation for your old man."

I rubbed my nose on his shirtfront. Left a little stain. "You're not old."

Ted gently released me. He picked up my sweaty Frappuccino, wrapped a napkin around it and placed it in my hand. All better. I sawed the straw up and down and slurped.

Grady took the floor. He cleared his throat first, took Ida's hand and then said, "When we got to the Sunken Balls we thought it would be a good idea to split up. You know, cover more territory that way. So we hovered, tried to catch some conversation, just to see if anyone was talking about Otis."

"No luck," Bob said.

"We regrouped and tried to work on our next plan of action. I thought we should just start questioning everyone. Ask them what they knew about Otis Culpepper. Ted suggested we act like we were private investigators or cops, but I didn't think that would be too smart."

"Considering the seedy clientele, you would have cleared out the place in under ten seconds." I nodded.

"Of course, we couldn't just blend in and pretend we were regulars there, so we took the opposite approach." Bob licked the fork he'd saved and then rubbed it on his shirtfront.

"That's mine," Ida said and took the fork from Bob. She dropped it in her purse.

I looked at my seafood sandwich. By golly, it was her fork. They didn't serve sandwiches with forks. Napkins, yeah, but not forks. I was getting distracted again.

"So what did you do?" A dull humming was starting in my

head, but I forced it away. A nap would have been good if I could have afforded the luxury. No chance for that, so I took a long, cleansing suck of my Frap, waited for the brain freeze—waited, waited, there!

Ted noticed my distress and rubbed the back of my neck while explaining. "We put out feelers. Grady was pretty sure he could find enough guys to get a poker game together, and he was right. We targeted the older guys, the ones who looked like they'd been around the block a few times, flashed some cash, and, before you know it, we're escorted into a little private room complete with cards, table, free drinks, and chairs for six."

"It felt like I'd come home again." Grady smiled, showing the gap between his teeth. For a minute, he looked twenty years younger.

"You'd never know Grade hadn't done this kind of thing in ages." Bob scratched under his waistband.

Grady continued. "Somehow, we got the other three guys talking about Otis. This made them all really edgy. And really angry. Otis was the biggest con man this side of the Mississippi. There wasn't anything he wouldn't bet on, and he won almost every time. At first he paid off his debts when he lost, but after a while he was working the guys to try and win his money back. He just got deeper and deeper in debt. These guys didn't care much at first because they all have plenty to throw around. But after comparing notes, they discovered he was in so deep that there was no way he could pay them back. That even if he won every hand, every pool game, every shell game for the next ten years, he would still be owing them."

"Bad Otie," Ida said.

"That blows the cash cow theory," I mused. "No reason to keep him alive if he can't get their money back to them."

"Right," Grady said, "but he told them there were other ways to get his hands on money. He was going to sell his condo, and he casually mentioned he had a life insurance policy. Double indemnity if his death was accidental. And he hinted around that he could pull it off."

"Pull it off? Pull what off?" Ida gasped. "That's how Mrs. Culpepper lost her legs!"

"He also said he could use his wife's disability money, too, if they'd only let him back in the game."

"We didn't get this information easily," Ted said. "The details came out in dribbles. The most talkative was this guy named Peter Benbow. He would mention something, and then watch the other two, as if looking to see if the other guys would get nervous. Then another guy named Forbes would say something and look around. The third guy, Kirk, didn't say much, but he sure wasn't fond of Otis. He mentioned a problem he'd had with the guy and then kind of waited for the others to say something. It was strange how they kept looking at each other."

"Like they were all wondering which one snuffed Otis?" I was getting excited. We were knee-deep in motive. Now, what about opportunity? "Did you ask when Otis left the night he disappeared? Did they talk about that night?"

"Oh, yeah. They were all very quick to say they'd seen Otis leave, alone, and they all gave versions of where they'd gone afterwards."

"Establishing alibis," I whispered.

"Pretty shaky ones, right guys?" Bob and Grady both nodded. "They're all bachelors, live alone, any one of them could have followed Otie home. Who knows?"

"Well," I said. "We know Otis never made it to his bed that night. His wife said that much. If one of the voices the neighbor heard was his, then he made it to his front porch, but then what? No other sounds of a struggle that we know of, at least not that anyone heard."

"Wasn't the second voice a woman?" Ida asked.

"Right!" I slammed my fist into my palm. Ouch. That was the fishhook palm. Shouldn't have done that.

"Who was the woman? If it wasn't the wifey, then who?" Grady asked.

"Wasn't he cattin' around with some other woman?" Bob asked.

"The girlfriend!" Ida and I said together.

TWENTY

"OH MY GOSH. We forgot Fanny!" I grabbed Ted's wrist and I twisted around to get a look at his watch. He grimaced. It was nearing six, and we hadn't checked on Fanny, whose job it was to "interrogate" the girlfriend. We'd been so busy all day...

"Who was the other woman, Grade?" I jumped from my chair. "I can't believe we forgot about Fanny."

"Oh don't worry about skinny bones," Bob said. "She spent the afternoon at the golf course, remember? It wouldn't surprise me if she plum forgot about driving to that lady's house. She's probably still whacking balls on the driving range, even as we speak."

Grady agreed, then added, "The woman's name is Sandy Jones. Otis wasn't too good at keeping that a secret."

At least not from Viagra-popping grandpas. Probably bragged about it and shared details, too. Humph. Men.

"A real looker, that gal," Grady said. "She doesn't live on the Estate grounds, has a little house over on Cranberry. As a matter of fact, not far from where Fanny lives. She likes to garden in shorts and the skimpiest little tank tops you've ever seen, hardly any tan lines, and those thighs..."

Ida grabbed Grady's nose and squeezed hard. I guess we were all getting punchy. Grady rubbed his bruised nose, and looked at Ted for affirmation.

Bob sat up straight, suddenly in very good spirits. "Why don't we run on over to the house on Cranberry street and talk to Sandy ourselves? If Fanny has come and gone, we'll just say we're looking for her and go to the driving range."

You could almost hear his thoughts—*and get a peek at those shorts.*

"I don't think so, Bob," I said. "We might make her nervous, all of us crowding in like that. I think it would be better for Fanny to talk to her one-on-one. I think Otis's girlfriend would be more likely to open up and tell us some things about Otis that way."

"Good point," Bob said. "But maybe we should go. If Fanny isn't there yet, we'll just say we're looking for her and go to the driving range. Matter of fact, I could hit a few myself." Bob stood and went into a putter's stance.

"No time for that, Bob." Grady wagged his finger. "It's getting dark, and I want to beat the rain. But I don't think it can hurt to pay Miss Sandy a friendly visit, can it? Just to check on Fanny?"

Sure, Grade. Just Fanny-checking.

"We can't stay long," Grady added. "If there's a squall we might be in trouble."

Bob turned his air putter into an imaginary shovel. "No fun digging in the mud, huh?"

"Makes the dirt really heavy and unwieldy," Grady said.

I groaned. "We're really going to dig up Otis's grave?"

"Shhh." Ida said.

ON THE WAY TO Cranberry Street, Ted patted my knee, rubbed my back, kissed my cheek. He was making up.

I was a rock. Let him suffer.

We had the back of the Suburban to ourselves, so I managed to squirm out of my pantyhose without any prying eyes. Ted's eyes glazed over at this, and he smiled.

"Forget it, bud, it's not what you're thinking. They were cutting off my circulation."

Ted looked crestfallen, and I had to admit I was good. Take him to the edge—swat him back. Give him hope—keep him waiting. I was horrible. I guess it wasn't really fair for me to torture him like I was.

Enough of these games. I pulled the hem of my skirt over one bare knee. Ted sat up, ramrod straight as if he'd been zapped with a cattle prod. His eyes were wide and questioning. I nodded and glanced from my knee to his eyes, and then down to my knee. I nodded again. Ted started to breathe quickly. He glanced around. We were in the clear.

Ted crept his hand over to my knee. He tested it with one long forefinger. Not bad, nice touch, maybe a little tentative, but okay. Ted placed another finger beside the first. I hiked my skirt up another inch. Ted looked so happy.

"Hey, watcha doing?" Ida twisted and flopped her arms across the back of the seat in front of us. She stared at my white, mottled thigh.

Ted snatched his hand away. I threw my skirt down.

"Nothing," I said in a very high voice.

Ida got on her knees and put her chin on the seat back. She settled in. I think I saw a tear in the corner of Ted's eye. He'd been so close.

"Hey, Ted," Ida said. "Why were those poker guys chasing you out of the Sunken Balls, anyway? They looked furious!"

"Bob's fault," Ted answered. "After Grady started winning every hand and the guys got distracted—and pretty angry— Bob started dropping hints that one of the guys might have had something to do with Otis's death. Practically came right out and accused them each of murder. That got 'em going. I slipped away to get the Suburban open while Grady tried to get them calmed down."

"Are you joking?" I clapped my hands over my eyes and rubbed vigorously. "I don't believe this! Bob, how could you? Now they know we know!"

"I wouldn't worry too much, May," Ted said. "They might have had motive and opportunity, but we still don't have any proof that they did anything to Otis, or to the fake Otis, but at least it proved one thing. Those guys could be killers if they wanted to be. Hair-trigger tempers. But I'm not betting on a conspiracy theory here."

"You're not betting on anything else again in your life. From now on, I'm keeping the checkbook."

A fat wallet hit me in the head.

"Take what you need to cover your losses, Doc." Grady

talked into the rear view mirror. All I could see were his hazel eyes twinkling with mischief beneath two bushy eyebrows.

I opened the wallet. "Wow, Grade, no wonder they were ticked. You've got at least two thousand dollars in here." I ran my thumb over the bills. "I don't suggest you go swimming any time soon."

"Grady doesn't like to swim anymore," Ida spoke quietly. "He says the water's too cold. It counteracts the Viagras." Ida twisted around again and played with her seat belt.

That did it. I got a bad case of silent giggles. I tried to keep quiet, but every time I gained control I'd see Ted's twitching lips and fall apart again. By the time we pulled onto Cranberry Street, my eyes were streaming and my stomach muscles had traded places.

"THAT'S FANNY'S CAR," Bob said.

I peered over the seat. Sure enough, her pink Cadillac was parked next to a green Toyota in front of a small, but quaint, yellow house.

"I wonder how long she's been here?" I said, getting over my giggles long enough to dab my eyes with Ted's sleeve. Dark mascara stains spotted his cuff. I apologized.

"Wonder what she's doing in there?" Grady sat with his hands on the steering wheel. He turned to Bob.

"Maybe she's dead." Ida leaned over Grady's shoulder. A blue light flickered behind the curtains of the front window.

"Are we going to sit here all night?" I unhooked my seat belt.

"She's right. We've got to go see what's happening in there," Bob agreed. "Ida, did you remember to bring some of those pecan sandies?"

"I think May has one in her purse," Ida said.

"Sorry, no. We'll just have to go in cold." I gave Ted a gentle push.

Bob went first, Grady and Ida walked hand-in-hand, and I took Ted's elbow. Bob pushed the doorbell. The sound of chimes echoed through the house.

Nothing.

Bob leaned on the button.

"For the love of Pete!" I heard Fanny yell from the opposite side of the door.

"She's not dead," Ida said.

The door opened a crack. Fanny stood behind it. When she saw us, she opened the door wide and put her hands on her hips. "Your timing couldn't be any worse. Hurry up! They're just about to tell us where the carpet fibers came from."

"Fanny. Where in the heck are your clothes?" I asked.

Fanny was sporting a pair of red satin nightie shorts with a matching sleeveless pajama shirt, showing a lot of her bony chest. The outfit was at least three sizes too big. Her legs looked like two broomsticks and on her feet she wore clear plastic high-heeled slippers. White feathered tufts covered the insteps.

"These ain't mine. I had to borrow." Fanny turned her back to us without explaining further and hurried off in the direction of the blue light. The hallway was quite dark, so we followed the sound of her clicking heels and the blue halo of her hair.

When we got to the living room, I saw who I presumed was Sandy Jones, stretched out on a couch. Her attention was fixed on a television set, a bowl of popcorn was on the floor by her elbow, and she was munching. She turned her face toward us while keeping her eyes on the tube.

"Come in, come in. They're about to say it, Fanny, hurry!"

The television went to commercial. Fanny and Sandy groaned loudly. Sandy threw popcorn at the screen.

Grady cleared his throat.

"Oh my gawd, where are my manners?" Sandy spoke with a thick Southern accent. She rose slowly to her feet, taking a while to reach her full height. This lady was tall. Nearly six feet would be my guess, about fifty years old, wearing a long black slippery nightgown over a near-perfect figure. She wore rings on most of her long, tapered fingers; the nails were manicured with bright red polish. Her blonde hair was long and flowing. She was knockout gorgeous.

I hated her on sight.

Bob started to drool, Grady was speechless, and Ted looked at the woman with too much appreciation. I wanted to jab him, but reminded myself that I was to blame after all, for having primed the pump. He was just a victim of his hormones.

The ever-congenial Ida broke the spell. She put her hand out and introduced herself, then the rest of us. Sandy floated up to accept the outstretched hand, taking Ida's in both of hers. Warmth and charisma oozed like pinesap.

When Sandy took my hand I could smell her perfume, light and pleasant. Her touch was gentle. My initial feelings for her were beginning to fade. Bob actually bowed from the waist when he closed his beefy hand over hers. Sandy lightly touched Ted's arm, then smiled at Grady. The boys were falling all over themselves.

I wanted to put Sandy in my enemy category, but she was making it tough, waving toward her furniture, offering us places to sit. The commercial ended, and she held up a finger.

Fanny hushed us. She sat rocking on the edge of the couch, leaning in toward the TV with her fists pressed against her mouth.

"New Detectives," Bob explained.

The television showed a man in a lab coat bent over a microscope. The voice-over was explaining something about the individuality of certain carpet fibers.

"A match! I knew it! Didn't I tell ya it was the husband, Sandy? It's always the husband." Fanny jumped to her feet and danced a jig in her oversized shorties. The program went to credits, and Sandy pressed the remote, turning the screen black. She walked gracefully to the wall and flipped on the overhead light.

My pupils constricted painfully.

"Ah darn it, Sandy, can't we watch another Forensic Files?" Fanny lifted a black videotape from a stack on the coffee table. There were dozens of them—on the floor, in a bookshelf, spilling out everywhere—out of place in the otherwise feminine Victorian furnishings of Sandy's home.

"She records all my favorites. Can you believe it?" Fanny lifted a can of soda and tipped it back. "Empty," she said and tossed the can in a pile with several others. "You guys want one? Maybe we can get Sandy to play her latest CSI."

"That's Crime Scene Investigation," Bob explained. He pulled a soda from a six-pack and popped the top.

"Fanny, how many of those have you had?" I indicated the empty cans.

"I don't know, what is it, Sandy? Six? Seven? I lost count."

I figured Fanny would be smoking up a carton by night's end. I raised my eyebrows in question. What had happened to her reconnoitering? Wasn't she there to pump the beauty queen for information?

I looked at Sandy again and wondered how in the world she'd managed to hook up with a guy like Otis. Old bloatie, no floatie Otie. Had he been one of those guys with irresistible charm? The type impossible to refuse, captivating in a mystical sort of way? He certainly didn't have the looks or physique to grace the cover of a romance novel. I remembered his backbend at the funeral. He must have been at least six inches shorter than this woman and a little on the geeky side. But wait. That was the fake Otis. Maybe the real Otis looked like Tom Cruise or Magnum P.I. No, they were close enough in looks to fool Mrs. Culpepper.

That is, if she'd been fooled at all.

"That's a lovely skirt," Sandy said to me. She sounded sincere. I blushed and fidgeted. "This old thing?" I couldn't help myself. I've always been a sucker for compliments, genuine or not.

"And Bob." Sandy gazed at my smitten friend with her Marilyn Monroe eyes. "I've heard good things about you. Sounds like you're really whipping those residents into shape in your magnificent dayance classes. Simply *everyone* is talking about them around town. All the rage, from what I gather." Sandy patted her slender hips. "I could stand to exercise a bit more myself."

"No ma'am, you put us all to shame."

Geez, Bob.

Grady's eyes were perusing the pretty Sandy, and I was getting worried that Ted would ask her if she had any feminine problems she'd care to discuss with the good doctor. It was obvious Fanny wouldn't be of any help in the information-gathering department; she was punching another black tape into the VCR. I wanted to get Sandy talking about Otis, but how? One doesn't just come out and ask about the man a woman's been having an illicit affair with, does one? It's just not proper.

I had to be clever.

"Too bad your little Otis boyfriend is dead," Ida said. She was busily cleaning up the place, folding blankets, patting pillows, picking up cans.

"I'm so sorry!" I gasped, and glared at Ida. She smiled sweetly and waved.

"She don't care," Fanny said over her shoulder. She was thumbing the remote, fast tracking past the commercials. "Everybody knew they was doin' it."

I quaked. "Fanny!" I looked apologetically at Sandy, but her expression remained pleasant. She didn't look at all disturbed by Fanny's statement. She thanked Ida for her concern. Ida told her she was welcome. Sandy sighed prettily and brushed the hair out of her eyes.

"It's true, I did love my Otis," Sandy said. She sat slowly on the couch and patted the place beside it. I guess that meant I was to sit down, so I did. She crossed her long legs and leaned her arm on the back of the couch. The boys tripped over themselves to get the chair directly across from Sandy's knees. I tried to take the same relaxed, graceful pose but ended up looking like I was recovering after hip surgery, so I sat up and put my hands in my lap.

Bob won the battle of the chair, so Ted found a beanbag couch and molded into it. He was close to the floor so his knees were up around his ears. He tried to look stately, but with his eyes barely peeking over the top of the coffee table he looked ridiculous. That made me happy.

Ida and Grady squeezed into a white love seat. Ida's leg was draped over Grady's lap, but they looked comfortable enough.

Sandy played absently with an earring.

"It really is a sad thing," I said. "About Otis drowning and everything.

A moment of silence.

"So how'd you two get together anyway?" Bob popped another soda and tipped it back.

"Um, Bob? Don't you think you should slow down a little?" I opened my eyes wide, hoping he'd catch the double meaning. We didn't want to scare this little bunny down the rabbit hole by bombarding her with so many questions. Easy does it.

Why did I even worry? Sandy launched into her life's story without any further encouragement. Some things are just that simple.

"Oh, it was serendipity I suppose," Sandy said.

Serendipity? Who says that anyway? Right up there with coiffures. It's serendipitous that I have pink coiffures. Pay attention, May.

"I moved up from Dallas several months ago, hoping to make a fresh start after managing an interior decorating business that was failing. Also, I'd been in a series of bad relationships. Poor choices on my part." Sandy's Southern accent grew more pronounced as she talked. It was charming and added to her sensuality.

She paused when Fanny's program came back on. We asked her to turn down the volume, which she did, and then we lost her to Forensic Files. Entranced by a murder-for-hire story, Fanny sat cross-legged on the floor, inches in front of the screen. From the back, her little legs in silhouette looked like angel wings. "Dipshit!" she hollered at the TV detective. "Check the dog's mouth!" The cherubic vision burst like a pricked balloon.

Sandy looked at me with emotion-filled eyes. She once again talked about Otis with hardly any probing from us. She seemed eager to purge her pent-up anguish.

"After I moved here, I was livin' day by day. I didn't have a friend in the world. I was stayin' in the Red Brick Hotel downtown looking for work, wondering if I'd made a horrible mistake, and I guess bein' lonely and depressed made me vulnerable."

I could appreciate Sandy's feelings. I remembered my sense of isolation the year before until I met the people sitting with me in that room. Nothing is worse than being utterly alone. I leaned over, touched Sandy's shoulder and said that I could certainly understand. Her shoulder felt frail under my hand, fragile enough to break with one high-pressured squeeze. Good thing I liked this gal.

When I drew away, I could smell the sweet scent of her perfume again. Fanny cursed loudly and said something to the TV about testing the blood spatter evidence. I urged Sandy to continue.

"I was feeling really low, you know? Deprayessed and all, thinking life just couldn't get any worse, when one day I was at the little grocery store down on Main and I started to cry. I didn't mean to, it just happened when I was standing in front of that little bulletin board where people tack up ads on note cards and sticky-notes, you know? Sad little note cards with flaps of paper with phone numbers on them. People trying to find their dawgs, or looking for a job, or advertising their car for sale, or looking for their missing kids, thayet sort of thang. I was standing there, staring at all of those pathetic white and yellow cards and posters. I was just tryin' to find a place to live, you know? But everything was so far beyond my budget that I simply broke down and started weepin' like a baby."

I heard Ida sniff back tears of her own.

Bob cleared his throat.

"And then this little man, this darling little man came up behind me. He didn't say anything, he just pressed a handkerchief into my palm and walked away."

"Otis?" I asked, already knowing the answer.

"Yes. Otis. I chased after him and used whatever I had left in my wallet to buy him a cup of coffee. I just didn't want to be alone. We ended up talkin' for three hours that day, and he wasn't at all like the other guys I'd been with. He was interestin', and funny, and the gentlest man I'd ever known. He was quite a few years older than me, but he had the energy of a young man, so alive, you know? I could see myself with him for a long, long time. By the time we went our separate ways, I knew I was falling in love."

What I'd learned about Otis Culpepper was a far cry from the wonderful man Sandy was describing, but I wasn't tactless enough to mention this. Thankfully, Fanny was so involved in her forensic show that she was quiet and didn't throw out any cheeky opinions about the late, no-floatie Otie.

Sandy uncrossed, then recrossed her legs. All the guys leaned in.

"I went back to the bulletin board every day for a week after that, hoping I'd catch a glimpse of him. I didn't know where he lived, I only knew his first name, and we hadn't exchanged phone numbers. I was so angry with myself for not finding out more about him."

I was angry with Ted. He moved out of his beanbag and came over to take the arm of the couch. The arm beside Sandy. He slid a comforting arm around her. I gave him a killer look. He acted surprised and then quickly moved over to my chair arm. I vice-gripped his thigh. We waited for Sandy to continue.

"Finally, I found this house here. The rent was manageable, and I was writing down the name of the landlord when I saw Otis come through the door. He was polite and kind, and said he was happy that I'd found a nice place to live. When he started to go into the store I stopped him. I wasn't going to lose him again, so I asked if he'd look at the house with me. He was such a big help. He even managed to talk the landlord down a hundred dollars off my lease and got the security deposit waived."

Figures, I thought.

"He helped me move in, and I fixed a dinner for him the next night. We talked about everything. I wasn't ashamed to tell him about my miserable love life, the guys who had used me then tossed me aside like yesterday's trash, and he told me about growing up in Oregon, his family, how painful it was to lose his mother to cancer. He treated me with respect. He never talked to me like I was a dumb blonde, and he never took advantage of me."

"No, of course not. Who would do a thing like that?" the boys chorused, trying to look considerate—like they would have been so principled. Ted grabbed my gripping hand before I could show him I knew he was lying to himself.

"We had sex that night," Sandy said, with a pleasant look in her eyes.

What? I wanted to bang my head against Bob's soda can. Was she listening to herself? Otis—the kind, caring, sympathetic listener—was *not* taking advantage? Well, I guess once a con, always a con. Oh yes, I almost forgot. They were *in love*.

"Sandy," Grady said every so gently, "did you know Otis was married?"

A tear slipped from Sandy's eye and she brushed it away. Was that a tear of guilt? Sorrow? Regret?

Sandy squeezed her nose with a tissue. "No, not at first, but after we started seeing each other regularly, he admitted it to me. He was deeply sorry to keep it from me, but his wife was not in good shape, and she couldn't be a real wife to him—in *that* way. She was very sick, he said, and didn't have long to live."

"On her last leg?" Bob murmured.

"She couldn't pleasure him like I could," Sandy said.

Eeek, this was awful. Sandy wiped away another tear. One of her fingernails was ragged, and I thought it might be good for her to give herself a little scratch right under the eye. It might bring her to her senses.

"But you didn't break it off?" I asked. I quickly glanced at Ida, hoping she didn't think I was alluding to Grace's nubs.

"Oh, it was so awful!" Sandy groaned. "Here I was in love with the most dear, dear, man in the world, but I knew it was wrong. I just couldn't help myself. I kept telling him we should stop seeing each other, but it was impossible. Every minute away from him was like an eternity." Another tear coursed down Sandy's cheek and dropped onto her lap. Poor, naïve woman.

"When I heard Otis had died, my whole world just stopped spinning. I was so overcome with grief, and there was nobody I could talk to about it. In fact, I only learned of his death when I read the paper. At first, when they reported him missing, I thought he'd finally done it. He'd left his wife, and we would be together—unattached just like we had wanted for so long. He would show up on my doorstep, and we'd run away together. But then, I learned he'd drowned in the pool where he lived, and my dreams vanished. I was alone again. I could hardly take the pain."

Sandy was crying outright now. Her face was in her hands; her shoulders were jumping and quaking.

All of us rushed to her aid. I shoved more tissues at her, and we embraced her in a group hug. I think the guys enjoyed this more than they were willing to admit, but we eventually got Sandy calmed down, and Ida went off to the kitchen to fix her a cup of tea.

"Sandy, did Otis ever tell his wife about you?" I had changed into my detective hat. We'd almost forgotten we were on a mission.

"Yes. At least he said he did. I don't know how she couldn't have known anyway, since Otis spent so many nights with me. That's probably why she didn't report him missing right away, she was accustomed to his spending time away from his bed." Sandy wailed out again. "How could I have been so despicable? This feeble, sickly wife at home while I'm doin' her husband! I didn't even go to his funeral because I just couldn't have faced what I had done. Now, I suppose God is punishing me for my wicked ways."

Oh, shucks. Sandy collapsed backward onto the couch, her hand over her forehead. But even as she blubbered into her tissue she was lovely.

"Pipe down!" Fanny hollered. "They've almost got the latents!" Her nose was inches from the TV screen, and she was fogging up her glasses. Some sleuth Fanny had turned out to be. By the number of empty soda cans, I'd say she'd been here quite a while.

Apparently Otis hadn't told Sandy everything. Mrs. Culpepper was missing a few limbs, but she certainly wasn't feeble or bedridden, and she didn't look like she was teetering on the edge of death, either. Our Mr. Otis had been keeping a few things from his ladylove.

"I can't imagine how I can go on now that Otis is gone. I spend all day watching Court TV, Forensic Files, Young Detectives, you know, just light stuff. I don't even have the energy to shop. I miss him so much, and we had such high hopes for our future." The waterworks were on again. I stroked Sandy's silk covered leg. Darn, this lady was toned. No wonder Otis was two-timing. But why had he played the game for so long? Why not just divorce his wife and settle down with Sandy?

The guys at the pool hall had mentioned Otis needed his wife's disability money, and that he was talking about selling his condo. My guess was that he needed his wife to keep him afloat while the sharks were nipping at his heels. He might have done better to keep a life preserver handy.

"Sandy, I hate to bring this up, but did you know anything about Otis and his extracurricular activities?" I tried to be gentle.

Sandy sat up and dabbed at her pink nose. "I knew he gambled quite a bit, if that's what you mean. He said he had some money trouble, but that he was taking care of it. He had a brother somewhere who was going to help him out. I guess he never got to make that call." Sandy broke off into more sobs.

I listened to Sandy blubber while a sneaking suspicion formed in my mind. It crept up on me ever so subtly. It was so delicious I couldn't wait to tell the rest of the gang.

TWENTY-ONE

It was time to leave Sandy. Hugs all around, and Ida settled the sniffling woman on the couch with a cup of tea. Fanny put in another video for her new friend while I straightened up the living room. There was party litter everywhere, and I busied myself by picking up cans, fluffing pillows and carrying empty glasses to the kitchen sink.

Keeping an ear on what was happening back on the couch, I had water going but couldn't find the dish soap. The most logical place to keep such a thing was under the sink, and I got an absurd sick sense of satisfaction when I pushed aside a box of trash bags and noticed an old, grimy pair of shoes tucked toward the back of the cupboard. Mud covered the soles.

Sandy looked all together, a woman to envy, but here were her shoes covered in muck, and her carpet looked as if it could use a good scrub as well. I had to tell myself, though, that when people are in the throes of depression, it's not uncommon for things to get a little untidy. I looked down at my own feet still covered in Ida's house slippers. Okay, even when you're not in the throes of depression.

Well, I wasn't above doing a good deed or two, so I grabbed the shoes and rinsed them off, running the little hose thing over them. The mud ran down the drain and, as I wiped up with a sponge, I noticed something glittering at the bottom of the sink. Several green sequins. Strange. Hmmm. Oh well, I rinsed those down as well, shook off the shoes and turned them upside down in the drain tray. After I finished with the dishes, Ted came to me and whispered in my ear that we needed to go.

It was getting late. Not much time before we'd make our

scheduled trip to the cemetery. Where were my nerves of steel? Even as I gathered my courage to do the dastardly deed, I was thinking hard, trying every way I could manage to keep us from digging up an old rotting corpse.

I didn't tell the gang about the idea I'd had earlier, how Otis had been less than forthcoming about his wife, and how I was sure Sandy knew more than she was letting on. We needed to make one more stop, and then I was certain my suspicions would be confirmed. It had something to do with our Mr. Otis's abrupt disappearance, and Grace's now-exposed lies.

"Stop by the Culpepper's Condo. We have to talk to Grace again," I ordered quietly.

Fanny gathered her clothes under her arm. "Mind if I borrow these?" She pointed to her nightie ensemble. Sandy told her to keep them.

"You look really cute, Fanny," I said—anything to get her away from her New Detectives. I propelled her toward the door. There was no time to waste. Grace might be loading the moving truck even as we spoke.

THANKFULLY, the lights were still blazing in Grace's condo when we pulled the Suburban into the carport across the street. I moved out with a purpose, followed by the rest of the gang.

After testing the cement in the sidewalk, I was satisfied that it was dry enough to walk on. I quickly signaled the others to follow me. At the door I lifted my fist and rapped quickly.

We stood quietly, waiting for the sound of Grace's chair. What I heard made the hair on the back of my neck come to full attention.

"Ted, did you hear that?" I hissed.

"Sounded like footsteps."

"Running footsteps."

"Someone is in there with Grace!" Fanny said. "I think she's in trouble. It's much too late for visitors." Fanny reared back and lifted her leg. She was preparing to kick the door in.

Bob grabbed her ankle and vigorously shook her foot and his head. "Wait. Listen."

The mechanical whine of Grace's chair approached the other side of the door. Several locks clicked, then the door opened slowly, but just far enough for us to see Grace's pale face peeking through.

"Who is it?" she asked, her voice trembling.

Fanny put her shoulder to the door and pushed. "Get out of the way, Grace!"

Grace backed up giving us clearance. Her face was shock white, and she looked utterly petrified. "Please hurry and come in. Close and lock the door behind you," she said.

We did as we were told, crowding the narrow hall while Ted pushed the door and threw the locks. I wondered if this was smart, thinking we would be trapped if an intruder was hiding somewhere within the confines of Grace's home. Surely we had them outnumbered, but that didn't matter much if we found ourselves looking down the business end of a loaded gun.

Bob leaned down and grabbed Grace's shoulders. "We heard someone in here with you. Are they threatening you? Are you in danger? Are they hiding somewhere? You just nod in their direction, and I'll take care of the rest." Bob stood up and rubbed his clenched knuckles.

Grace groaned in dismay and spun her chair around. She batted at the little handle and shot herself down the hall pulling as many G-forces as that little chair would allow. She careened around the corner on two wheels.

"Go after her, Ted," I screamed. "She's up to something!"

We all raced down the hall. When we got to the den, Grace was where I'd seen her the night before, her back to us with her elbows moving in a blur.

"Grace, what are you doing?" I asked, moving quickly to the back of her chair.

"It's almost done, just a few more rows, and it will be done, orange, black, orange, black, see? Isn't it coming along nicely?" Grace peered over her shoulder and lifted the longest most awful looking afghan I'd ever seen. She must have been working on it non-stop since that morning. There were dark patches under Grace's eyes, and it looked as if she hadn't slept in days. I was satisfied we were alone in the condo, and the fear I'd had earlier dissipated. But Grace was acting strangely. It was probably from all of the trauma of the last few days.

"Stop, Grace, just stop." I quieted her hands with my own.

"I don't know a thing, really, not a thing." Grace lifted her yarn, and I grabbed at it. We had a little tug-o-war before she relented and sat back, exhausted.

"She really isn't taking this well at all." Ida clucked her tongue. "Poor dear, I'll go make her some tea."

That was Ida. She could fix anything with tea.

"Hold on a minute, Ida," I said.

I took a turn around Grace's chair and faced her. I asked her directly. "There isn't anyone else in the apartment is there, Grace?"

Grace squirmed. She opened her mouth, and something came out that might have been melodic if it hadn't been so creepy—a warbling, high-pitched up and down sound. Slowly, she shook her head.

"I didn't think so."

The boys started to relax, then looked confused. I'd been right about one thing, after all.

"Is there something you'd like to tell us, Grace, or—as the case may be—show us?"

Grace slumped. The afghan slithered off of her lap onto the floor.

"I just can't stand it another minute," Grace said. "All the lies, the deceit, the treachery! I'm so sick of the whole sham."

"You made some shams, too?" Ida looked admiringly at Grace. "Sweetheart, you shouldn't overdo."

Normally, Grady would have patted his wife's hand, but it seemed the scene had him wholly mesmerized. The gang stood there like they had wandered into a minefield, unsure of where to place their feet.

"It was Otis's idea. All of it," Grace said, fighting tears.

"Go on." I crossed my arms.

"Ah, hell." Grace sighed and turned her chair to face the

gang. She pressed her palms against the arms of the chair and lifted herself up about twelve inches. Then like a butterfly emerging from its cocoon, she slowly, carefully, unfolded one leg and then a second, healthy, complete limb. She lowered herself into the chair with a thud. She rubbed at her reddened, tender skin. "You know how much it hurts to sit like that?"

Ida fainted dead away.

GRACE TOLD US an incredible story while we all sat around the edges of her bed. We'd brought Ida back around, and she was looking better stretched across the bed with her head resting on a pillow and her feet propped on some magazines. Fanny was comfortable in her shortie jammies.

Grace sat close to Ida, her knees drawn up, her arms wrapped around them. She rocked slowly back and forth.

"We're going to stay here until you tell us everything," I said firmly, and then I switched over to good cop. "I know this has all been hard for you, but it will be better just to get it off your chest."

It didn't take much psychological manipulation; the details came out in a rush.

"I never wanted to lie to anyone, but Otis was in real trouble," she explained. "He'd been hustling guys over at the pool hall, and at first it was no big deal. But after a while he made some of the guys angry, and they didn't want him around after that, so he changed his game. He started gambling, losing some, then winning some back, then losing just to keep them off balance. Eventually, though, he was winning all the time, but he'd just turn around and gamble that money on the horses, or Keno, or whatever. And so he had to get more deals together. It all snowballed.

"Otis had big debts all over town. He'd borrowed some money from some loan shark, a guy named Peter, I think, and he couldn't pay it back. The other people he owed money to were calling and threatening. He was at his wits' end, and so was I. There was nothing I could do to help."

I thought of a few things, like shoving him out on his keester, but I didn't mention that. Apparently, Grace had loved her husband very much. Enough to share him? I wondered.

"When it all started, we lived in town. But when Otis thought about getting some disability money, we had to move in here. It would have looked strange for me to have legs one day, no legs the next. So he paid off a doctor, got a false medical report, and voila! I even got the chair on Medicaid."

"That explains why we hardly ever saw you out of your apartment," Grady said.

"Or at night swim," Ida added feebly. She looked much better.

"Yeah, it was a sacrifice," Grace said.

Well, if that wasn't the understatement of the year.

"I can't believe what some doctors will do." Ted sounded angry.

"Well, I can," Fanny huffed. "Just you sit one minute in those cold metal stirrups, I tell you…"

"Fanny." I cut her off with a fierce look. "Please continue, Grace."

"Otis talked about putting the condo up for sale, but that would have taken time, and the bad guys were breathing down our necks. They were making phone calls in the middle of the night. Hang up calls. Once they left a dead squirrel on our doorstep, and another time they stole all of our mail. Otis started staying out all night just to avoid them."

I quickly glanced at Ted. Could she not have known about Sandy?

"Eventually, Otis did the only thing he could think of. He called his brother. It was the last thing he wanted to do, because he and his brother weren't particularly close, and he hadn't talked to him in quite a while. He just hated asking him for money, but there wasn't anything else we could think of."

"Where did his brother live?" I asked.

"Portland. Portland, Oregon. Not Maine."

Bingo!

"Hey, that's where the fishing line was from." Ida sat up in bed.

"So you know about that." Grace said it more as a statement than a question. "Otis's brother, Eldon, agreed to lend Otis the money, but he said he would deliver it personally. He wanted to do some fishing down here anyway, and he thought it would be nice to drop in on his big brother. Eldon had every right to turn Otis down. After all, what had Otis ever done for him? But he didn't. He even said he was looking forward to some time with Otis."

"Let me guess." I felt really smug. "He came down here on a bus."

"Well, yes. How did you know that?"

"Just a hunch." I sniffed. I was feeling pretty cocky. "It was Eldon's tackle box the cops found on the front porch, not Otis's, wasn't it?"

"Yes." Grace sighed. She looked completely worn out.

Ted looked at me and gave me a "good job" wink. My detective work ran out there, though, but I wanted Grace to think I was all knowing, so I put on my best poker face and waited.

"Eldon made good time getting down here. Unfortunately, when he got to our condo, Otis was out, and I was running his bath so I didn't hear the doorbell. Eldon just set his tackle box down on the front porch and went for a walk. He didn't have much with him, just a backpack, so he took that with him. Maybe if he'd left that, too, Otis would have noticed it, and things might have turned out differently. We'll just never know."

I was worried about losing the momentum and pushed Grace along. "So, you were running a bath for Otis. Do you usually do this?" *And what in tarnation were those pool chemicals doing in your bathroom?*

"Oh yes, every night. I'd run his bath, put a glass of milk by the side of the tub and come upstairs to bed. Sometimes he's late getting home and his bath is cold, but I figured that was his problem, not mine."

"That's really nice," Ida said. "Men really appreciate that sort of thing."

Grady put his hand on Ida's knee.

"That night, I heard Otis come to the door. I was accustomed to waiting for him, and I knew the sounds he made when he

came home. But before he even got the key in the door I heard
a car pull up, heard a door slam, and I heard a woman's voice.
I went to the window and opened it just a crack." Grace's eyes
grew moist. "I heard everything."

I winced. So, Grace learns about Sandy in a most demoral-
izing way. Through an open window.

"This woman was just rippin' Otis a new one. She was yelling at him, accusing him of lying about leaving his wife—me.
I guess he'd been having an affair for quite a while. Otis was
trying to calm her down, but then he got really loud. He said,
'Why would you think that? I told you I'd leave her, it's just
not a good time right now.' And she said, 'It will never be a
good time. It's always the same story with you,' stuff like that.
I was heartbroken at first, and then I was livid. I heard Otis say
something about checking on me first, that it would be unusual
if he didn't come in and take his bath, and then after I was
asleep he'd come back to her place, and they'd work everything
out."

Grace took a deep breath. "That's all I needed to hear. I got
out of bed and ran downstairs. At that minute I was so angry
with Otis, that if I'd had a gun they'd both be dead. Instead, I
went into the bathroom and found some sleeping pills in the
medicine cabinet. I figured if Otis drank enough sleeping pills,
he'd doze off in the tub and wouldn't go to his girlfriend that
night. The next morning I was going to confront him and tell
him to break it off, or I'd break something of his off. I put the
sleeping pills in his milk and went back to bed."

"Enter Eldon," I said.

"Yes." Grace was clearly upset when she said this. She
scooted up on the bed and stretched out beside Ida. An old
Army tune went through my head.

*Two old ladies, lying in bed, one rolled over to the other and
said... I want to be an airborne ranger...*

Grace brought me out of my fugue.

"When I went back upstairs and closed the window, I couldn't
hear anything else. I suppose I didn't *want* to hear anything else.
What I learned later, was that as soon as Otis's girlfriend left,

Eldon came around the corner. He surprised Otis, but it was a good surprise. The brothers were happy to see each other. Otis told me his brother had traveled all day, and he was stinking pretty good, so he got him in the house and offered him the bath and the milk. I didn't know Eldon had a low tolerance to sleeping pills. How could I?"

"How could you?" Ida echoed. She threw her arms around Grace.

After politely wrestling herself free of Ida's embrace, Grace continued. "I dozed off and woke up again when I heard Otis at the door one more time. I looked at my clock and was surprised to see it was nearly four in the morning. I thought that was strange, but I found out later that Otis never made it to the tub. He'd chased after his home-wrecker to tell her he was breaking up with her."

"It must have taken him a long time to get his point across." Bob huffed under his breath.

"So where was Eldon?" Fanny had been patient, I had to give her that. Now, though, she beat her heels vigorously against the side of the bed, and it looked as if she was ready to explode. "Where the heck was Eldon?"

Grace closed her eyes. She furrowed her brow and rubbed the back of her neck. "He was in the bathtub."

"Still? Wouldn't he have been a little pruny by that time?" Fanny asked.

"Worse," Grace said.

"Worse than prunes? Nothing's worse than prunes," Ida said. "I have to eat them every day for my colon, and by the time you go through four or five bags, you just want to—"

"Shut your trap, Ida." Fanny got rude. "Let the woman talk."

"Much worse than prunes." Grace looked at Ida. "He was dead."

Ida put her hand over her mouth. "Oh! Prunes can do that?"

"Just a dumb question, Grace," I said. "Did Eldon look at all like Otis?"

"Spittin' image. They were only a year apart, but they could have passed as twins. In fact, I think they did a few times when they were kids, always playing pranks and fooling people."

"Pretty convenient, no?" I was getting spunky again. I narrowed my eyes at Grace.

"I guess you could say it was the answer to our prayers. When Otis woke me up with the news, he was already thinking ahead. You know he's got a job at the pool, don't you?"

We all nodded.

"He ran and got some of those pool chemicals, then he just dumped a mix of them in the bathtub. I got a toilet plunger and we started pumping up and down on Eldon's chest, to get the chemicals in his lungs."

"Pretty smart," Fanny said. She looked admiringly at Grace. "I noticed you were careful not to leave suction marks. Good work."

I'll bet Fanny had never seen anything like that on any of her New Detective shows.

"Well, after that, Otis got one of those towel bins from the sports complex linen closet—he's in charge of washing and drying the towels—and then he parks the bin with the clean ones by the pool and takes the dirty ones."

"We've got it, I think," Grady said, hurrying Grace along.

"We dressed Eldon in Otis's swim trunks, then we got him into the bin. Then Otis covered him with towels. We decided Otis would roll him over to the edge of the pool later and dump him in between scuba and night swim. We had to hide him in the linen closet for hours, and thank goodness the day shift guy is a lazy bum. He always leaves the towels for Otis."

"So that's how you did it." Grady whistled.

"Just to be sure he didn't float to the top too soon, I'd gotten a piece of fishing line from Eldon's tackle box and tied it around his ankle. I don't know how he did it, but Otis got his brother tied to the pool ladder seconds before the lights came on. And you know what's crazy?"

"All of it?" Fanny snorted.

"Nobody noticed at all! Nobody noticed that one minute

Otis was pushing a load of towels across the floor, and the next minute he's dead in the pool."

"So you called the police before that to say Otis was missing. To set it up," I said.

Grace nodded. "I thought if I mentioned the trouble Otis was having with the loan shark and the goons at the pool hall they would be looking in the other direction when Eldon was found. I needed to keep the cops from probing around the Waning Years Estates."

"And when Eldon surfaced, you were called to the county morgue, and identified the body as your husband's." I sighed heavily.

"It was such a perfect plan. Of course, Otis would have to disappear for a while. He said he'd wait until after the funeral, and then he'd be in touch with me. He told me to put the condo up for sale, to get all of his insurance paperwork in order, get a post office box where I could get his insurance money, and then he'd call me. He said we'd go away to a nice little place where we could finally be free."

"Just waltz out into the sunset," Fanny said.

Grace sat up again and grabbed her knees. "But I haven't seen him since! He hasn't called me, I don't know where he's staying, and I can't exactly put out a missing person's report on my dead husband now, can I?" Suddenly, a phone rang. Grace leaned over Ida and snatched up a little black phone from the bedside table. "Joyce gave me this cell phone, but I don't know how to use it. Every time it rings there's this really angry woman on the other line yelling at me about some doctor with bad breath."

"Hey," Ted said, "you found my phone, and it isn't even busted! Thanks." Ted took the phone and pocketed it.

"So where's Otis?" I asked aloud. Fanny got up and paced.

"Yeah, where the heck is Otis?"

TWENTY-TWO

GRACE COULDN'T GO to the police with the news that she'd buried the wrong brother, but we could. She could claim temporary insanity later. If Otis had fallen victim to foul play, there was no time to waste in notifying the police of his possible abduction, or as Fanny was quick to remind us, his probable murder.

If we could prove Otis was still missing, and that it was Eldon in the grave, the police would have to do something to help us. There was only one thing to do under the circumstances. We had to get to the cemetery, dig up Eldon and get his fingerprints. We could take these to the police as proof positive they had the wrong corpse in the grave. We told Grace to hold off on the move until we could sort everything out, and then we left her, legs and all.

So with our incredibly ridiculous plan established, the gang split up in order to get ready for the evening. Fanny went with Ida and Grady, Bob went to his apartment, and Ted and I went to our cabana.

I couldn't wait to get out of my skirt. It seemed like Otis's funeral had been so long ago.

"It sounded like you had everything figured out before Grace explained her part in this Otis-Eldon thing," Ted said.

"Most of it, but not everything. When Brad told me he'd picked up Otis on the bus, it got me thinking. Sandy mentioned Otis had a brother from Oregon and that's when I put two and two together. The guy on the bus was Otis's brother, he had been carrying a tackle box, and the fishing line was a brand they only sold in Portland. That part was easy enough."

"You knew about the pool chemicals, too. That was darn good detective work."

"But I didn't know what it meant until Grace told us what they'd done with them. I'm assuming they wanted to be sure Eldon had those chemicals in his lungs in case of an autopsy, to convince the police he'd drowned in the pool."

"Right."

"But you pointed out the sleeping pills, the fact that there had been some in his system, and they were like the ones I'd found in the medicine cabinet. That was good." I pointed an "atta-boy" finger at Ted.

"Thanks."

"And it was Fanny who found the fishing line. That was a nice catch," I said.

"And you put that together with the guy on the bus. Really smart."

I blushed under Ted's compliments.

"But there's one thing you figured out, and for the life of me I have no idea how you did it."

"What was that?" I was a little bit worried that Ted would discover I hadn't been completely sure of everything. I wanted him to believe I was incredibly clever. If my top was drooping and my bottom was sagging, at least I wanted him to know I still had a brain.

"How in the heck did you know Grace wasn't a double amputee? She put on a darn good act."

I relaxed. Piece of cake. "Didn't you hear someone running when we got to her house? It had to be her. That's why she took so long to get to the door, and that's why she looked so frightened when we pushed our way in. Didn't you think it a bit unusual that she would race off to get that hideous looking afghan over her lap if there were intruders in her house?"

"Oh yeah. I was so sure someone else was in the apartment that I guess the notion that it was her footsteps we heard didn't even occur to me. I'll have to admit I was pretty keyed up."

"Well, she'd been lying about a lot of things. It was just natural for me to think she had a lot more to hide than her brother-in-law's body. And one more thing," I hated to admit I hadn't been that clever, but I had to be honest, "when we came through the front door I saw a pair of pink fuzzy slippers in the entry way. They looked just like mine."

Ted laughed. "I missed that."

I walked over to the dresser and pawed through my clothes. Silly me, I'd forgotten to pack anything appropriate for grave-digging. I settled for a navy blue jogging suit and told Ted to find something comfortable. Something disposable would be good. I draped my clothes over one arm and turned to Ted.

"And now we know who was in the pool, and who's in Otis's grave. But we still don't know where Otis is," I said.

"If we hadn't paid a visit to his girlfriend, I'd have guessed he'd changed his mind about breaking it off." Ted slid the belt out of his pants. "I would have expected him to be on a plane with her to Tahiti, and the kicker is, his wife couldn't have done a thing about it. Grace couldn't have gone to the police after lying about his death, and she couldn't have put Otis's face on the back of any milk cartons. He was in the clear. Even the goons didn't know he was still alive. A perfect escape plan."

"Now hold on, Ted, how can you be so sure about the goons?" I felt an unsettling in my stomach. It could have been the seafood sandwich, but I didn't think so. "I mean, if we could figure this stuff out, why couldn't they? Maybe they have suspicions of their own. We've been asking a lot of questions. What if they've been watching us?"

"The goons? Yes." Ted kicked off his pants. "They might be watching."

That made me worry. I really had expected him to shake his head and tell me there was nothing to worry about, and that Otis was just holed up in some hotel somewhere until the heat cooled off. "Yes," he repeated. "We need to be more careful."

Be more careful? I was putting on grave-digger clothes, and Ted had just told me we needed to be more careful. What was more gutsy and foolhardy than uncovering a corpse?

"This could get really dangerous." I looked at my husband. "Those guys from the pool hall might be watching us right now.

They might be waiting to jump us as soon as we walk out the door. They might want to torture some information out of us." I was revving up for a full-blown panic. *Please Ted, tell me we don't have to do this.*

"We could go to the police," Ted said.

"Yes, we could. We could go to the police, we could tell them what we know, and let them take it from there."

"Hmmm. Okay, what exactly are you going to tell them?"

I crumpled. What would I tell them? The guy in Otis's grave wasn't really Otis and that the real Otis had disappeared? Maybe if we could get Grace to go downtown with us, she could confirm this. But she'd already identified the body as her husband, and, besides, I was quite certain she wouldn't implicate herself in a cover up, a misuse of a dead body, or anything else so odious. She needed to help her husband, and the only way was to get his insurance money. Without that, Otis was goon fodder.

It was then that I thought of something so awful, yet so plausible that I had to run it through my mind several times before mentioning it to Ted. I took his hands and looked into his eyes. I needed his full attention.

"Ted, did Grace seem sincere about her story? Do you think she was telling the truth?"

"I think so, why?"

"She was in a real hurry to get out of her apartment. She already had the moving guys scheduled for tomorrow, but she still doesn't know where her husband is. Doesn't that seem a little strange?"

"She said he told her to do that."

"That's what she *said,* but how do we know? And another thing. How upset did she seem about this affair Otis had been having? She acted like she didn't know about Sandy until the scene outside of her bedroom window. That just doesn't sound right to me."

"You know what they say, the wife is always the last to know. Besides, people act in different ways. You just can't predict a thing like that."

"Well, I know what I would do if I caught you with another woman," I said.

"Take my car and drive half way across the country?" Ted grinned.

"I was just stupid back then, but suspicious. I didn't know for sure that you were having an affair."

"Because I wasn't," Ted said calmly.

"I know that now, but when I thought something was going on, I was just reacting. Maybe if I were sure, and it had hit me right between the eyes like what happened to Grace, I would have behaved differently."

"What? You'd have killed me?"

"Maybe." I was thinking.

Ted's eyebrows shot up. "Really?"

"Of course not. But I've heard about these crimes of passion. Some women are so overcome with jealousy they just erupt violently. It's not an impossible theory."

"So you think maybe Otis isn't missing? That Grace saw her chance to kill her husband after burying the brother, take his insurance money and get off completely free?"

"What do you think?"

"I don't know. It could have happened that way, but if I were a betting man, I'd put my money on one of the goons."

"Right. Like five hundred dollars worth?"

"Just proves I'm not a bettin' man."

"Ted, I think we have made a terrible mistake confronting Grace like we did. Now we've alerted her. If she killed Otis, then she won't have any compunction about killing all of us."

"Come on, May, now you're just getting yourself worked up about nothing. Even if she did kill her husband, how do you propose she'd go about taking all of us out? Sniper fire?"

"Well, Ted, how about a car bomb? Or maybe a couple of house fires in the middle of the night? She could do it! She's probably trying to get us all together as we speak!"

"Do you remember if anyone mentioned we were going to the cemetery? That wouldn't be good." Ted stroked his chin. I think my panic was rubbing off.

I pinched my eyebrows and groaned. "Maybe I mentioned it. I don't know."

"I've just thought of something else," Ted said. "If the goons knocked off Otis, then they'll want to get their hands on Grace's insurance money, and they certainly won't stand by while we muddy up the waters. They might even be scoping out this cabana as we speak."

"Oh, Ted!" I clutched my husband. He double-clutched me.

"Hurry up. Let's finish getting changed. We can't waste any more time. As soon as we get those fingerprints, we'll go straight to the police. We'll camp out at the station until they take us seriously.

A sudden noise outside our door froze us both.

"Ted, did you hear that?" He put his finger to his lips, then whispered, "Turn off the lights."

I hit the switch and we were bathed in darkness, listening, listening. I could hear the thumping of my heartbeat.

Clunk.

"Ted!"

Snap.

My lower lip trembled. I had nothing to throw if we were attacked.

A shadow flitted behind the patio curtains.

"There's someone outside!" I whispered.

The silence exploded.

Knock! Knock! Knock!

"Someone is at the door!" I threw myself at Ted. We clung to each other, quivering, staring toward the front of the cabana.

"Shhhhh," Ted whispered in my ear.

A shadow passed by the bedroom patio doors, and I felt my knees start to wobble. Ted tightened his grip around my ribcage, keeping me upright. The shadow stopped in front of the glass doors. Through the curtains I saw a second shadow join the first.

I nearly swallowed my tongue.

"May! Dr. List!" Fanny's voice. She rapped against the glass doors and jiggled the handle. "Whatever you're doing, knock it off and get out here!"

It took all of my will power and a warning from Ted to keep me from beating an old lady senseless. I got the door open, and the gang rushed in.

"Why in tarnation are all of the lights out?" Fanny asked.

"Maybe we interrupted something?" Grady gave Ted the old thumbs up and a wink. I was tempted to break his darn thumbs off.

FANNY, GRADY, BOB and Ida huddled in the cabana bedroom. In the soft yellow light of the moon, I noticed they'd all changed into dark apparel. Fanny wore a funky ski cap and a shirt that went to her knees, probably loaners from Ida and Grady. Bob was squeezed into spandex tights with his dragon robe tied by a cloth belt, knotted under his belly. Fanny dug around in the bag hanging from her walker and came up with some metal tubes that looked like fat lipsticks. When she popped the tops off, though, they were greasy camouflage sticks.

"Here." She passed them around. "Rub 'em on all the shiny places. Cheekbones, foreheads, noses, and under your eyes. Go on now."

Ida complied, Bob licked one for some reason, and Grady waited his turn. Ted went to the light switch.

"Wait," Fanny ordered. "Leave it off. Just turn on the lamp by the bed. No use drawing attention."

Attention to what? Had they seen someone outside?

It looked like I was the only one with the jitters. Ida was having a good time, nothing left of her face but two bright eyes, shining in the lamplight. Grady rubbed camouflage stick on his nose. Bob dabbed at his fleshy cheeks. He might need another stick before he was finished.

"Shovels are outside," Fanny said, folding up her walker. "Don't need to carry this thing, too."

"Shovels? Oh yes, good." Ted was getting into it.

I wasn't.

"This is an excellent plan." I cleared my throat. "But maybe we're being too hasty. Really, we haven't discussed any alternatives to the grave dig, have we?"

I told myself I wasn't really scared, not really, not at all anxious about the job. No, I was just being practical. I crossed my arms and sat on the bed. Once the plan became reality, it didn't sound so good. My head was starting to hurt again. Where was the morphine drip when you needed it?

"May is waffling," Fanny said. She tapped her foot. I could tell she was getting angry.

"Perhaps we can think of another way." Ted wanted to help. He was showing his spousal support and tried to make me feel better by asking the gang to reconsider. But he didn't know these guys like I did. Once they got an idea, it was next to impossible to dissuade them.

But I tried.

"We could all go to jail you know. They have laws against this sort of thing. What if we get caught?" I said, staring at the wall. In the back of my mind I was thinking, *and what if the goons are out there.* I turned to look at them. Maybe I could act intimidating. No such luck.

"You don't think we'd go into this without a backup plan, do ya?" Fanny had a little round tin. She scooped out a finger of black paste and smeared it around on her face, under her glasses. "Don't forget your hands, gang." She was rubbing it around like lotion. "The guys will dig, and the ladies will be the lookouts. If someone comes, Ida will have an asthma attack. You give the signal, May, and the guys will scoot."

"How are you going to explain us all being out at the cemetery?" *And why was I even asking the question? It was preposterous.*

"My poor, dead mother." Fanny clutched her hands to her breast. "It was midnight twenty years ago today that she died."

"And you're paying respects on the anniversary of her death," I said, sardonically.

"Midnight when she died," Fanny repeated. She put her hand up to her black forehead. "How I miss my poor, dead mama."

"It must be really hard for you." Ida crossed over and patted Fanny's shoulder. "But the pain will go away in time."

Fanny looked at Ida as if she'd lost her mind. Well, maybe she had.

"Here." Grady stuck the fat lipstick thing in my hand. "Grease up. It's gonna be a long night."

TWENTY-THREE

AND SO, THERE WE WERE. Geriatrics of the underworld crouched and moving in a huddled mass of greasy faces, spandex, navy sweats, blue hairs, ski caps and pain meds, on our way to dig up Otis's dead brother. I was pretty proud of Ted. He was fitting in nicely.

We'd taken the Suburban most of the way, but parked it a quarter mile from the county cemetery just in case. Grady backed it under some leafy trees and Fanny instructed the men to snap off branches and place them over the hood.

"Breaks up the lines of the car," she'd said. "So's nobody'll notice and come investigating."

After we were finished with the vehicle concealment, it still looked pretty much like a Suburban to me, but I didn't mention it. We were all issued shovels and flashlights, but were cautioned not to use the lights unless it was absolutely necessary. Good thing there was a full moon. Still, there was a lot of tripping and grunting going on as we hustled along the gravelly shoulder of the road toward the burial grounds.

Ida was breathing heavily. Not accustomed to such strenuous activities, I'd imagine. I was sweating a good deal under my splotchy makeup despite a cool evening breeze. We were all staying close and kept bumping each other, clanking our shovels.

We were a few yards from the cemetery gates when Fanny shouted "Car!"

I could see the headlights cresting a hill.

"Scatter, everyone! Get in the bushes!" I cried.

Ida stumbled over me, threw her shovel aside, dove and hit

with a grunt. I went to my knees and crawled into some wet bushes. Ted found a clump of pompous grass and disappeared. I didn't see what happened to Bob or Grady or Fanny, but I assumed they took cover, because the car passed without slowing.

Ted emerged and lifted me by the arm. "We're almost there! Come on!" He scooped up Fanny and Ida's discarded shovels.

Then we were running, if that's what you could call it, elbows, knees, chins, shovels pulsing forward. Ida's wide girth was thumping along atop plump legs. Fanny was bent and shuffling, head down, tiny feet and balled fists a blur. Bob moved diagonally as well as horizontally, his belly bouncing with each step, his tennis shoes slapped the pavement. The tail of his robe flew out like a kite. Grady and Ted were faster than the rest of us, and I wished I'd thought to wear one of my sports bras. I was stretching.

The cemetery gates were at least eight feet tall, iron and spiky at the top, chained and padlocked. The rest of the fence surrounding the cemetery was a stout wire affair with smaller spikes positioned about every ten feet.

"Abort the mission?" Ida asked, hopefully. She was finding it hard to get into a normal breathing rhythm. *Wheeze, wheeze.*

"Not on your life, missy. We've come too far," Fanny said. Bob leaned on his shovel and sucked at his teeth.

"I'm hungry," Ida said. "Do you think Denny's is still open?"

We were at a loss. There was no way to get over the fence. Ted checked the chain, and it was as solid as I expected it to be. Fanny, though, was walking along the barrier, running her hand along it and patting it like she was checking for defects.

"Here," she said. "Look." We all hustled over. "There's a little space under the fence here. We'll scoot under."

Bob started laughing.

"Shut it, Bob," Fanny said forcefully. "I know what you're thinking. Use your shovel and clear out a space big enough for your big lard ass. We ain't goin' home without those prints."

Bob started to argue, but Fanny was down and pushing her-

self along like a seal before he could think of a good come-
back. I turned on my flashlight. Fanny had her head under the
fence, but the opening was small, even for her ninety pounds.
She squirmed and kicked, and clawed the ground.

"A little help here!" she hollered.

Ted and Grady hurried to pull at the fence offering a bit
more clearance. More scrabbling and twisting.

Fanny was in.

I looked at Ted, looked at the space under the fence and
shook my head. "There's no way."

Bob sighed and stuck his shovel in the ground. Fanny had
wandered off. I could see her light moving around. She was
probably looking for fresh dirt mounds and reading tombstones. Ted and Grady joined in the digging. I aimed the flashlight, while Ida strolled back and forth humming *Starry, Starry
Night*.

After about ten minutes, Bob dropped his shovel and said,
"Here goes nothing."

"I think May should go first. She's smallest," Grady said.

"But, but, if Bob can get through then the rest of us should
be able to do it." I really didn't want to go under the fence. I
could be lookout from there.

"She's right. I'll go."

Thank you, Bob.

Bob squirmed and kicked as Fanny had done. He pushed
and grunted, as Fanny had done. He got his head through, wiggled his shoulders and arms through, but that's where it all ended. No matter how hard Grady and Ted pulled at the fence,
there just wasn't enough clearance.

"Back out, Bob," Grady said, straining and pulling at the
heavy wire.

"Back out, Bob," Ted said.

"Back out, Bob," Ida said, squatting near Bob's head.

Ida was squatting near Bob's head?

"Ida? How did you get in there?"

Ida poked at Bob's shoulders with splayed fingers.
"Through the gate," she said simply. "It's not locked. But if

you'd rather come through this way, you're gonna need to dig some more. I think Bob's stuck."

It wasn't locked. The chain was solid, and the padlock was there, but someone had forgotten to close it. Once we got around to Bob's head, we pulled together and got him through. He wasn't in a good mood. I imagine there'd been a good deal of chaffing as we tugged and hauled him across the ground.

"So you lost a little skin. Remember, Bob, it's for the mission," Grady said.

"It's not that," Bob said. "I've torn my robe."

"Pssst." Fanny hailed us with her flashlight. "I've found it. Get your shovels and shake your buns. He's right over there." She moved off and we followed the bobbing light.

In a grove of small trees, we found fresh dirt, slightly rounded. Ida produced a can of her favorite soda from a little waist purse, and the men were sharing. Energy for the job ahead. We'd switched off our flashlights and had to rely on moonlight and sparsely positioned security lamps, but it was enough to work with, and even gave the evening a soft, pleasant look. Crickets were singing, I heard an owl in one of the taller trees and a breeze ruffled my pink hair. The smell of rain was in the air, so we couldn't waste any time getting started.

Wait a minute.

I was standing on the grave of Otis Culpepper, or, I should say, the grave of his brother, preparing to dig up his body just to get a few fingerprints. What was I thinking?

"What are we doing?" I hissed. "Have we all gone completely nuts?"

"She's losing it again," Fanny said to Ida.

"Where did you have it last, May?" Ida asked.

Fanny shuffled over and smacked me in the back of the head. "Hold it together, May Bell."

"Knock that off, Fanny," I said.

"Get some giblets, girlie." Fanny swatted my pink hair again. "If we don't get his fingers rolling in ink, we can't prove anything to the coppers. It's what we got to do. There are lives at stake."

"Lives? What lives?" I smoothed down my hair. My face was starting to itch. That darned paint was cracking in my wrinkles.

"Lives! Somebody's life, yours maybe, Ted's, who knows?"

"She's right, Mayfly." Ted surprised me. "We've got to do this."

"I just don't want to be a part of this." I was starting to feel like the kid who wouldn't take the dare. Everyone would think I was a party pooper and so much for my popularity.

"It's okay. You have to be our lookout, anyway. Take Ida and Fanny, and stand by the gate. We'll do the rest." After putting the fingerprint kit in his pocket, Grady moved us off.

I was more than happy to take orders.

When we got to our post, Ida said, "Let's sit. Do you want to sing a duet?"

"No singing," Fanny said. She pulled her glasses off and huffed on them, then rubbed them around on her sleeve. "Cop a squat, ladies, this might take a while."

We all sat. I could hear the thudding of shovels jabbing into dirt, and I wished the boys weren't so loud.

A dog barked in the distance.

"I hope this doesn't take too long," I said. My voice quivered.

Fanny had her arm over her head, doing some stretches.

"What do you think happened to Otis?"

"He's probably dead." Fanny said it so easily.

"Why do you think that?"

"Plenty of people wanted him dead. Plenty of motive."

"Let's talk about that for a minute. What motive?" The shovels gouged away.

"A motive for murder?" Fanny pulled her feet up toward her crotch and leaned forward. She started down the list. "To conceal a crime, for revenge, accident, for some monetary gain, or just the joy of killing."

I grimaced. "The joy of killing?"

"Oh, yeah. Some people get off on that sort of thing." Fanny grabbed one skinny leg and hefted it up over her shoulder. I couldn't see her eyes in the dark, but I imagined they were clear and glistening. Probably sinister when she said, "Could you ever do something like that, just to see if you could get away with it?"

I gasped. "No! Certainly not."

"No? You don't just wonder what it would be like?"

"Fanny, you're giving me the willies. Please stop."

"No, I suppose not. Me neither," she said. "Not in my character."

"That's nice to know." I listened to the shovels. *Hurry up!*

"But what about your husband?" Fanny said. "Do you have a big life insurance policy gathering dust? Do you have an inheritance? Does he just get tired of you some days? Maybe he wants to get you out of the way so he can try out some new blood."

"Good grief, Fanny! Don't say stuff like that!" She was really getting under my skin. But I couldn't stop the thoughts that crept in.

May Bell. You've been under so much stress lately. I've brought you something to help you sleep. I know the bottle says just take two, but I'm a doctor, after all, and it's perfectly safe to take twelve. Believe me. Here's a glass of water. I can't stay; my new temp is waiting for me at the clinic. Pleasant dreams, my dear!

I shook my head. Knock it off, May.

"Would you look at that?" Ida said.

Fanny and I turned to see her tracing the stars with a finger. "Is that the Big Dipper? I think it is, maybe it's Caseopizza. And lookie there! Someone's shooting fireworks. So pretty— red and blue, white swirling lights.

"Crap!" Fanny jumped to her feet. "Coppers!"

In the distance a car crept down the road, approaching the cemetery with red lights revolving. A darting, white searchlight probed the bushes and grass alongside the burial grounds.

"They're almost here. We need a distraction." Fanny grabbed her flashlight and headed for the gate. "Run back to the guys and tell 'em to make a run for it!"

"What are you going to do?" I hauled Ida to her feet.

"Never mind me, just go!"

Fanny went out the gate waving her flashlight around. Ida was creaking. Her joints had locked up and the police car was almost upon us. Forget running back to the guys, Ida wasn't going anywhere.

"Get down!" I hit the ground, pulling Ida down with me.

"Uh," Ida grunted.

We lay prone on the grass. I lifted my head slightly to see where Fanny had gone.

Where was she? I lifted my head a little higher. I couldn't see Fanny anywhere, and the police car was nearly in front of us. The searchlight swept the gate, and I ducked. Its beam stroked the back of Ida's head. I hoped she could breathe with her face in the dirt like that. I strained to hear the sounds of digging, but they had stopped. Had the guys noticed the lights?

Where the heck was Fanny?

The police car slow-rolled to a stop.

I could smell exhaust, could feel the engine rumble, could see the red and blue lights arching and swirling. They didn't turn on those lights unless there was trouble. I knew that.

Ida whimpered.

"Shhhh, Ida, stay down!"

A car door opened. I heard a police dispatcher talking in stilted monotone. Radio blurbs, numbers, codes, and static. I pressed myself into the dirt, working up something to tell the cop if he came over and nudged me with his SIG Sauer, or whatever they were using these days. This was so bad, so improper! And where was Fanny? She was supposed to be the one with the dead mother.

A scream shattered the midnight calm and sent a flock of nesting birds scattering in blind panic. "What was that?" Ida turned to me, her eyes wide in terror. Another scream turned the blood in my veins to ice.

"Aliens! Aliens! They got me!"

I scooted closer to Ida. "It's Fanny! Look!"

Ida lifted her head close to mine. We peeked over the top of the grass. Fanny was in the middle of the road running toward the police car's headlights. She had her clothes off and waved her arms wildly over her head.

Ida gasped.

"It's for the cause," I said soberly.

"Of course," Ida said.

We could hear Fanny clearly. "They came down right back there and swooped me up in their craft with some kind of laser! I was probed!"

Oh, Fanny. I closed my eyes and bit at my lip to keep from laughing.

"They stripped me and then took my liver!" Fanny was at the car. She put a foot on the front bumper and climbed onto its hood. A tall man in a hat and uniform stepped out of the car and came around behind her. He took her by the feet and pulled her off. He wasn't rough about it, just gently slid her backward down to the road. Her skin rubbed in a fleshy vibrato as she slid over the metal. It sounded like *screeee*. I could hear the man talking in low, soothing tones, but I couldn't make out the words.

"What's she going to do?" Ida was starting to have some trouble breathing, and I worried that she'd give us away if she went into a full-blown asthma attack.

"Take me in right now!" Fanny shouted for our benefit. "I want to file a report STAT!"

"She's getting them away from here," I said in disbelief. Fanny would stop at nothing.

The policeman's partner was out of the car holding up a blanket. Poor old demented woman, poor black-faced thing wandering around, confused, crazy, didn't even know she wasn't wearing any clothes. Get her in the car, get her to headquarters, and find a nice psychiatric ward or nursing home.

Fanny dove into the back seat shouting, "Go, go, go!"

The cops sped away with their ward, just like that, and we were in the clear.

"They're gone." I took Ida's arm again, but didn't give her a chance to limber up. We had to get to the guys. How we were going to spring Fanny, I didn't know, but she'd saved us for the time being. Good old girl.

I flew through the graveyard. Ida was behind me, huffing and puffing. We had our flashlights on, but it didn't keep me from slamming my thighs against a couple of tombstones as I raced along. The slivers of light weren't of much use.

"Over here!" Ted called out and flashed his light on and off. I'd gotten turned around somehow. Wasn't the grave over there? No, it was in the crop of trees to my left. Where was Ida? There she was, a shadow making time, chasing Ted's light. I fell in behind her.

At the edge of the grave, Ida and I stopped, bent over and gasped for air. It took me a few minutes to recover. When I straightened up, my knees were spongy. I was very uncomfortable, and the greasy paint stuff dripped from my face and down into my collar.

"We saw the cops," Ted said. "We almost took off, but then we saw the car leave. Where's Fanny?"

"Aliens got her," Ida said, gasping for oxygen.

"I'll explain later," I said, swallowing the coppery taste in my mouth. So much for my pilates classes. Nothing had prepared me to keep up this kind of pace.

"Well, we did it." Grady sounded disappointed. He was sitting on a huge pile of dirt with his shovel across his lap. I heard Bob somewhere at my feet. No, he was under my feet. Down in the Otis hole. I leaned over and peered in. Then I looked at Ted, then at Grady. The guys all looked exhausted under the pale moonlight.

"Great! That's great!"

"Just one little problem," Grady said.

"And what's that?" I flipped on my light and knelt by the grave. "Couldn't get the lid off the coffin?"

Bob looked up, shielding his eyes.

"Sorry." I turned off the light.

"We got the lid off, awright."

I started to turn the light on again and thought better of it, but it was so dark down there, I could barely make out the top of Bob's head. What was he standing on, anyway?

"Ah, gee, he was decomposed?" I felt so defeated. All that

work. All that planning for nothing. Maybe we could take him out in pieces. Or maybe we could just get his hands. Maybe if I ran back to the Suburban I could find some plastic bags...

"Not exactly," Bob said. "Have a look-see for yourself."

I looked at Ted, a habit I had—looking at my husband for reassurance. He always knew what to do. Ted nodded.

Bob grunted and pulled at something. I heard a heavy, wooden sound, creaking hinges, and then a heavy thud. I tried to see what was happening down in the hole, but couldn't make out a thing. It was still so dark down there.

"Get on your belly and hang your head over the edge," Bob said. "Then point your light down."

I did as I was told. Ida leaned over my shoulder, her breath hot on my neck.

"It's Otis!" Ida shouted.

"Ted, I thought you said that couldn't be Otis?" I jabbed the light around at the open coffin. What? I leaned down further. "It *is* Otis! And Eldon!"

There were two bodies in the coffin.

"What in the world?"

"Sacrilege!" Ida squealed.

Otis stared up at me. He was on his back stretched across the top of his dead brother. In the middle of his forehead was a neat, round, black hole, and another in his right cheek.

Ouch.

I got to my knees and dusted off. "Close it up." I took command. "Close it up. We've got to get the cops out here somehow without letting them know how we found Otis."

Ida was making some funny sounds and when I looked at her, I saw she was staring down at Otis. Her mouth was formed into a tight funnel, and her tongue was sticking out like a wiener. She bobbed her head forward and back like a turkey.

"Look away, Ida. Think about something else." It was all I could do to keep my own reflexes in check. I gritted my teeth, swallowed convulsively and helped Ida to her feet.

At least we had our answer. Otis hadn't gone missing after all. He didn't die of accidental drowning, heart attack or old age. Now we knew why nobody had seen Otis around. Our dear Mr. Culpepper had indeed been murdered—shot right through the face.

As the shovels pushed the dirt back into the hole, I had to wonder. *Who had pulled the trigger?*

TWENTY-FOUR

IDA AND I HELD HANDS while the boys returned the grave to its pre-desecrated state. A foggy mist settled down around us, followed by an eerie, silent breeze. I shivered and pulled my greasy collar up under my chin. The haze softened the security lights, turning us all into shadowy ghosts. As we made our way toward the giant cemetery gates, we were startled by a sudden noise.

"What was that?" I clutched Ted's arm.

"It's just the sprinkler system," Bob said. "Must be on a timer. Come on. Let's get out of here." Shovels over his shoulder, Bob moved out ahead of us. We dodged and ducked, but got soaked by the sprinklers by the time we got out onto the street.

Back at the Suburban, we dripped and pushed branches out of the way. We discussed how to tell the police we knew where to find the dead Otis.

I brushed leaves off the windshield. "It's going to be pretty interesting since they aren't even looking for him. They think he's dead."

"He is dead, sweetheart," Ted said.

"Oh yeah." My brain was turning to mush. "It would look pretty silly for me to tell the police they could find Otis's dead body in his own grave!"

"Take it easy, May Bell." Ted tried to calm me, but I shrugged him off.

"She's right," Grady said, and grunted when a stubborn branch gave him some trouble. He pried it away from the hood of the car and tossed it aside. "If we go to the police without the smoking gun, we'll get a quick trip to Bellevue for sure."

Ted was quick to play devil's advocate. "But if we keep trying to solve this thing on our own, whoever killed Otis might just make us tenants in the next available burial plot."

Bob rubbed at his torn robe. "Is anyone hungry? All that digging really made me hungry."

Ida took Bob's hand and opened the door of the Suburban. She leaned in and rummaged through the glove box. While Bob and Ida were scavenging, Ted, Grady and I decided, after much discussion and some regret, that, regardless of their reaction, it was time to turn this case over to the authorities.

"Ted's right," I said. "It's just too dangerous to keep this up. A good soldier knows when to call in reinforcements. Or even," I added quietly, "when to retreat."

Ted looked at me, and an unnatural expression passed over his face. I think it was a look of pride, or of affection, or maybe a look that said he knew how much all of this meant to me, and that he was impressed with my strength and courage. That look could carry me through a wall of fire and bring me out safely on the other side.

I knew what we had to do.

"But not yet," I said with a newfound sense of confidence. "Let's go over the facts one more time. We might have missed something."

The guys seemed surprised by my sudden show of bravado. But I didn't want to give up on this case without turning over every stone, regardless of the danger. They nodded enthusiastically.

It would have been so easy. Just go to the police, tell them what we knew and let them do their job. I'd been so eager to hand it over.

It was the look in my husband's eyes that caused me to reconsider. For a rare moment in my life, he'd shown a glimmer of respect when we were on the case. He'd complimented me earlier on my detective skills, and, in the brief second after I said we should go to the police, I saw the love and the admiration in his eyes. But I also saw something else, the look of disappointment.

I didn't like it.

"Let's go," I said, and crawled into the Suburban.

I needed a shower. A hot, steamy, cleansing shower free of cats or corpses. The inside of the Suburban was stinking up pretty good by all of the dirt, muddy clothes, sweat and grease paint. Grady dropped us off at our respective homes and went in search of Fanny.

We would have to wait before going over the facts. It was quite disheartening for us all that the sun was coming up, and, even after all that expert sleuthing, we were no closer to the truth than we'd been the night before.

THE SHOWER WAS heavenly. The black paint ran from my face and swirled down the drain. It took a great deal of soap until the water finally ran clear, and by then I'd gone over almost everything I'd learned since coming "home" to the Waning Years Estates.

Suddenly I heard the bathroom door creak. Through the steam and suds a human form approached the shower door.

"Ted. Is that you?" I croaked

It was the size and shape of Ted, but taking slow, careful steps. It clutched a dark object in its hand, and the thing was pointed directly at my chest. I rubbed at the soap in my eyes— that only made things worse—I'd made myself soap-blind. Where could I go? I was trapped inside a shower stall. I had learned too much. I should have known.

Would I be joining Otis and Eldon?

When the shower door opened, I was ready. Shampoo in one hand, the conditioner in the other, I battered the invading monster like a windmill.

"May! What in the name of all that's holy are you doing?" Ted ducked and dodged, and spilled the cup of coffee in his hand.

"Ted! You brought me coffee?" I smiled wide. Good husband. "Can you get me a towel?"

I took my time drying off. My cheeks were pink from scrubbing and from embarrassment, and I needed a second before emerging. I had to stop imagining horrible things. I wrapped myself in a white bathrobe, pulled on a pair of socks, sipped at my cooling and near empty cup of coffee and took a deep breath.

"You need sleep," Ted said. "I can tell."

"I suppose you're right. There's just been so much excitement these last couple of days." Maybe Ted would buy that as an excuse for me giving him the shampoo treatment. "You should see yourself," I said. Ted was still in his grave-digger clothes; his face was three different colors; and his hair stood up in stiff tufts.

"My turn for the shower." Ted started off, then turned. "If you want to bring me some coffee, I promise not to hit you with a loofah."

I blushed again. "You've got it."

Ted spent a long time in the shower. That grease paint was tenacious. I paced, waiting for him, thinking about the case. When he emerged, I could tell it took a great deal of work to get his skin clean. The first layer was red, practically rubbed off.

"Do you want to go over the facts of the case?" I said wearily.

"No coffee?"

"Oh, Ted, I'm so sorry, I forgot. You still want some?"

Ted tossed his towel at the bathroom door and shook his head. "That bed looks really good right now, and I can barely stand as it is. Move over, Babe, I'm goin' in."

It was noon before Ted jerked and startled me awake. The minute my eyes opened, I thought of Fanny. Was she serving time in the pokey, or had Grady managed to spring her?

Coffee. Black and thick.

I poured a cup from the morning carafe, nuked it a minute and took the mug over to the breakfast table, moving like my joints were full of rust. Every muscle in my body screamed for mercy, and my bruises had bruises.

Ted walked in shortly after, looking like he was still asleep. He moved stiffly, too. His eyes were puffy, and since he'd gone to bed with his hair wet, it was flat on one side. He took juice from the refrigerator and sat across from me. He sipped at his juice and then poured himself a bowl of cereal.

"Did we really do what I think we did last night?" Ted asked.

"Not if the cops ask," I answered.

"I can hardly move this morning. Are you as sore as I am?"

I nodded, wishing our cabana came with a maid. There were clothes strewn around everywhere, and everything was covered in muck. Thankfully the rain had merely threatened, and then had passed, but the cemetery sprinkler system had turned the soil to sticky clay. Our dirty grave clothes would have to be laundered, or they'd be a sure giveaway. *Evidence,* Fanny would say.

"You can't exactly call it grave-robbing when we didn't take the body." Ted swigged his juice and poured another glass. He poked at his grape nuts with a spoon.

"Bodies," I reminded him.

After our mid-day breakfast, Ted got on the phone while I made quick work of the laundry. There was enough dirt on our cloths to start a small vegetable garden. I gathered up the soggy mess we'd worn the night before and pushed them into the washing machine. As I did, something tapped at my memory cells. I couldn't put my finger on it, but it had the feeling of déjà vu, a fleeting memory upon waking—there for a second then gone. I pushed the clothes down farther in the machine.

There it was again. What was it? Like something missing or something that shouldn't have been, and, as hard as I tried, I couldn't figure out what was bothering me. So, I finished loading the machine, rinsed off my shoes and then rinsed Ted's. Gosh, what filth.

Ted came up to stand beside me. "They're all over at Grady and Ida's. They want us to come over as soon as possible."

"Fanny, too?" I turned off the water and placed our shoes on a towel to dry.

"Grady bailed her out last night. Just in time, too. They were getting ready to transport her to some place called Trembling Acres."

"The mental hospital?"

"Yep. Apparently, she refused to give them her real name or tell them where she lives. They didn't have a choice."

"I hope she didn't make any enemies. As much as I hate to admit it, we're going to have to turn this case over to the police eventually."

"That's what the gang wants to talk about. But I think they want to visit the girlfriend one more time."

"What for?"

"For one thing," Ted said, "Grady agreed with you on the issue of Otis's wife. She really was in a hurry to leave town, and she might have been lying about a few things. We want to talk to Sandy and ask her if Grace had ever seen her and Otis together, or if she had called some time when Grace answered the phone—just anything to discredit Grace's story that she knew nothing of the affair. If Grace is lying about that, we might have just found our murderess. For all we know, Otis could have come home to tell her he was leaving. We don't know that he didn't, except for what Grace told us. That would have given her enough reason to kill him. She would still be eligible for his life insurance money."

"Right. And wasn't his car still in the carport? If he'd taken off, surely he would have driven, but then again, if it was like Grace said, he wouldn't have wanted to draw attention to his car. The cops could have tracked him down that way. I don't know. It's a long shot to think she killed her own husband, but she *could* have done it, now that we know she's fully limbed."

"Wait. How would she get him in the grave? And when?"

"Hmmm. I didn't think about that. Okay, let's change directions. Sandy knew about some guys who'd been threatening Otis. We need to get those names. Whatever we can offer the police will be good."

I grabbed my purse and swung it over my arm. I felt very

confident. Ted followed me to the door and we stepped out, in a hurry to get to Ida and Grady's condo.

"Um, May, dear?" Ted stopped. "We're not wearing any shoes."

"Oh, bother. They're soaked."

"You still have Ida's slippers?"

"They'll have to do. I'll just go put on an extra pair of socks. It's a short walk to the condo, and then we'll mostly be in the Suburban. Piece of cake."

WE GOT TO Sandy's house around one o'clock. Bob had changed into a neatly ironed white shirt and slacks. I could smell a good dose of aftershave on his clean cheeks. He was even being careful with the bag of Doritos on his lap. He brushed away crumbs and wiped his mouth with a napkin after each bite.

Fanny sniffed the air and wrinkled her nose. "Good grief, Bob, did you use the whole bottle of cologne?"

Bob deliberately wiped his hands on the napkin and closed the bag. "It's *Dude,*" he said.

"Do I look all right?"

"You look very nice, Bob," Ida said.

Fanny snorted. "You ain't Sandy's type."

Bob tried to hide his blush and went on the defensive. "Oh? What makes you so sure?"

"Well, let's see," Fanny started folding down her fingers. "You ain't a gambler, you don't have a price on your head, you ain't in debt up to your eyeballs, you ain't a woman-hater, or a girl-beater, and you ain't married. I think that just about covers it. Oh yeah, and you're about six inches too tall. Any more questions?"

Bob looked deflated.

"You forgot one thing," Ida said seriously to Fanny. "He's not dead."

"Never mind her, Bob." I glared at Fanny. "Sandy told us she'd been a poor judge of character where men were concerned. I'd say she's ripe for a change."

"You think so?" Bob licked a finger and ran it over his eyebrows, which turned a pale orange from the spit and Dorito dust, but not that you could tell if you weren't looking.

"Sure. Someone with class—like you."

I sat back in my seat, happy with myself. As far as I knew, Bob hadn't been with a woman for a long time, not counting his brief interlude with our old apartment manager, and that really didn't count at all. It would have been nice if Sandy saw in him the things we appreciated.

Bob shifted slightly to his left. Soon it wasn't just his aftershave I smelled.

"Excuuuse me!" Bob said.

Fanny started waving her arms through the Suburban air, cursing loudly.

"We're here," Ted said. "Time to play ball."

"Rack 'em up!" Ida cried.

SANDY MUST HAVE BEEN in her garden when we rang the front doorbell. She came around the corner of her house with her hands in gloves, a trowel by her hip, and a wide-brimmed hat low on her forehead. She wore skintight white shorts, sandals, and a bikini top. Her knees were dirty and a leaf clung to her long hair.

She smiled brightly.

Bob started coughing, Fanny banged between his shoulder blades much more vigorously than necessary. I think she enjoyed doing that a little too much.

"I thought I heard the bell. Why don't you come around to the back? I'm just finishing up." Sandy's long, lean legs led the way. Her shorts rode high enough for us to get a good view of some major cheek leak. Wow! This woman was ruthless.

Fanny had left her walker in the Suburban and wandered about with her hands behind her back. I admired the lovely garden. Bougainvillea trailed up a wooden trellis, and flowers of every variety scented the air.

Sandy pointed out the various plants, naming them all, telling us which ones were perennials and which ones were annuals.

"How do you keep everything so green?" Bob asked. It was the first time I'd seen him interested in anything besides food or ballet, but then again, there was this gorgeous woman bending over to pluck a dandelion out of her violet patch. Bob's aftershave was steaming up.

"I had a sprinkler system installed. Nothing fancy, but it really helps out. It's on a timer and runs about an hour every evening." Sandy stood up and put her hand on Bob's arm.

"Umm, Bob, you smell as good as my roses." Sandy held his gaze a minute before turning to me. "Careful, May, that ground is still a little bit soggy."

I looked at my feet. Shucks. I'd messed up Ida's slippers. I shook my foot and mud flew.

"You'll be okay if you stay on the trail," Sandy said. "I had some landscaping bark put down." Sandy led us off, and we continued the tour.

The men were ever so complimentary on the placement of hedges and decorative grasses. Ida loved the bird feeders and fountains; Fanny kept glancing at the house. She was probably dying to get to Sandy's detective tapes.

We had yet to tell Sandy about our cemetery discovery, and, thankfully, the gang's code of silence was holding up well. I wanted Sandy to go on believing her Otis had died at night swim, not by twin gunfire to the face, and not because I was feeling particularly altruistic. I'd noticed something about Sandy's garden that gave me cause to keep our information secret, but as yet, I didn't know what it could be. I had to rely on my instincts.

"Sandy," I said, something was buzzing in my head. Something about my ruined shoes, Ida's slippers, something, something. "What kind of dirt would you say this is?"

"Hmm?" Sandy and the rest of the group looked at me.

"I mean—did you use potting soil or something? Or did you just use the dirt that was here when you bought the house?" I acted nonchalant, just making conversation, but my words were coming out too quickly. I willed myself to stay calm.

"The soil here is so acidic I had some guys bring in a load of top soil. Otherwise my plants wouldn't grow at all."

"That's what I was thinking," I said quietly. Now I knew what had been bothering me.

"Can we go look at some of your new tapes now?" Fanny was waving us toward the house. She looked like a flight attendant, waving with two fingers extended—*This way to the exits.*

Ted looked at me. I looked quickly toward the Suburban. I knew we hadn't interrogated Sandy the way we had planned, but it just didn't matter.

"Sandy, thank you so much for sharing your garden. We just wanted to be sure you were okay. We really don't want to take up any more of your time." I pulled at Ted's sleeve.

"Yes, Sandy, if there's anything we can do, please let us know." Ted caught Grady's eye, and Grady took Ida's arm, leading her back to the drive.

Bob and Fanny stood with their mouths open. They looked like two kids ordered into time-out.

"Let's go, Bob," Grady said firmly. Bob pouted, but he turned and followed.

Fanny cursed all the way to the Suburban. She kept "accidentally" stepping on the back of my slippers.

"I've figured it out," I said when we were pulling away from Sandy's driveway. "And we've got to get to the police station. Now!"

TWENTY-FIVE

AT THE POLICE STATION, the desk sergeant jerked out of a doze when we entered. We were all speaking at once. The officer looked at Ida over his glasses, then at the rest of us in turn. I imagined what he must have been thinking. Here was Ida with her blazing hair offering pound cake from her purse, Fanny with a history of bare boobies and alien liver extractions, Bob reeking of *Dude*, and Grady leading the pack with grease paint in the creases under his eyes. My pink hair and inside-out dress didn't help matters. I'd only noticed the dress thing when I was in the Suburban. Ted was the only one who looked anything close to normal.

"Why don't you all just take a seat? I'll see what I can do." The cop smiled at us solicitously, and it reminded me of someone placating a bunch of crazed lunatics before handing out the meds. I really couldn't blame him.

"I'll need you to fill out some paperwork."

At least he was doing something.

While the officer dug around in a drawer for some forms and clipboards, Fanny, Ida and I shared a hard wooden bench. Grady and Bob stood, since all of the other chairs were occupied. A man with bulging biceps dug around in an ashtray for butts. Fanny gave him a silent signal and he tossed one over.

"Fanny! What are you doing?" I hissed. "That's disgusting!"

"Killjoy," she said, and shot the butt back into the ashtray. The bicep man chuckled and put his second-hand cigarette to his mouth. His wrists were shackled, chained to a belt around his waist. Yikes.

"Anybody got a light?" the man bellowed. Fanny reached into her cloth bag.

"Fanny!"

"I can at least give him a light," she said brusquely.

I didn't fight it. A uniformed officer was coming through the door.

"Someone here about a murder?" The officer looked around the room. I lifted my hand. "Why don't you come with me?" He signaled me to follow him.

"Can my friends come, too, Officer, er, Crouch?" I'd caught a glimpse of his nametag. As I stood up, I looked to Grady and clutched at Ted. So much for nerves of steel. I considered fighting Fanny for her walker. My knees kept folding on me.

Crouch the grouch. The officer took the paperwork from the desk sergeant and grunted, which I took for a yes, and we all crowded in behind him on our way to his desk. I heard several of the other officers snickering as we passed, but I kept my attention on the back of our guy. The seat of his dark pants sagged, pulled by the various cop things hanging on his belt. He kept fiddling at a long stick banging against his left leg. I just couldn't imagine this guy chasing any perps on Top Cops the way his waistline bubbled over on each side. My guess was, he'd just as soon draw his gun and shoot anyone trying to get away. That much sooner to the doughnuts.

"Your name please?" The cop pulled out a chair on wheels and plunked down. Although he didn't offer, I took the chair beside the desk. The rest of the gang rounded up chairs and scooted in as best they could.

I gave him my name, enunciating carefully, "May Bell List."

The cop hunted in his drawer for a pen, then clicked it several times while I waited impatiently. "Go on," he said.

"You mind?" Bob pointed at a white cardboard box of assorted danishes lodged between two stacks of papers.

"Be my guest," the detective said with mock cordiality. Bob didn't care. He scooped out an éclair.

"May, you'd better tell them about Eldon first, so he'll get the whole picture. Then you can tell him about the murder," Bob said. He looked down at his shirtfront and dabbed at some spilled cream filling.

The cop squinted like there was smoke in his eyes. "A murder you say? Somewhere around here?"

"At the Waning Years Estates swimming pool to be exact," Ida said. "Otis Culpepper."

"No, no, that's not right," Fanny said. "Criminally! It wasn't even Otis. It was his brother." She lifted a framed picture from the desk. The cop took it from her and put it back.

"Now you're saying two guys were murdered? That's funny. I don't remember that." Crouch shouted across the room to another cop throwing darts at a bulletin board cluttered with America's Most Wanted posters. "Hey Chuck! You know anything about two murders over at the Waning Years Estates?"

"Can't say I do. Too busy picking up alien abductees." The cop tossed another dart, and I could see him smirking. Now would be a good time for one of Fanny's head smacks, but the guy was too far away.

"I can explain that," Fanny growled.

"I thought you looked familiar." Officer Crouch gave Fanny a sidelong glance, probably worried that she'd start peeling off her clothes.

"We were trying to dig up Otis, only it wasn't Otis in his grave, it was his brother Eldon." Fanny stood up and put her hands on the detective's desk. "But, guess what? Otis somehow showed up in his grave later, lying right there on top of his brother. And where were all of you guys when people are digging up graves, huh?" Fanny was revving up.

"I guess we're hauling in old crazies claiming they've taken a ride on a flying saucer." The cop leaned toward Fanny, and Fanny leaned toward the cop. Things were getting out of control.

I pulled Fanny back. "We didn't know Otis was in his own grave. Not until after we found Eldon," I said, not making much sense, and I didn't have the slightest idea how I was going to start over. Two officers walked by, grinned at Crouch, and twirled fingers around their ears as they passed. I felt my face grow hot.

Bob finished the éclair. He rummaged through the box, then settled on a mashed thing with colored sprinkles.

"Lady," the detective said, "you're talking about murder. We've got no reports of that, no bodies, no emergency calls, nothing."

I was holding my temper in check. "No, you wouldn't, because it was a very clever murder. Maybe two murders. Just look in Otis Culpepper's grave. Only there are two guys in Otis's grave. We thought it was Otis at first when we saw him floating in the pool during night swim. It was actually Otis's brother, because he didn't have a tattoo."

"The Mona Lisa," Ida said sweetly.

"He almost didn't make it, though," Bob said. "He fought it all the way to the grave."

"Yes, I checked the body myself," Ted said. "He slid halfway out of his coffin. I confirmed the death and absence of tattoo when I was getting a feel of the body."

"I was lucky enough to have moist towelettes in my purse," I said. "But that's not the point."

"What is the point?" Crouch looked amused.

"The real issue is, who killed Otis? At first I thought it was the goons or maybe the wife. But then I changed my mind. It could have been the wife when I figured out that she still had her legs, but my guess is the girlfriend did it. I wasn't sure at first until I noticed her muddy shoes." I thought I was making some headway. This bit of crucial evidence would get the guy's attention.

Crouch wasn't looking at me any more. He was checking his fingernails and biting his lip.

"I'll tell you what." He sighed and then gave me a thin smile. "As soon as I see a dead body I'll look into it." The cop's patience must have run out. He closed his notebook and waved us away.

AS WE ALL WALKED slowly from the precinct, I felt as if I'd been beaten and then wrung through an old timey dryer.

"He didn't believe me. He thought I was nuts," I said, fighting tears.

"I coulda told you that," Fanny said. "With all that rambling in there you sounded like a flaming psychotic." She ka-chunked along the sidewalk.

"I guess your stunts didn't exactly pave the way for good will," Bob said to Fanny. He'd made off with the remaining doughnuts. The white box was tucked under his arm.

"Now what are we going to do?" My voice was high, and I was bordering on desperation.

"It's clear to me," Fanny said. She hefted her walker and threw it over her shoulder. "He wants a dead body? Well, then, we'll give him a dead body."

"What?" I asked.

"Yeah. I say we wait 'til dark, get back over to the cemetery and haul 'em both out. Drag 'em on over here, then let the coppers say we're crazy. Humph!"

"Yes! Roll their old bones over here and dump them on that guy's desk." Ida squealed.

"I think we have room in the Suburban," Grady mused.

"You'll want to put tarps down," Ted said.

Gads! There weren't enough towelettes in my purse to handle a job this big. But it did look like the only way.

"Mind if we make a stop at Starbucks first?" I asked.

ONCE WE WERE SETTLED under the umbrellas at the coffee shop, I had a chance to explain my shoe theory. Everyone had been asking, but I wanted to think it through one more time, to get the words right. I sure didn't want to sound like a flaming psychotic. As I explained, I was certain my suspicions were correct.

"Remember when I walked through the cement at Grace's house, Ida? My shoes were covered in that wet gray cement. I had to throw them out. Then, my second pair of shoes, and Ted's, were covered in that brown muck from the cemetery, and I had to borrow Ida's slippers again." Ida looked at my feet. "Oh, there they are!"

"When we were at Sandy's house last night, I noticed a pair of her shoes under the kitchen sink. I was looking for dish soap, and there they were, covered in this brown, moist dirt. I remembered she liked to garden, and didn't think much of it, but when we were at her house today, I paid close attention to the soil. It was rich, dark brown—almost black. Not at all like the stuff on my shoes, or the shoes I found in her house. The dirt on her shoes was the same stuff we brought home from the cemetery."

Bob stroked his chin. "You're right. I had to soak my shoes in the sink before I got them clean. The cemetery sprinklers made everything damp and muddy. Probably comes on every few hours."

"I thought of that, too," I went on. "When Sandy mentioned her sprinkler system, that got me thinking about the dirt in the cemetery and the stuff on our shoes—on her shoes. It was exactly the same stuff. And one more thing, when I was rinsing them off, there were green sequins stuck in the mud. Ted, do you remember what Joyce was wearing at the funeral? Remember? She caught her skirt on a branch and ripped it off."

Ted looked blank.

"It was a beautiful, green dress with lots of green sequins. Hand sewn, I would imagine. Lovely work."

"How the heck do you remember that?"

"Am I thinking what you're thinking?" Ida asked.

"The little princess was out at the cemetery," Bob said.

"*Before* we got there," I added. "Before we dug up Otis's grave. Now who do you suppose put Otis in there?"

"Eldon?" Ida asked, bless her heart.

"No, dear, Eldon was already in there." Grady patted her hand.

"Otis put Eldon in there?" Ida looked at her husband.

"No, Eldon was already dead." Grady had the patience of Job.

"Oh, that's good. I thought you said Otis was dead."

"He is dead, numb wad," Fanny jabbed.

"Oh. That's right," Ida said.

Ted put his elbows on the table. "Okay. So let's say Sandy was at the grave. The shoes prove it. But it took all three of us digging like we were fools to get down to the casket." Ted paused a moment, letting this all sink in, then began anew, "I know the woman is really fit, but I doubt very seriously she could dig up a grave, haul a body over, dump it in, and then cover everything up again, all before her slumber party with Fanny, not to mention she'd have had to do it in broad daylight. It would be next to physically impossible and, if I may be candid, quite ludicrous."

Everyone grew quiet. Of course. It would be impossible. My bright idea grew dim.

"And besides, why would she shoot Otis? She was in love with him, remember?" Grady said.

"She was pissed!" Fanny shouted.

"Oh, that's so embarrassing," Ida said. "And I should know. But not too bad if your Depends are on just right. It makes me think of the time when I was playing Bingo last year, I had finished off about three glasses of sweet tea…."

Grady handed Ida her drink.

"You know, Fanny could be right," Ted said. "Maybe Sandy was ticked off. Maybe Otis never had any intention of leaving his wife. Why would he? Grace was too valuable. And maybe he did love her. He saw his way out after Eldon died. Just leave town, collect the insurance, and disappear. Sandy had no rights to his money, and he couldn't exactly move in with her. Did any of you see any sign that she was getting ready to leave town?" We all shook our heads.

I remembered what Grace had said. "So Otis goes back to Sandy to break it off. Then he comes home, disposes of his brother Eldon, and tells Grace he's going to lay low, but he's never heard from again. What did he do during that time? Where did he go?"

"I know where I'd go," Bob said.

"I know where you'd go, too," I answered, catching a whiff of his aftershave on a cool breeze.

"One last joy ride on the Sandy express," Grady said.

TWENTY-SIX

WE LEFT THE COFFEE SHOP, certain we'd figured out who'd killed Otis.

Sandy.

While Eldon had been the victim of an unfortunate accident, the holes in Otis's face was unmistakable proof of a cold, calculated murder.

Now, all we had to do was prove it was Sandy who'd popped Otis's cap (Fanny's words), and hopefully answer the big question: Why?

But that would have to wait. It was nearing three o'clock. Bob had a dance class to teach soon; Ida and Grady were hinting they needed personal time; and Fanny had a golf game. So Ted and I headed to the Ramirez Rose to do some shopping. We couldn't very well go pulling up dead bodies in broad daylight, so we had to just bide our time. It was painful to wait, but necessary.

The tinkle of a bell announced our entrance into the gift shop.

"Missy List! I heard you wuz in town and here you are!" Mr. Ramirez, a small brown man with a gold tooth glinting from under his top lip smiled widely and rushed to give me a warm hug. He smelled of WD-40 and extra-strength glue.

"What brings you here?" Mr. Ramirez was pumping my hand, and calling to his wife before I had a chance to answer his question. "Anita! Lookee-see who's here!"

Anita Ramirez scurried around a carousel of postcards. When she saw me she covered her eyes with her hands and screamed. Then she spun on her heels and dashed behind the postcards again.

"She so excited! Wait here." Mr. Ramirez hustled after Anita.

Ted and I looked at each other, perplexed.

"I heard you were coming!" Mrs. Ramirez came back, this time with a foil wrap in her hands. It could mean just one thing.

Tamales. Just like the old days.

"I made these Saturday. See?" Anita poked open the foil.

Yup, the smell was unmistakable.

"All for you." Anita shoved the tamales into my hands.

"Thank you so much, Anita, I haven't had any good Mexican food since we moved to Spokane. They smell delicious." My eyes were tearing, and not from emotion. Mrs. Ramirez made the best doggone tamales I'd ever tasted, even if I did have to deaden my tongue to get them down. Spicy.

"I kept them in the back jus' in case you came. I knew you'd come! Didn't I say she'd come?" Anita looked at her husband, who nodded an affirmative.

"Pardon my manners," I exclaimed. "Ted, let me introduce you to Mr. and Mrs. Ramirez. They were my neighbors. Remember, I told you about them?"

Ted shook their hands in turn. He was cordial, and didn't let on that he knew Mr. Ramirez had demolished a building or two with his contraptions.

I wondered if the novice inventor was still tinkering with explosives.

"What a beautiful place you have here. Looks like you're doing quite well." I looked around the quaint little store. "Are those the things Ida made?" In a corner, a rack held brightly colored leotards, leggings, tutus—all sorts of dancewear.

"Come see!" Anita waved us over. "Come, come!"

I was admiring the beautifully tailored outfits when a noise from one of the dressing rooms made me pause. Someone was moaning and grunting in there. Occasionally, I heard a pained whimper.

"Ted. I think someone's in trouble!"

It wouldn't be unusual for one of my senior brothers or sisters to have an attack of one kind or another. So many things could go at our age. Thankfully, Ted had his professional face on—and he was going in.

Ted batted away the curtain and shot through its folds, ready to do good. Mr. and Mrs. Ramirez just stood together smiling. Why weren't they concerned?

"Hey, Ted! How the heck are ya, man?"

"Bob?" I heard Ted say.

"Bob?" I pushed the curtain aside and peeked.

Bob had his back to me, but even from that vantage point I could tell it was our large friend. A pink crinoline tutu was up under his armpits and the elastic band was digging a good two inches into his flesh. His neck was a brilliant shade of red, growing close to purple as I gawked.

"We have an emergency here," Ted said, very seriously. "It's cutting off his circulation."

"Hard...to...breathe...," Bob gasped.

"Well, for Pete's sake," I said and then shouted back to Anita that we needed a pair of scissors post haste.

"He always try to squeeze. I tell him, Bob, you no size six no more!" Mr. Ramirez chuckled.

Ted pressed two fingers against Bob's bulging vein on his neck. Bob struggled, but Ted was determined to get a pulse. I think Bob was trying to motion to my husband that he'd just managed to block his only source of blood flow to his brain.

"Help is on the way!" I cried.

Bob raised his hands in the air and went *en pointe*. I was hoping he wouldn't do a pirouette, because, besides a pair of fluffy gray leggings, the only thing he had on was that stuck tutu. I tried not to focus on his bare backside, but couldn't stop myself from looking. Darn, he's muscled up pretty good since his last strip tease at the activity center.

"We're losing him!" Ted cried.

Bob was shaking his head around. His mouth opened and closed like a beached fish. His eyes were starting to roll. Anita thrust a pair of scissors in my hands. I slapped them into Ted's outstretched palm. With a quick snip, Bob was free.

Bob slumped against Ted. "Thanks, man."

MINUTES LATER, Bob emerged from the dressing room encased in some green lycra affair. It was one piece with skintight shorts and skinny straps over his wide shoulders. A tuft of gray chest hair peeked over a scooped neckline.

"Ahhh, much better," he said, and then after explaining how he was impossibly late for dance class, he left us.

"That," I said pointing at Bob's disappearing form, "is the real Bob."

"I see," Ted said.

"Now," Mr. Ramirez had my elbow, "you come see my new invention. It's nearly done. So exciting."

I nervously allowed Mr. Ramirez to take me around to the back of the Ramirez Rose.

It was a junkyard of scrap metal, boxes, wood and tools. Everything was strewn around, but in the midst of it all, Mr. Ramirez had set up a work bench. I could tell he spent a great deal of time tinkering. He pointed to a small contraption on the ground.

"I make this for police. You see them shows when the police have to knock down someone's door? Sometimes it takes two or three bangs, and sometimes they have to use they feet. With this, no more feet, no more two bangs. Just flip the switch."

Ted stood beside me, watching. Mr. Ramirez bent down over his contraption. In front of us several wooden doors were propped up against sawhorses. Mr. Ramirez directed the nozzle of his contraption at the doors. When he pushed down a red switch, it whirred like a jet engine starting up. The noise quickly grew in intensity. I took a step backward. The sound was incredible, nearly loud enough to perforate my eardrums, so I shoved the bag of tamales against one while ear while pushing a finger into the other.

Suddenly a spit of fire shot out of the back of the machine followed by an explosion. Something large and heavy flew out the nozzle and crashed through one of the wooden doors. It left a smoldering hole, the size of a basketball, but the door remained standing.

"Hmm." Mr. Ramirez scratched his head. "Should have

just knocked it down. Needs a few adjustments, I guess." He smiled at us.

I smiled back. My ears were ringing, but I could still hear well enough.

Ted smiled.

"What do you call it?" I asked.

"The B & E?" Ted said under his breath. I jabbed him.

"I don't know yet. So far I just call it my X-12."

"Oh? Why?"

"It just sounds good, kinda official. No reason." Mr. Ramirez squatted and lifted the machine with a grunt. It looked heavy, and it was smoking, so Mr. Ramirez hot potatoed it for a while until it cooled. He turned the machine over in his hands. He stared down the nozzle. Since Mr. R was absorbed in thought, I decided this would be a good time to make our departure.

We bought a few postcards, thanked Anita for the tamales, and walked with Ted back to our cabana. "The B & E, Ted?"

"For Breaking and Entering. If our Mr. Ramirez gets that thing working right, every crook will want one. He might make his million after all."

"He means well," I said.

I took Ted's arm in mine as we walked casually along the sidewalk in our stockinged feet. I rested my head on his shoulder. Anita had bagged the tamales along with a few postcards I'd bought at the store. The plastic sack was tucked under my free arm. The smell was making me a little bit hungry.

"This is nice, Ted," I said dreamily.

"Umm," Ted agreed.

We rounded a corner and stopped to admire the meandering stream.

"It still smells like it might rain," I said.

"Yes, the sky is getting dark."

"Might put a crimp in our plans." I stared up at the gathering gray clouds.

"You planning to dig up Otis again?" A voice from behind a nearby bush caused me to freeze. I dropped the bag of tamales.

Sandy emerged from behind the large bush. She held a gun

aimed at my stomach. Ted quickly stepped in front of me and held up a hand.

"Hold on, ma'am," was all he could say before she interrupted.

"I knew I should have gotten rid of those darned shoes," she said. "When Miss Smarty Pants started asking about my dirt today, I realized she'd figured out I'd been to the cemetery."

"What are you talking about?" I peeked from behind Ted. Surely she wasn't that smart. Good looking, yes, but smart, too?

"Along with something else Fanny said while we were watching Forensic Files last night. She's the one who gave me the idea, actually." Sandy smirked and came closer.

"Said you can't kill a dead man. That's when I knew you'd figured it out. You knew it was someone else in his grave, not Otis."

"Who's Eldon?" I acted surprised, but Sandy didn't buy it.

"Don't play dumb with me, puleese. At least give me that."

I clamped my mouth shut when Sandy widened her stance and steadied the gun with her other hand.

"I just knew you weren't going to let it go and that you'd be out there trying to figure it all out. You were asking too many questions. The questions about the dirt just verified it for me."

Me and my big mouth, I thought. Ted played innocent.

"We don't know what you mean. Will you put down that gun and explain?"

"I was at the cemetery yesterday, that much is true, before you came to my house. I was looking around, pretending to pay Otis my last respects, just thinking of what to do. I went back later, but by then you must have seen my shoes. Couldn't have seen that coming, but it doesn't really matter, does it? The next time I went to the cemetery—last night—it was dark, and, after I did what I did, you all showed up with your shovels. Oh my gosh, I nearly had a heart attack because I thought you saw me! I got out, though, thanks to Fanny's strip tease. Still wish I'd have gotten rid of the shoes. If I had, we wouldn't be having this conversation now."

"You were there?" Ted said.

Great Ted. So much for acting innocent.

"I'd just finished up when you started shining those flashlights around. Like I said, don't know how you missed me."

I came from behind Ted; angry now, angry that she had a gun pointed at my husband, and that she'd snuffed our poor, dear Mr. Otis.

"So you killed him. Why?"

Sandy shook her head. "No, I didn't kill him, but you wouldn't have believed that. You were going to tell the police I killed him weren't you?"

"No," I said, not very convincingly, since that's exactly what we had tried to tell them.

"But if you didn't kill him, then why are you pointing a gun at us?"

"I'm going to escort you all out of town, and then I'm going to convince the rest of your friends to shut their traps. Otis is dead and buried. Why don't we just keep it that way?"

"This doesn't make sense. Sandy, if you didn't kill Otis, then you have nothing to worry about. That will all come out at the trial," I said. Oh dear, that wasn't the best thing to say. Sandy grew pale and rigid. Her bottom lip quivered.

When her eyes pooled up and her hand started to shake, Ted stepped forward and gently took the gun from her. She didn't resist. She merely collapsed into sobs.

"I'm so sorry," she wailed. "I'm so scared. I didn't know what to do,"

"Shhh," I said, quickly. Someone was coming down the path. I heard the thunder of feet. We stepped onto the grass and saw a herd of elderly men fast approaching. They were a serious bunch. Eyebrows were drawn down, jowls were flapping, and shorts were bunching. At the lead was Lanky, shouting out instructions to "Lift your knees, men, kick your butts if you have to." On the fronts of their white T-shirts were the words *Waning Years Runners Club*.

"Hi, officer!" Lanky called out. "We got our own runners club now, see?" He swung his arm out to wave just as another member of the team must have spotted Sandy and felt the testosterone-driven need to make an impression. He lifted his chin and started to dash past Lanky, but was caught right under the nose.

Now, most anyone would have gone down after a bludgeoning like that, but not this guy. With his nose gushing blood, he just picked up the pace and sped off down the walk.

"I get that sort of thing a lot," Sandy said. Her tears had stopped for the time being, thankfully. We sure didn't need a lot of consoling, comforting men right then.

Two men at the back of the pack had fallen behind. They struggled to catch the others but were barely moving when they came alongside us. Sweat coursed from their foreheads. One stopped when he saw Sandy, and then bent over and grabbed his chest. His friend turned, looking worried. The first man held up a finger and stood panting. I could see he was giving Sandy the up and down.

Good grief.

I took the gun from Ted and waved it at him.

"Security. Get a move on, boys," I said sternly. "No loitering here."

The two men came to attention, panting and blowing they wasted no time racing down the path. Soon they were out of sight.

"Sandy, what did you mean, you didn't know what to do?" I asked, handing the gun back to Ted.

"Otis told me everything about his brother, what happened, his wife, everything. I knew what happened. After he put Eldon in the pool, he came to my house and showed me that gun," Sandy said, pointing to the gun in Ted's hand. "He was terrified, because he thought someone might have seen him dump his brother in the pool. He asked me if he could stay at my house until the coast was clear and he could slip out of town."

"Did he tell you he was going to leave his wife?"

"No, and I accepted that. Honest, you guys, I truly just wanted him to be safe. There were these really bad men after him, and he saw this as his chance to make a clean getaway."

Sandy began to slobber and wail again. "But I found him

dead! Someone shot him in my house when I was out buying us some champagne, and I knew everyone would blame me!"

"So you buried him?"

"Yes!" More bawling, her mouth wide open, her eyes closed and streaming. She was clearly losing control.

"Somebody shot him right there in my living room! I cleaned up everything, because I just knew the police would think I did it! I had to get rid of the body, so, so I buried him in his grave."

Ted and I looked at each other.

"But that's impossible, Sandy," Ted said. His tone was challenging. "You couldn't have possibly dug up that grave by yourself."

I felt the blood in my veins turn cold. Was this a setup? I looked around. Nothing but trees, bushes, and the babbling brook.

"Oh yes, I did," Sandy said. "I used the backhoe."

The backhoe?

"When I was at the funeral I saw it parked by that little building on the grounds. Later, when I went back to the cemetery, I snuck a look at it thinking it might come in handy. The keys were still in it, so I didn't think anyone would mind if I borrowed it. The sprinklers came on while I was there and the groundskeeper was lurking around, so I decided to go home and wait for it to get dark. And you all showed up, and you saw my shoes…and, well…."

"Sandy, you told us you didn't go to the funeral," I said.

Sandy faltered. "Well, I didn't, exactly. I stood off to the side, way in the back where Mrs. Culpepper couldn't see me. That's how I noticed the backhoe. I used a wheelbarrow to put Otis in the trunk of my car and then another one I found at the cemetery to take him to the grave. It wasn't easy."

"I wouldn't think so," I agreed. As I tried to give comfort to Sandy, my horse manure meter was pegging. Something Sandy had said didn't sit right with me. She could have been at the funeral; she could have stayed far back out of sight like she said, and, incredibly as it was, she could have pulled off the whole burial thing. But still, a component of her story made me wary—*something* made me believe Sandy wasn't being completely honest with us. What was it?

"Oh, shucks. It's raining," Ted said. "Come on you two, let's get back to the cabana before we soak our socks." He picked up my tamale parcel and shoved the gun in the bag. "We'll figure out what to do from there."

TWENTY-SEVEN

I GOT SANDY and Ted settled at the table with chips and sodas before I went to the bedroom to call Grady. I quickly explained what had happened, and what Sandy had told us. The rain was building outside, coming down in torrents, and we both agreed we would need to get to the cemetery in a hurry before the whole project was a wash.

Grady also cautioned that whoever had shot Otis was probably not far away, and that we would need to be very careful. Maybe they were watching us at that very minute, and the sooner we got Otis and Eldon to the police station the better it would be for all of us.

"Fanny's here, and she's in a pretty foul mood."

"How did she do on the golf course?" I asked.

"They had to haul her off the last hole after lightning struck some guy's putter."

"Sounds painful," I said.

"And here's Bob now," Grady said. "He's just getting back from a dance class."

"Don't take too long getting over here." I was feeling edgy and wanted to get this over with.

I WAITED BY the patio doors while keeping one ear on the conversation in the kitchen. The pattering rain made their words unintelligible, but I could tell Sandy had recovered from her initial siege of emotions, and she was chatting calmly with Ted. Her Southern accent was dripping with charm. Ted knew the penalty for wayward thoughts, so I didn't worry too much. Still, there was something unsettling about that woman, and I was sure it wasn't just because she had pointed a gun at me. It was something she'd said.

Something.

When the gang appeared, I held the doors open for them, then struggled against a fierce wet wind to get them closed. Ida had a swim cap on over her flaming hair, and Fanny looked like a drowned mouse with fat rain drops stuck to her glasses. Bob was still in dance togs, and Grady wore a splattered rain coat.

"Here. Let's get going." Fanny pulled out her little bag and started searching for the grease paint.

"That won't be necessary," Sandy said.

"We know what we're doing. We've done it before." Fanny didn't look surprised that Sandy was there. Apparently, Grady had filled her in on the whole story of our Sandy confrontation. "Only this time we're using that backhoe you found, Sandy, and if any cops come, May, it's your turn to strip." Fanny was up to her elbows in the cloth bag.

"We heard about the backhoe," Ida added while she wrestled with her swim cap. It was suctioned pretty well. Bob helped her get it free. After the tussle, Ida's hair stood up like wild, red weeds.

Bob wandered into the kitchen and helped himself to a soda. He popped the top and took a long draw followed by a thunderous belch. The rest of us crowded around the table.

"Sandy, we heard you were at the gravesite just before we got there," Grady said. "How did you get out without us hearing you? Just curious."

"Out the back. There's a whole section of the fence down."

"And to think I tore my robe for nothing." Bob glared at Fanny.

We all looked sheepish. Should have done a little more investigating.

"So how'd you get Otis out to the cemetery?" Fanny asked. I guess Grady hadn't told her everything.

"I put him in the trunk of my car."

Ida gasped.

Bob burped.

"Ingenious!" Fanny said, snapping her fingers. "I should have thought of that."

"Fanny?"

"I mean, if I'd been in her place, I would have thought of something like that."

That sense of unease was tickling my stomach again, not a fine and pleasant feeling, a sense of something not quite right there. I noticed Fanny was preoccupied with her cloth bag again.

I grew bold. Ted was looking at me curiously. He must have seen the look in my eyes.

"By the way, Sandy, how did you get him in the trunk of your car? I hardly think you can lift a man like Otis. He wasn't very big I know, but…"

It was Ted who answered the question. "Remember, May Bell, she said she used a wheelbarrow."

"And some rope, a few boards, it's really quite amazing what you can do when you have to," Sandy said.

The men nodded in agreement. Sheesh, I sure didn't remember any of them acting like Bob Vila. It took a woman to think of a wheelbarrow and a backhoe, didn't it?

Ted and I changed quickly into our grave-digger clothes. I could hear Fanny on the other side of the door explaining how to apply the grease paint. She sounded like a drill sergeant. The wind and rain still battered the windows, and I couldn't hide my unease from Ted.

"It will be okay, May. This will soon be over. It's the least we can do for Otis. Are you ready?"

Fanny threw open the doors. I was still in my underwear and took refuge behind the bed.

"I sure hope so," Fanny said, clearly annoyed. "You're gonna blow this whole operation. Shake your buns, lady." Then she marched past me and out through the patio doors. I could hear her walker, *kachunk, kachunk, kachunk,* growing ever more faint in the distance.

"Don't let her get away. She's liable to throw the corpses

over her shoulder and make off with them." Bob laughed, his
thumbs hooked in his spandex straps. Better than Speedos at
any rate. I finished dressing squatted behind the bed.

"Where's the Suburban?" I walked out into the rain, shielding my eyes. Luckily my shoes were dry, but not for long. The
rain was gaining strength.

"Back at Grady's. He forgot to put gas in it, and we have
just enough to get to the cemetery and then to the police station."

"Grady," I moaned.

Such bad timing. Such bad planning.

"Sorry." Grady looked sheepish.

IT WAS GETTING DARK quickly. We moved along the sidewalk
toward the Suburban, hurrying through the shadowed places,
ambling through the lighted spots. We wanted to look casual,
just in case anyone else happened to be taking an evening
stroll. I kept waiting to hear the pitter-splatter of runner's shoes,
but thankfully we were all alone. The rain had moved everyone indoors. All I could hear were the splashes as our feet went
through the puddles. Most of our peers sacked out by eight
o'clock anyway, which was good for us.

It didn't take long to get to the carport. We all climbed into
the Suburban and sat wet and shivering while Grady got the
doors closed behind us. Fanny leaned her walker against the
carport wall before climbing in.

"Don't need that," she said. "Free parking at the cemetery."

Sandy raised her eyebrows, but I lacked the energy to explain. I noticed Bob had taken a seat beside our guest. Ida was
in the passenger side and Ted and I shared the back with Fanny.
If we kept this up, we'd soon need a bus.

"Just in case any of you get hungry, I brought May's tamales," Bob said. He lifted my soggy bag. I thought I'd detected a sharp odor drifting around in front of me.

"And I brought pecan sandies!" Ida called out from the
front.

I was tempted to start a round of *Row, Row, Row Your*

Boat. It was all sounding so much like a field trip. I massaged my temples.

The dark strip of road fell away, and soon we were zipping out through the Waning Years Estates gates and onto the highway. I kept thinking about the cargo we'd soon be carrying in the back, and hoped Otis and Eldon wouldn't be too disturbed by such impropriety. I wondered if Grady had thought to bring tarps.

THE DOWNED FENCE wasn't hard to find. Grady pulled off the road, and we crept onto the cemetery grounds. The rain had abated, but we didn't know for how long, so we moved in a hurry. Ted instructed Grady and Bob to find a wheelbarrow, and, with a thumb's up, they hustled off in the direction of the cemetery equipment building.

"I'll get the backhoe; you girls are lookouts." Ted barked instructions.

"Again with the lookouts. Why can't I drive the backhoe?" Fanny sulked.

"Okay, fine. Go ahead."

"Ted." I tried to see if my husband was kidding. He wasn't.

"Yeah!" Fanny said, punching the air with her fists. She shuffled away into the night. Fanny was hardly gone a minute before we heard the thunder of running feet. I tensed, wondering what would happen next, but it was just Grady and Bob, back with the wheelbarrow.

We raced toward the sound of the backhoe. Fanny had made good time getting it over to Otis's grave.

Ida huffed and panted as we ran. Bob drove the wheelbarrow.

FANNY SAT HIGH atop the digging machine, a dark form in the hazy light of the security lamps. She was grabbing gears like a pro. A giant blade scooped away dirt and deposited it in growing mounds. When we heard the sound of metal on wood, Ted held up his hand.

"Okay, boys, haul 'em up!"

Bob and Grady scrambled down into the hole.

It took all of us to get the two men up and onto the wet ground. They were slippery, and not just from the rain and mud.

"All right, now into the wheelbarrow!" Ted grabbed Otis under his arms and tugged. We dropped him in, and then Eldon was placed crossways over the top of his brother. Bob took off for the Suburban at a dead run.

He didn't get two feet before the two bodies slithered out and onto the grass. We got them back in and rolling in no time.

A light on the backhoe helped us find our way back to the downed fence. Fanny spun the backhoe around, and she was pushing dirt back into the Otis hole by the time we had the Suburban's doors open.

Bob was sucking air. He parked the wheelbarrow and wiped his forehead.

"Much more efficient," Ted said, pointing to the backhoe. Where had Fanny learned to do that?

"I just hope she hurries," Grady said. He and Ted were shoving and folding the flopping bodies of Eldon and Otis into the back of the Suburban while Bob held the wheelbarrow steady. Ida just looked into the sky with her mouth open, catching drops. Even though the rain had let up, it didn't really matter. We were all soaked to the bone.

"I think that just about does it, guys." Fanny trotted up to the back of the Suburban. She inspected and gave her approval. "Might want to throw something over the bodies, though. Just in case."

Ida peeked into the back of the Suburban. "Hey, that's Otis!" she said. "Is Sandy in there, too? Because I don't see her. Hey, Grady, where's Sandy?"

Grady closed up the back of the Suburban. We had to get moving.

"What did she say? She has some more pecan sandies?" Bob glanced around rubbing his belly.

"No. Where's Sandy?" I looked around, annoyed, because we really had to go. Now.

"Sandy?" Bob called out. "She was here a minute ago. Maybe she got in the Suburban." Bob leaned his head in. "Nope, she's not there, but I've got some tamales if anyone's hungry." Bob started rummaging in the bag.

"I'm right here," Sandy said, and she was not alone. Two uniformed police officers were flanking her.

"Ted, I hope you don't mind that I used your phone?" Sandy waved Ted's cell phone at him. He instinctively touched his belt where the phone should have been.

"I'll take that." One of the officers stepped up and took the tamale bag from Bob.

We all could have been knocked down with proverbial feathers.

"Sandy? You called the police?" Ted looked pained. Bob looked disappointed. Not only was his heartthrob a turncoat, but he'd just had his tamales confiscated by the local fuzz, too.

"See, officers? I told you they were up to something, and if I'm not mistaken, you'll find the gun that killed Mr. Culpepper in that little bag there."

Sandy was pointing at the tamale bag. I felt my heart leap into my throat. My gosh! Ted put Sandy's gun in there!

"And if you check for prints, you'll find hers," Sandy pointed at me. "Or his. Either one of them could have pulled the trigger."

My mind was racing. Had I touched the trigger? Had Ted? We had both handled the gun after Sandy. Oh, this was so bad!

"I pretended to go along with them," Sandy said, "acting like I didn't know they'd killed Otis. See, they thought they could just shoot him and bury him in that grave. That other guy is his brother. Everyone thought it was Otis, so they figured they could commit a perfect crime and get away with it. I talked them into coming out here to dig them up, though, see, because I pretended like they'd been found out, and they had to move the bodies."

Sandy was pouring on the Southern charm. She stood slightly behind one officer with her hand on his shoulder. Even with her hair wet from the rain she looked stunning. My opinion of her had solidified—I despised the woman.

"What are you talking about, woman!" Fanny stepped up until she was inches from one of the officers. He took a step back and put his hand on his gun.

"Hold it right there, lady. In fact, all of you just get down on the ground and spread eagle."

"Spread eagle?" Fanny put her hands on her hips. "Spread eagle? I won't even spread crow! She knew what we were doing. We were taking these guys over to the precinct, that's what, because you bozos wouldn't get off your doughnut holes and come see for yourself!"

"All right, ma'am, that's quite enough." The officer with the tamale bag took a quick glance inside. He whistled. "It's here, all right."

"The gun?" the partner asked.

"Just like the lady said. And some lovely postcards, too."

I was clinging to Ted, shocked and confused. Why had Sandy called the cops? Sandy caught my perplexed look and smiled wickedly. One of her hands had found its way to the officer's waist. He didn't seem to mind—seemed to enjoy it, actually.

"Ted!" I whispered, "I just figured it out."

"Not now, May."

"I just figured out what's been bothering me. When Sandy had us at gunpoint, she said 'you guys.' Nobody from Dallas would say 'you guys.'"

Ted talked out of the side of his mouth. "What are you getting at?"

"She's not from Dallas, that's for sure. She's been lying to us all along. My guess is, that she was lying to Otis, too. That accent is as phony as she is, and we've been set up. She had this whole thing planned all along. The gun, the trip to the cemetery, all of it."

Fanny was railing at the police officers, and they seemed unsure of what to do with her.

"It's obvious she's got it in for us," I whispered. "But why, Ted?"

"If you're right, she found out we were going to take the

bodies to the police, and she had to cover her tail. Now I'm sure she's the killer," Ted answered. "But it's going to be pretty hard to prove that now." Ted sounded as scared as I felt.

I looked from Grady to Bob, but Ida was nowhere to be found. Was she hiding behind Grady? No, out of the corner of my eye, I saw her sitting in the Suburban. She'd apparently had enough of the rain. Fanny kept up her tirade, which gave me a chance to turn my head slightly. Ida was in the driver's seat rocking side to side. She was singing something, I think the song was Bingo—B-I-N-G-O—but I wasn't sure. It was hard to hear, what with Fanny shouting, the rain coming down and the general confusion.

The cops had tired of Fanny's sparring, and they grew forceful. The one with the tamale bag ordered all of us to stand beside the Suburban while he and his partner inspected our cargo. Since I didn't see a police car, I suspected they had snuck in under cover of rain, darkness, and the sound of the backhoe. I chided myself for being so careless. A good spy would have had a lookout.

The cops ordered Grady to open the back of the Suburban. "Let's just see what we've got here."

"Yup, looks like both of them just like you said." The cop beside Sandy gave her an appreciative look.

She smiled so sweetly at him. I wanted to give her a punch in the solar plexus. That would wipe the smile right off of her ruby red lips.

"That one's Eldon, and the one crumpled underneath with the bullet wounds is Otis, his brother." Sandy pointed to each corpse in turn.

"She shot him!" Fanny screamed. "Shot him, buried him in the grave on top of Eldon, and now she's trying to pin it on us!"

"The last time I saw him he was alive and well." Sandy shot Fanny a look. "In fact, we were in the shower together."

The police officers looked enviously at the little dead man in the back of the Suburban.

"Oh, for Pete's sake, she's the one who dumped him in the casket! I'm telling you, she shot him!" Fanny stomped her foot.

"No, he was in the shower like I said. I left him, went to the store, and when I got back, he was gone. I haven't seen him since. Not until now." Sandy looked at Otis, and started to sniffle. One of the officers produced a hanky.

The tamale officer shined his flashlight around on the bodies. I watched. Then I gasped.

"Wait, officer, do that again!" I moved toward the policeman, and Ted stuck out his hand to stop me. I shrugged him off. "Go over Otis again with your light!"

The officer scanned the body again.

"There! Look at that!" I pointed to the front of Otis's shirt. It was a flannel work shirt, soiled with the grave dirt, and snagged in some threads was a very small, but very telling bit of evidence.

The policeman leaned in.

I leaned in.

We all leaned in.

"Well, I'll be," the officer said.

"Check her hands," I ordered. "Check her hands, and you'll see where that came from."

The policeman reached out and plucked at Otis's shirt. He came away with a lacquered sliver of fingernail. He held it up in the light. The polish color, dark red, matched Sandy's other nails perfectly, and if he'd had the chance to check, the ragged edge would have corresponded exactly.

But he didn't get that chance.

Sandy's syrupy southern accent disappeared. Her voice lowered. The vituperations that came from her mouth were anything but feminine. She lunged toward the officer and grabbed the tamale gun from his hand before he could react.

"I guess we're just going to have to do this the hard way," Sandy said.

She ordered the officers to reach for the sky.

"I was hoping it wouldn't turn out like this. You all had given me the perfect out." She cursed again. "I'm going to fire that Joyce. These stupid acrylic nails never do hold up in a crisis."

"Whoo, boy," Bob said. He glanced at me.

The policemen raised their hands and backed away from Sandy. I was a little bit pleased. They'd been duped, too, after all. I wanted to put my thumb on my nose and wiggle my fingers at them, but thought better of it.

"Now your guns and radios. Right here." Sandy pointed to the ground with her toe. The officers cursed something less impressive than what Sandy had done, but complied reluctantly. Sandy kicked the guns and radios into the bushes.

She kept her pistol trained on us while she punched numbers into Ted's phone. The lighting was bad, so she did it slowly. I was hoping she would be distracted long enough for us to make a move.

No such luck.

"There's been a change," she said into the phone. "Go to plan B. Get over there, and hurry up. We're on our way now."

"Ted," I whispered, "how did she know what prefix to use? Our service is out of Spokane." I was flummoxed.

Although I didn't look at my husband, I could feel him squirm when he admitted giving her his business card while they were chatting at the cabana. Darn Ted. He'd pay for that later.

"You won't get away with this," Fanny said. She had her hands clenched into little fists.

"Oh, Fanny, do you have to use that old cliché? You know all of the victims say that at one time or another. I mean really, you've surely seen enough of those stupid crime shows to know that much."

Fanny was so angry she vibrated. "Why, I oughta!" she yelled.

"What? You oughta what? Take my fingerprints?" Sandy laughed. "You're all so pathetic. Wouldn't know how to solve a case if it was a snake that bit you."

That really stung. I wasn't so sure of Sandy's use of the metaphor, or simile, or whatever it was, but she really knew how to hurt an old woman. Fanny was so angry I thought her head might explode.

"Seems you've lost your Southern accent," I said.

"Yeah, I noticed that, too," Bob said.

"Don't tell me you just now figured out I'm not really from Dallas. Pathetic. The lot of you. So pathetic."

"I knew," I said, but it sounded like I was making it all up. Then I took a long shot. "I'm guessing you're not from Dallas at all, but from Portland, Oregon. Am I right?" I wanted to sound really confident.

"Give the girl a gold star!" Sandy said.

Under different circumstances that would have gotten some pats on the back or a few glad hands from my friends, but they were too busy holding their arms in the air. Mine were getting pretty tired. Ted tried to be helpful, and put his hands under my elbows.

"Watch it, bud," Sandy said, moving the gun over to him.

I felt the Suburban rock ever so slightly.

"Portland, huh? I wouldn't guess you happened to know Eldon Culpepper while you were up there?" Fanny said.

"And she gets the blue ribbon!" Sandy said.

The Suburban roared to life.

"What the…?" Sandy was taken completely by surprise. The cops lunged at her, but not fast enough. She backpedaled, keeping the gun drawn. Ida had found the gearshift and stomped on the gas. We were pelted with rocks as she squealed away.

"Go, honey! Go!" Grady shouted.

The Suburban was gone.

Sandy screamed with rage. She cursed and jumped up and down. Everyone ducked and dodged, because her gun hand was waving all over the place. "Move!" she shouted and pointed back down the road, I was guessing to where the cops had secreted their car.

I was right.

"She's going for backup," one of the policemen said, looking over his shoulder at Ida's retreating taillights. He sounded downright giddy, but that didn't last long.

Sandy grinned at us, and her gun hand steadied. "By the time she figures out where we are, it will be too late for all of you," she said.

"Ted," I whispered, once we were squished in the cop car, "she's got Otis and Eldon in there, and the back is open."

"I just hope she takes it easy over the pot holes."

TWENTY-EIGHT

SANDY HELD HER GUN to the back of Bob's head while he drove the squad car. She flipped on the bubble-gum lights, and the siren cleared the light traffic. We were headed in the direction of the Waning Years Estates.

We were going much too fast, the rain was coming down again in sheets, and it was too dark for anyone to notice the odd fact that there were a bunch of civilians stuffed in the police car. The cops wouldn't have been noticed anyway. They were in the trunk.

"Where are we going?" I asked Ted, as if he would know. He shook his head and clasped my hand. He grimaced a little because I was sitting on his lap. Sandy answered my question.

"Over there," she ordered. We pulled up into the parking lot of the athletic complex. "Now, I don't suppose anyone would happen to have a key? Oh, looky here. I just happen to have one on my little key ring. Isn't that perfect? In case you're wondering, I copied Otis's key when he wasn't looking."

"Why are we here?" Bob asked soberly.

"That's for me to know and for you to find out," Sandy said.

What a brat. I would have socked her if the gun weren't so close to Bob's chin.

Where was Ida? For all we knew, she'd driven home, parked the Suburban and gone in her house to start on some fudge, or a pot roast or something.

"Well, what do you know?" Sandy tugged on the front door and it opened. She still had her gun pointed at Bob who reluctantly stood by while she moved us in ahead of her. "Looks like someone else got here first."

We were ordered down the dark, empty hallway toward the lounge area. Sandy wrapped her arm around Bob's neck and kept the gun close. As we passed the checker tables, Fanny scooped up a black checker and heaved it at Sandy, smacking the tall woman between the eyes. Sandy squinted, and then pointed the gun at my little friend.

"Watch it, sister!" she yelled.

Fanny stuck out her tongue.

I vigorously shook my head. "Cool it, Fanny."

When we got down into the lounge, the pool lights were on. The place was lit well enough to see that we were indeed, not alone.

"Mr. and Mrs. Ramirez!" I gasped. The two were on the floor with their hands tied behind their backs. Their mouths were covered in duct tape. When they saw us come through the doors, they struggled and mumbled behind the silver tape.

"Pipe down," Sandy shouted at the couple. She pushed Bob away and looked around, as if she were expecting to see someone besides the Ramirez couple.

A man walked out of the shadows. He looked at Ted, and said, "Thanks for the check, Doc, you'll be happy to know it didn't bounce."

I recognized the rough-looking man as one who had charged after the boys at the Sunken Balls. Since he had a swollen bruise over one eye, it looked like he hadn't fared well against the bikers. I was sorry they hadn't worked him over a bit longer.

"Hello, Peter," Ted said, as furious as I'd ever seen him. "Friend of yours?" He jerked his head toward Sandy.

"I'd like to think we're much more than that." Peter came over and nuzzled Sandy's neck.

She giggled.

"Gag me," I said, and then wanted to take it back. I hope she hadn't taken that literally.

I glanced around, looking for an avenue of escape. Sandy's first plan had failed. Now that there was no possibility of her pinning the murder on us, she was left with only one alternative.

We would all have to die.

Everyone else was thinking the same thing by the looks on their faces and the tomb-like silence in the lounge. Even Fanny was quiet.

Oh, if only Ida had found help. But even if she had, what could she do? She had no idea where we were. I clung to Ted, thinking it might be the last time I felt his body against mine. I worried about my daughter doing missionary work in Belize, hoped the news of our demise was delivered gently, and I even felt bad about leaving Trixie at the Poochie Hooch. Poor Grady would die alone, and the last thing Bob would see was the back of Fanny's little head. He had his arms around her protectively, and surprisingly, Fanny didn't fight it.

No. We had to do something. I tried my negotiating skills.

"If you don't kill us, we won't say a word." My voice was quivering.

Sandy laughed hysterically. "You hear that, Peter? They won't say a word. Is that right, officer?" Sandy stepped up to one of the policemen.

The cop turned his fingers in front of his lips and tossed an invisible key over his shoulder. Normally, I would have thought him a coward. But considering the circumstances, I was grateful his belly was yellow.

Peter ordered all of us to sit on the floor by the Ramirez couple. The smell of stale beer and old pretzels drifted up around us. Bob kept Fanny encircled in his arms; Ted and I held hands; Grady hugged his knees. The cops looked humiliated as they sank to the floor.

Sandy slowly raised her gun. She steadied it with her opposite hand and drew a bead. We all held our breaths, leaned back and cringed.

"Say, Peter, did Otis do that before you shot him?" Sandy brought the gun down to her side.

"You shot Otis?" Fanny could keep quiet no longer. She was

almost to her feet before Bob reached up and hauled her back down by the seat of her pants.

"Once or twice," Peter said, he leaned down for something under one of the tables. "Not sure, exactly." When he came up again he had a large metallic object in his hands. It looked heavy. Mr. Ramirez started to squirm wildly beside me. He was trying to shout behind his mouth tape.

"He's got the B & E," Ted said soberly. Then he looked toward the wide expanse of glass. The blue lights of the pool threw his face in shimmering color.

"Oh, my heavens," I said. If there was any blood left in my face, it had just drained into my socks. "They're going to shoot the pool out!"

"That's why they kidnapped the Ramirezes," Ted said.

"Tell him what he wins, Peter," Sandy was much too happy. She danced around on her long legs, did some Kung Fu kicks, and spun.

"You'd get a lot more height if you bent that back leg just a little," Bob said. Fanny snapped her head back, clocking Bob's chin. Bob grunted.

"You all brought this on yourselves," Peter said, placing the X-12 in front of the pool wall. He adjusted it so the nozzle aimed center mass of the glass. "If you hadn't stuck your noses where they didn't belong, we'd be rich, you'd all be sipping tea and eating croutons, and Otis would be out of our hair."

"I believe you mean crumpets," Bob corrected.

"Whatever," Peter said.

"Why don't you humor an old woman." Fanny was calmly making a last request.

It wasn't like her. She was more prone to make a flying leap than to engage in idle conversation. Then I figured it out. She was stalling for time. Give Ida an opportunity to reach help.

I joined in.

"Yes," I said, "Sandy, you said you knew Eldon in Portland, right? I don't get it. What's the connection here?"

"Otis wasn't the only guy who liked to gamble," she said. "Eldon had his brother's propensity for losing big. Too bad I was his girlfriend."

"Oh," Bob said, "two for the price of one."

Sort of like double pneumonia, I thought.

"When Otis called Eldon the first time asking for money, Eldon didn't say no right away, but he didn't say yes either. They weren't exactly buddies, and he didn't want to seem too eager—wouldn't have looked right. Besides, after that first phone call, Eldon and I needed some time to get our heads together and come up with a plan. We knew Otis had a huge insurance policy, and it would be ours for the taking if we played our cards right. When we finally figured out what to do it was so perfect, we didn't know how we could go wrong."

Peter continued to work over the X-12. It didn't look complicated, but the guy didn't look too bright, either.

"So what was the big plan?" Fanny sounded bored.

"Otis knew his brother had a girlfriend, but he'd never met me."

"So you rushed down here, seduced the brother and got him caught up in an affair. What were you hoping to do? Blackmail the guy?" I asked. *Stall, stall.*

"Think, girlie!" Fanny was getting feisty again. "Otis didn't have any money, why the heck do you think he was calling his brother?"

"They could have thought about blackmail, because Eldon needed money, too, Fanny, and quit yelling at me," I shot back. My head was starting to throb, and I was trying hard not to cry. It was impossible to think clearly with the B & E aimed at all of that water.

"Come on, guys, it's simple," Sandy said in a patronizing tone. "I knew it would be no problem getting Otis in my bed." She flipped her hair over her shoulder.

I caught Ted nodding beside me and leaned my sharp elbow on his thigh.

"Once he was in love, I was sure he'd leave his wife, get a quickie divorce and marry me in a hurry. He'd sign over his life insurance policy, I'd call Eldon, and he'd come down and knock off his brother. Neat and tidy. We planned to make it look like his wife did it. Can't remember how, exactly. Doesn't really matter now anyway, because it got all fouled up."

"He didn't leave his wife, he didn't get the quickie divorce, and he never planned to marry you." I wanted to gouge away, but my words had as much of an impression as a butter knife on granite.

"Yeah," Sandy said, looking baffled. "Go figure. When Eldon got here, it was really unfortunate that he drowned in Otis's bathtub, but it all worked out for the best, you see, because everyone thought it was Otis in the swimming pool. Poor guy didn't even know he was making things easier—paving the way for his own murder."

I shook my head. Poor Otis never saw it coming.

Peter stood, apparently satisfied with his B&E placement. He said, "His own wife couldn't even say anything after I popped Otis. She had no idea where he was, where he'd gone, and that he'd ended up cuddled inside the casket with his bro."

"I didn't think Sandy could get Otis in the grave all by herself." Fanny smirked.

"I helped," Sandy defended, "but I broke a nail. I needed Peter to lift him. That stuff about the ropes and boards, all lies." She smiled and batted her eyelashes.

"Peter, how did you get involved in all of this?" Ted asked.

"Come on, guys." Peter went to Sandy and ran his hand up and down her backside. "Would you turn down someone like this? Remember, I had a right to Otis's money as much as anybody. He'd practically bled me dry. Sandy found me hanging around one day after I'd caught Otis sneaking into Sandy's house one night—*after* his death—-and I was threatening to rough up Otis and to expose the fraud. Well, Sandy took me aside and made me an offer. Take out the old man, and then we'd work on the widow for the insurance. I didn't see how we could lose. It all worked out so much better than we thought. In fact, Otis was sitting in Sandy's recliner snoozing when I waxed 'im. He didn't even flinch." Peter looked smug.

Yikes.

"It was a perfect solution to a big problem," Peter added.

"Until now." Sandy looked at us all. Her eyes were flickering.

Darn. We'd just run out of time.

"Now we have an appointment with the wife of the late Mr. Otis Culpepper. I don't think it will take much to convince her to turn over the insurance money when it comes in, especially after we threaten to tell the police that she overdosed Eldon with sleeping pills, not to mention the disability fraud and all of her other lies." Sandy waved her gun around. "We don't want to keep her waiting, do we? By the way, Mrs. List, thanks for convincing her to stick around an extra day."

Sandy walked over to Mr. Ramirez and grabbed a corner of the duct tape. She ripped the tape off of his mouth with a flourish.

We all winced.

"Okay, little man, did you make the adjustments like we asked?"

"Yessum," Mr. Ramirez said. His eyes were wide, and he was shaking.

"How many minutes?"

"Five. I set it for five minutes."

"Gooood," Sandy said, and replaced the tape. She reached down and gave him a kiss on the forehead. Mrs. Ramirez struggled helplessly beside her husband.

"It's time to go, Peter," Sandy said. She held up her keys and jingled them at us. "Don't worry, we'll lock up when we leave."

Sandy's foot came up slowly. She brought it down slowly. The red switch on the X-12 went to the on position. The engines started to whine. Then she brought it down again forcefully and broke off the switch. She even had the presence of mind to pocket the piece that broke off.

Sandy and Peter waved their guns at us one last time and ran for the door. The sound of the lock slamming home was our death knell.

TWENTY-NINE

As SOON AS the door was latched, we were on our feet. The X-12 grew louder by the second. We all shouted at one another, for all the good that did. Our words were drowned out by the engine's shriek the minute they passed from our collective lips. The cops bolted for the door. They were kicking at it. Bob and Fanny were frantically trying to free the Ramirez couple. Ted and Grady raced around looking for another way out.

What! Were we dopes?

I looked at the X-12. My fingers were plugged into my ears. I was covered in a film of nervous sweat. Despite the cluster panic, I was thinking clearly. Nothing held the contraption to the floor. All I had to do was change its trajectory and we were outta there.

I was so smart.

Bob got the tape off of Mr. Ramirez's mouth. He struggled with the ropes.

Mr. Ramirez was shouting something. I had my hands around the X-12. We had at least four minutes.

Mr. Ramirez jumped up and down. I didn't have time to find out what for. I took a cleansing breath. I shook my hands. I rubbed my forehead. The thing looked really heavy. I imagined Ted's lecture. *Lift with your legs.*

Suddenly, I was hit by a fury of flying bones and wild white hair. I was lying on the ground and in pain. I looked up. A fan was up there rotating lazily. A nice, cool swim might not be bad after all.

"It's got a fail safe!" Mr. Ramirez screamed in my ear. He had positioned himself between the X-12 and everyone else.

"They made me rig it that way. It's got a mercury switch. You turn it, or move it, and it goes off!"

I would have gasped, but I still hadn't gotten enough air into my lungs.

Fanny was sitting on my chest, which didn't help any. She gripped my face in her knuckles and yelled, "You almost blew it, May Bell!"

We had to get a door open before it was too late. My calculations said we were speeding toward the unscheduled Night Swim.

"How long can you hold your breath?" Fanny yelled at me. She hadn't moved from my chest, and her bony hipbones were flattening my underwires.

"Get off!" I'd finally had enough wind to yell. "Get to the door. We'll all shove together."

Bob had freed Mrs. Ramirez of her tethers. She kicked off her ankle ropes. It was too late to disarm the B&E, so we grabbed at whatever we could lift and barreled toward the exit.

The cops were panting and rubbed their aching shoulders.

Fanny hefted a chair. "Outta my way, coppers!" she yelled.

I think one of them got a knick taken out of his ear when she swung. The chair glanced off of the heavy door.

I ducked.

"Wait, wait, wait." I patted the air with my hands. "The door swings in. We've got to pull."

I knew it was useless, senseless, and impossible. We weren't going to get that door open. Still, we laid on hands and tugged. We strained and made a few embarrassing sounds, but we were past concern about that. There was only room for two or three of us at a time, and mostly we just got in each other's way. Mrs. Ramirez was bawling.

"That's it," Bob shouted. He held up his watch. "Brace yourself, folks."

The cops hugged each other, and Fanny crawled onto the top of a table. I think she decided to surf her way out. Bob billowed out his cheeks, Grady closed his eyes, the Ramirez couple started chanting the Lord's Prayer, and Ted put his hand in mine.

Then the door opened slowly and Ida poked her head in. "I thought you'd be in here," she said, smiling brightly.

The X-12 shot out a blue flame and exploded.

"Ida! Everyone, get out! Get out!"

Ida squealed and bolted back the way she'd come. I grabbed Ted and pushed him ahead of me. He swung his arm around and scooped Fanny onto his hip. Bob tossed Mr. and Mrs. Ramirez over his shoulders and made for the stairs. The cops were already gone. So much for "to serve and to protect."

I was the last through the doors when something horrible and deafening happened behind me. I cautioned a glance. The X-12 had perforated the glass wall. There was a large hole, issuing gallons of water onto the lounge floor. Then the glass began to crack like a quickly forming spider web. The cracks ran out from the hole until they reached every corner.

That was the last thing I saw before vaulting the stairs. When I got to the upper floor, I felt the tremors as the wall gave way and turned the lounge into an underground reservoir.

We sprinted down the hall while all around us the walls moved, buckled and shuddered. The floor rumbled under our feet. Bob still had the Ramirez couple on his shoulders. Ted shouted for me and shifted Fanny around to his back. She rode him like he was the prize ram at a mutton bustin' contest.

The police officers had beaten us to the exterior doors. I'll bet they hadn't moved that fast since double dooughnut day at the precinct open house. They were yelling, urging us all to hurry, and waved us through and into the parking lot.

We didn't slow until we were a good fifty yards away where we congregated in the middle of a field and collapsed. None of us said a word. Every eye was on the sports complex. Every eye bore witness to disaster.

IT WAS AN IMPLOSION, really. It started with the area of the pool and then moved up toward the racquetball courts. Gathering speed, the building folded in, working through the racquetball courts, weight rooms, the basketball courts, and the locker rooms. Steel girders bent and moaned. Mortar and brick tumbled and crashed. Thick wooden boards splintered and toppled. It all went down like a giant elephant coming to ground.

A plume of dust and spray—and it was all gone.

"That was a hell of a thing," Bob said. He pulled a toothpick out of his breast pocket and stuck it between his teeth.

I crawled over to Ida and hugged her until she grunted. "How did you know where we were? You saved our lives, Ida, how did you know?"

"I knew she'd do it," Grady said. He wiped a proud tear from his eye.

"I didn't really know where you were," Ida said. Her red hair was clumped with mud. The field was wet and the rain was still coming down, but it had turned into a tame drizzle.

Ida didn't look at all bothered by it, though. "The Suburban ran out of gas. I don't know where I was going," she said, looking like she was searching her memory. She placed a finger to her chin. "I think I was supposed to go to the police station or something, can't quite remember why."

I looked at Ted. He didn't dare laugh.

"It conked out somewhere by the Sunken Balls," Ida said. "Then I remembered I wanted to give that girl the recipe. She's so nice. So I went inside. All of those other guys were there, too."

I raised my eyebrows. This was getting more bizarre by the minute.

"Oh, yes. I remember now. They were asking about all of you, really worried because they said some guy named Peter had just left, and he was acting dangerous or something." Ida turned to me. "That guy with the cigar was especially worried about you, May Bell. I think he likes you."

"That's nice," I said.

"Yes. I remember. They told me they'd heard Peter talking to somebody on the phone. That's when he started getting dangerous."

"Did they say who the somebody was?" Grady was very patient.

"It was Sandy."

"How do you know that?" I asked, thinking it would be easier to pull teeth from a chicken than to get a straight story from Ida, but I tried.

"I told them it was Sandy. Right after I told them about the gun."

"The gun?" I asked, worried that somehow Ida had found a spare gun flying around, but no, she was talking about Sandy's gun. The one she'd pointed at my head, the one Peter had probably used to puncture Otis's face.

"That's when they really got mad," Ida said, making her face look furious.

"I guess they figured out something was up," Bob said.

"Yes. Something was up," Ida agreed.

Grady reached over and took Ida's hands in his. He still looked proud.

"Then they all ran out and got on their motorcycles." Ida was remembering well.

"Ida, what did you do then?" I asked.

"Oh, I got on the back."

"Of a motorcycle?" My mouth dropped.

"No. It's called a hog." Ida frowned. "We drove all over town looking for you guys, then we came onto the estate. Those guys were worried about you all for some reason. I just hung on to that guy driving the hog.

"When we came past the sports complex, we saw a cop car. It nearly ran us over. That really made the guys mad, because Sandy was driving. She pointed her finger at them, and I think it must have been some kind of a gang sign because they were cursing, and, well, anyway. They told me I'd better get off."

"And that's when you realized we must be stuck in the lounge." Grady thrust his thumbs up in the air.

"No, no, I remembered I'd left some potholders in the lounge, and I wanted to get them for the girl, you know, to go with the recipes. Then, there you were. How did we get out here?" Ida looked around.

I flopped down in the mud and laughed. I made mud angels and roared. Ted ran his hands through his hair.

"Saved by the potholders," Bob said. He flipped his tooth-pick into the air.

The police officers got to their feet and had a brief counsel-ing session. Then they turned to us and explained that we would have to get to a phone. Their squad car was gone, their guns and radios were gone, and it was time for all of us to take a walk.

"Ida," I said gently, "where did you leave the Suburban?"

"Hmm?" Ida smiled at me.

"Where's the Suburban, Ida?" Ted knew what I was thinking.

"It's somewhere close to the Sunken Balls." Ida squinted her eyes, trying to recall where she's left it.

"Ida, did you close the back?" I held my breath.

"Oh, yes. I closed it up and locked it tight."

I let my breath out. "Good. And Otis, and Eldon?"

"Who?" Ida asked.

"Otis, and Eldon. Where they still in the back of the Subur-ban?"

"No, no, I don't remember, were they supposed to be?" Ida looked at Grady. He slumped.

"Great," Fanny said. "Now we have no proof."

"But you guys can verify everything, right?" I looked at the cops.

"Verify what? We need bodies," one of the cops said. I got the feeling they were well past their shift change.

"Come on, you guys!" I was sputtering.

"We need bodies," the other one said firmly.

I waved my hand toward the sports complex. "This isn't enough proof?"

"Proof of what?" The policeman shrugged.

"For the love of…" Fanny said. She got up, walked over to the policemen and smacked their heads together roughly. "You want bodies? We'll get you bodies. Let's go everyone, this night ain't over yet."

Fanny shuffled off through the mud. She was a little figure in the yellow lights of the parking lot. The cops rubbed the sides of their heads and followed. The rest of us trailed behind, wondering what we would do next.

THIRTY

AND NOW YOU KNOW why I said I should have listened to my husband when he said it probably wasn't a good idea for me to get involved in another murder. Even as we walked through the mud and out of the field, we weren't yet out of the proverbial woods. Sandy and Peter had probably found Otis and Eldon deposited beside the road, had more than likely absconded with the bodies, and were most definitely disposing of them as we trudged down the street, looking like a group of weary migrant workers. They might have even placed Eldon back in the grave to make it look official.

We were back to square one.

But wait.

All of their efforts would be for nothing if they couldn't get any of the insurance money from Grace. They thought we'd all been killed off by the B&E, so no reason for them to suspect we were in the clear. Sandy never considered Ida a real threat, and that would mean they'd be off their guard. We had to get to Grace's condo, and without a minute to spare.

I had an idea. "Grade, how far would you say it is to the stables?"

"It's about a half mile, I guess."

"Mr. and Mrs. Ramirez, you take the police back to your store," I said hurriedly. "And call for reinforcements. Get someone over to Grace Culpepper's house, and hurry!" I peeled off, and pointed everyone else toward the jogging trail. "We can make much better time if we go off-road. Are you with me?"

Everyone nodded enthusiastically. This is what it must feel

like to be the head of a highly disciplined commando unit, I thought. No hesitation, no wavering. We were all in this together, and we had to go right some wrongs.

The police were more than happy to comply. They raced toward the pink pig.

"We can make better time on horseback," Bob said. He jogged along, his belly bouncing.

"I'll saddle 'em up." Ted had his head down. He looked really determined although to my knowledge he'd never saddled a horse in his life.

"I don't know," Ida said. She was trying to keep up with Grady, who had increased his pace to a slow canter. "I didn't bring any Depends, and you know, with the chafing and all."

"Don't worry, honey, we still have a tub of aloe at home," Grady said.

Fanny moved in quick time. Her legs were a blur, her arms pumped like pistons. "Forget the saddles," she said. "No time for that. We'll have to do this bareback."

Ida whimpered.

"Wait." I put my hand up. "Listen."

We all stopped. Ida cupped her hands behind her ears.

"Hogs," she whispered.

It sounded like a bunch of buzzing flies at first, then louder, like bumblebees, then a whole chorus of growling, stinking, fuming Harleys broke through the brush. My cigar smoker was in the lead. The bikers shouted for us to get on.

Ida clapped her hands, and swung up and onto the back of the Harley like she'd been doing it all of her life. She waved for all of us to follow.

I looked at Ted, shrugged, and chose the spandex queen as my riding partner. Ted threw his leg over an imposing motorcycle, and settled in behind a man who looked like a ZZ Top wannabe. A guy I swear I recognized from one of those America's Most Wanted posters grabbed Grady and hauled him up.

Fanny took a running start and vaulted up behind a guy who was toothless and sported a long, gray ponytail.

"Sandy's with Peter!" Spandex screamed at me. "They stole

a police car and left it by the side of the road. Now we don't know where they are!"

"They killed Otis!" I cried.

"That's what we thought!" the girl shouted. "Ida told us some of it. We'll get 'em for ya, but we think they switched cars on us."

"Look for a moving truck! They've probably kidnapped Grace, and they're trying to get out of town!"

Spandex twisted her handlebars and did a wheelie.

I grabbed her waist and screamed.

"We almost had 'em on the golf course, but they gave us the slip," she said, shooting off toward the road. We broke out of the brush onto the well-lit pavement.

Ida must have told the bikers a lot more than she remembered. I didn't think Sandy's giving them the finger would have caused such a furor, or maybe Sandy and Peter had done much more than we knew to their pool hall buds. Then again, there was the matter of the scuffle at the Sunken Balls the last time we were there; maybe they just wanted to continue the feud. Who knew? It didn't really matter; we weren't going to have to take out a posse after all. Leave the cavalry to the professionals. For that, Ida would be eternally grateful. Aloe or no.

WE RODE IN PAIRS. In front of me I could see the backsides of Ted and Grady. Immediately to my right, Bob's expansive thighs pinioned his bike seat. The back tire looked dangerously low, but those were sturdy machines.

I craned around to see Ida, who peeked over the shoulder of her escort. She was smiling and smiling. The wind caught her lips, and they fluttered like paper.

Fanny was on the bike beside Ida's. She had taken a very unorthodox position on the motorcycle. Her arms were hooked under the pits of her chauffeur, and her little feet were hooked up on the seat behind her bottom. She rode like a jockey. Her perm had fallen out, despite the efforts of Joyce, and her sparse hair was thrashing around her head. Her glasses were down on her nose, and she kept trying to push them up by rubbing her face on the neck of her driver. He squirmed every time she did this, and kept swerving.

Behind Ida and Fanny, I could see at least a dozen Cyclops lights speeding behind us in close formation. It was all I could do to hang on to Spandex, but it only took a few minutes until I got the hang of things. When she leaned, I leaned. Once I accidentally leaned when she didn't, forcing an expert correction. After that, I paid attention.

We burst out through the Waning Years Estates gates and onto the highway. We picked up speed.

"There they are!" Spandex shouted and gestured wildly. I squinted into the wind. Taillights of a moving van headed in the direction of town.

"Go, go, go!" I beat on Spandex's leather jacket. She leaned over her handlebars and moved into the lead. I gaily wagged my fingers at Ted as we passed, and then hunkered down. We were gaining on them.

Not to be outdone, the guys revved their engines and followed in our wake. Fanny wasn't about to be left behind. When her hog came alongside of us, she was up on her feet in a half-crouch, holding on to the driver's ponytail like a rein. Slap a couple of boards on her feet and it would have looked like she was water-skiing down the road.

There wasn't much traffic on Main Street. We wasted no time closing the distance between the truck and us. When they stopped at a red light, we moved in for the kill.

I'M CLAIMING IT WAS all of the excitement, the poor visibility and the exhaust fumes that caused our tragic miscalculation. It wasn't a moving truck at all, but a family of four in a big van, just starting out a new life by the looks of the Utah license plates. Too bad we didn't notice sooner. By the time the Harley crew had the father face down in the intersection, it was too late. Those poor little kids. The expression on their faces wasn't something I'll soon forget. The wife experienced the least of the trauma; one look at the converging biker gang and she slumped to the floor of the truck in an unconscious swoon.

We apologized quickly, dusted off the agitated father and left the scene of the crime.

We combed the city streets, scouted every alley, went by Starbucks at least three times, and finally pulled up in front of the Sunken Balls to discuss our next plan of action.

"Sorry, May, we thought we had 'em." Cigar Face looked dejected. I patted his arm.

"Well, at least we've got the Suburban back," Grady said. He pointed to the burly truck parked halfway up on the sidewalk. There were three parking tickets stuck under the windshield wipers.

I licked the mud and bugs off of my lips and walked over on unsteady legs. The hogs were quiet, but it still felt like there were little ball bearings quivering around in my undies. I grabbed up the tickets and tossed them in the air.

"Look at this," I shouted. "There are dead bodies amok around Southern California and they're writing us traffic tickets!" I was angry with the police, and I was close to tears. All that work, and all that high drama and nothing to show for it.

"I guess we'd better find some gas and go see what happened to the Ramirezes," Grady said. "There's a can in the back."

"We'll give you a ride," Cigar said softly.

Fanny and Ted linked arms and came around to the side of the Suburban. The agony of defeat was written all over their faces.

Ida rubbed my back in a comforting way. "So sorry, May," she said. She reached in her pocket for the keys and handed them to Bob.

Bob walked around to the back of the Suburban and turned the latch. He opened the heavy doors and peered inside. "Well, I'll be damned!" he said.

"Oh crap," Grady said, shaking his head. "I forgot. I took out the gas can last week. I knew I should have put it back in." He snapped his fingers.

Fanny broke away and hustled over to Bob, mumbling. "Find something, you fool! Anything—a soda can or whatever. Whoooaahh!" she exclaimed.

"What is it, Fanny?" Ida shoved me aside. "Oh, there they are," she said, like she'd just found her missing wallet or the TV remote.

"Isn't that Otis?" Cigar Face had his hands on my shoulders and massaged distractedly.

"And Eldon," I confirmed. The massage felt really good, but it was short-lived. Ted moved in and put his arm around my waist. Cigar Face shoved his hands in his pants pockets.

Shucks.

"The cops said they needed bodies, and bodies is what they'll get," Fanny said. She had her hands on her hips. Her glasses reflected the streetlights and with the mud splatters and road muck, it was impossible to see her eyes, but I knew that tone of voice. She was taking charge.

"Saddle up, boys!" she hollered. "You there." She pointed to Ted's driver. He looked startled.

"Me?"

"Yeah, you. Find a hose and siphon some of your gas into the van. I've got a little business to take care of." With that, Fanny grabbed the doors and slammed them shut. She then took the keys from Grady and hustled to unlock the other Suburban doors. "May. You get in here. Ida, you get behind the wheel. Get ready to crank it as soon as there's enough gas to get us over to the police station."

The bikers were saluting and shouting, and tripping all over themselves to get gas caps off. Ted ran into the Sunken Balls to find some kind of hose. Anything would do, and I knew he'd be resourceful. I wasn't sure what "business" Fanny had to take care of, but I was on the job.

"Get back here," Fanny ordered. She already had her knees planted in the back seat and bent her torso over the top of the seat to be close to the bodies. There was a foul odor in the air, and I covered my mouth and nose. Oh, the stench!

"Wait," Fanny popped up. "You'd better use these." She dug

around in her pockets until she found some wads of tissues. "Ball 'em up and shove 'em up your nose and tell Ida to do the same."

I took the proffered tissues. Some had been used before, but that couldn't be helped. I tore off some for Ida. We rolled and shoved. I couldn't breathe out of my nose after that, so the smell was tolerable.

When I handed what was left to Fanny, she said, "I can't bother with the tissues; I need all my senses for this. Grab my ankles, will ya?"

I sat in the back seat and held Fanny's ankles. I didn't know what she was doing back there, so I just sat and waited. All I could see was her bottom and her skinny legs. Her feet kicked around some when she moved, so I had my work cut out for me.

"Hit the dome light. Can't see a thing back here." Fanny's voice was muffled. "And hand me my bag."

I reached up and flipped the light switch, then I lifted the other hand to search under the seat for her cloth bag. I almost lost Fanny, but got my hands back around her ankles before she tumbled over on top of the dead brothers.

My attention went out to Ted who emerged from the Sunken Balls with a thin line of plastic tubing. It looked like something that would belong in an aquarium, or maybe a soda decanter, but I wasn't sure. He shoved it in a Harley tank and sucked. It looked like we were in business.

My curiosity got the better of me, and I took a peek over the back of the seat. Fanny had little plastic baggies lined up across Otis's chest and she had a pair of tweezers in her hands. She was plucking things from his shirt, his head, and under his nails. She dropped these things carefully in the bags and closed them up.

"Evidence," she explained. "Don't want the cops to screw this up." She was very professional.

I took my position again and watched the boys work. They shouted to Ida to turn the key. She did, but the engine just sputtered. No good. The guys popped the hood. There were at least

ten heads under there shoving things around. I saw a wisp of
smoke swirl around my head. Maybe the engine was hot.

Wait. The smoke was inside the Suburban.

"Fanny!" I jumped up again and looked over the seat. "Why
are you smoking again?"

Fanny looked up at me, squinting. She had a cigarette hanging from the corner of her mouth.

"Hey," she said. Her cigarette bobbed. "You wanta get back
here and smell these rotting corpses? I'll be more than happy
to let ya!" She lifted her tweezers. Hanging between the tongs
was a flap of skin. I quickly shook my head. Let the lady
smoke.

Ida pumped the gas, and, finally, the Suburban roared to life.
Grady slammed the hood down. Unfortunately, one of the bikers hadn't pulled his head out in time. Grady apologized, yelled
for the all clear and slammed the hood again. It was a good slam.

Fanny continued to smoke and gather evidence. Ted and
Grady jumped into the front of the Suburban. The bikers
waited for us to get moving, and then provided an escort to
the police station.

It was quite a sight.

I had no idea where Sandy and Peter were. I didn't know if
they had abducted Grace, and I hadn't seen or heard from the
Ramirez couple or the two cops who had gone with them. But
I just didn't care. I was in no mood to worry about that at the
moment. We had the dead brothers, and we were getting ready
to blow this case wide open.

Let the cops laugh at us now.

THIRTY-ONE

THE LOOK ON the face of the desk sergeant was something I'll treasure for the rest of my life. When six senior citizens and sixteen bikers walked into the police station carting two dead bodies on a soiled brown tarp, the sergeant behind the desk moved much faster than he had last time we had been here.

Four of the bikers dumped Otis and Eldon on the officer's desk.

The sergeant shouted for backup.

The police station was small and grew smaller when every uniformed officer crowded into the room. Even the dispatcher left her post, but after one look at the discolored brothers, she threw up and had to be removed.

Patrol officers raced to the precinct. A couple of ladies near the front desk wore handcuffs, too much makeup and short skirts. They compared notes, apparently searching their memory to see if they had ever done business with either brother. One said something about being stiffed for a fifty. That must have been Otis. Or maybe she was saying the stiff looked fifty. That still could have been Otis. Even in his condition, with the holes in his head and his skin sloughing off, he looked pretty young for his age.

The coroner was called, the brothers were removed from the top of the sergeant's desk, and, after a while, the commotion settled down to a dull pandemonium.

The gang was brought to the back where we were asked to give statements. Fanny handed over a manila envelope full of her evidence. It was set aside to be logged in at a later time. Officer Crouch held pen and paper. He looked uncomfortable and embarrassed, as he should have.

"Before I begin," Crouch said quietly, "we're missing two of our officers and a squad car. They haven't answered their radio all night. Would you happen to know anything about this?" He fidgeted and his eyes darted about. I could tell it pained him to admit they had lost two good cops. I was tempted to tell him we had no idea, but then his discomfort was just too hard to watch, so I quickly explained where they had gone.

"They should have called by now," I said.

"Something went wrong," Ted said somberly.

"Do ya think so?" Fanny pointed her little chin at Ted, then removed her glasses and rubbed them on her sleeve. "Anybody got a cigarette?"

"Fanny, please. Not now."

"Okay then, how about an Elavil?"

Three hands reached for their pockets.

"Fanny, we need your whole brain on this. I'm worried. What if Sandy and Peter found them all walking along the road?"

"I shudder to think," Ida said. She put her hands over her mouth. She had been so quiet I didn't notice until then that she still had two nostrils full of tissue. Grady gently reached around and tugged them out. He palmed them. Good husband.

"Those two aren't ones to keep hostages," Bob said. He had found the doughnuts. His lower lip was dotted with sprinkles. "I'm guessing we're too late to help them." Bob looked into the white Danish box and flipped through the assortment like he was going through a Rolodex.

Ida's eyes pooled, and then spilled over. Grady helped her reinsert her tissues to staunch the nose flow that followed. "Those poor dears," she said, but with her nose plugged it sounded like, "dose pode ears."

The police officer jumped up. "I'll get your statements later. Right now we have to save two of our own!" Then he yelled, "Put out an APB on the squad car!" He grabbed his hat and keys and headed for the door.

He didn't get far. For one thing, the bikers were still congregated in the front of the precinct, chatting it up with a few of their buddies who were chained to the well-worn wooden bench, getting acquainted with the mini-skirted ladies, passing around a coffeepot and cups, and generally having a pleasant time. It was a labyrinth of leather jackets and holey blue jeans. The police officer was having one heck of a time getting around them.

For another thing, we weren't about to let him go it on his own, and the gang pressed in behind him, chattering about strategies, theories and lines of attack.

"Everybody out!" the cop roared.

Cigar Face over-poured his coffee. His face grew red, an unmistakable sign that something was about to happen. That would delay our mission, so I hurried over, pulled the zipper up and down seductively on his jacket and said gently, "Just go."

Ted looked at me with an expression of shock and maybe even a little bit of jealousy. I brushed past him in a huff. "That's for giving Sandy your phone number."

"Here." Bob tossed over his douhgnut box.

"Thanks," Cigar Face said, tucking the box under his arm. "Come on, ya'll. Let's ride."

The bikers were allowed to take the mini skirt girls with them. The guys on the bench were hauled off to lock-up, and then...a brief moment of calm. It was at that time that something amazing happened.

THE DOOR TO the precinct opened very slowly. A beautiful woman walked through, the epitome of grace and sophistication. She wore a long tweed jacket, an expensive scarf, and delicate pumps. She released the knot at her throat and the scarf slipped off of her long, blonde hair and came to rest on her delicate shoulders. Then she let the coat fall.

Ida sneezed sending tissue wads a good six feet. Then she found her voice. "Sandy?"

You could have blown me over with an atomizer. My jaw dropped like my face joints had just come unhinged.

I couldn't blame Bob, Ted and Grady. Sandy was, after all,

beautiful, and…she was stark naked. The guys just stood there salivating and stuttering.

Fanny was the first to break the spell.

"There she is! Arrest her! That's the one you want, what are you waiting for?" Crouch looked as if he'd zapped himself with his taser. The desk sergeant leaned too far over the front of his desk and tumbled onto the floor.

Fanny took matters into her own hands. She reached over and attempted to unlatch Crouch's holster. If the cop didn't make the arrest, she was certainly going to try.

The policeman batted away Fanny's hands.

Fanny slapped back. They started playing a slap game before Sandy spoke up and ordered them to knock it off. She had found her syrupy Southern accent again.

"Officer, I can see you have the perpetrators of a most heinous crime in custody. I was just about to give you a full account of what they've put me through this evening. I don't suppose they still have my clothes? No. Well, I commend you on apprehending them without my assistance."

This woman was incredible. She bent down and retrieved her coat, then slipped it on. She certainly knew how to capture her audience.

Fanny stared at Sandy. She was so angry I was afraid her glasses would melt. "What are you talking about, woman?"

Sandy lifted the corner of her scarf and dabbed at the droplets on her face. Even the rain hadn't smeared her carefully applied makeup. "I really thought you were my friend, Fanny. I thought we had something in common."

"Don't listen to her," Fanny said. She was boiling.

"Don't listen, officer," we all chorused. I could see, though, that the officer was off-balance. Who wouldn't be? Here we were, just a bunch of insane, geriatric, confused, filthy old folks teetering on the edge of Alzheimer's, and there was Sandy, a desirable younger woman wearing nothing more than her coat and a pitiable look on her face.

"Fanny, I'm so sorry, but all of those Forensic File tapes won't help you now."

How could this woman be so cold and callous? She knew how important Fanny's crime shows were; she knew how overjoyed Fanny had been to share a pajama party with someone who could really find the value of a good detective story. She'd even loaned her shortie babydolls to Fanny. She was evil, this one.

"Why don't we all go back into my office?" Crouch found his voice. "You give me your side of the story, and we'll sort all of this out." The cop was being very congenial and comforting to the teary-eyed vamp. He acted dazed, his comrades in distress apparently forgotten for the moment. I'm certain this is what Sandy had planned all along.

"Bubble butt," Fanny said, just loudly enough for Sandy to hear.

Sandy ignored her.

"Who paid for the collagen injections? Otis?" Fanny jabbed.

"Officer, don't you see what she's doing?" I was nearly frantic. "She's stalling! Peter's out there somewhere with your missing officers, and he's got the Ramirez couple, too!"

"Poor dear," Sandy said. "She's quite confused, sir. Don't be too hard on her though; she's had a traumatic evening. Digging up bodies, hanging out with bikers They're all probably off their medication."

"Fat face," Fanny said.

"I'm sure they can't be blamed, really. A good attorney will see that they get good representation, probably get them some easy time with an insanity defense."

"Thunder thighs," Fanny said.

Sandy rolled her eyes. "These? I think not." She flashed open her coat quickly, just for good measure.

Crouch was helpless. Sandy was using some pretty powerful ammunition.

"You might as well give up," Sandy said, addressing all of us. "Confess. Make it easy on yourselves."

"What is she talking about?" Ida looked at Grady.

"Where's Peter?" I asked. My concern for Grace and the Ramirez couple was growing by the minute.

"Peter? I don't know anyone named Peter, dear."

I suddenly knew why Sandy had made her appearance at the police station. She was trying to turn this case around on us again, and that could only mean one thing. She'd learned of our escape, and Peter had the cops and the Ramirez couple. That also meant they were in serious danger. They wouldn't have had to press Grace for cash just yet, so I wasn't worried about her. Sandy knew she had to get us out of the way first.

The desk sergeant was thoroughly confused. He kept flipping through his notes trying to find something—some sort of jurisprudence or standard operating procedure or recipe, or whatever was needed at a time like this.

"As you can tell, this is a pretty inventive bunch. I had a long talk with Fanny over there when she was a guest in my home. She said they had all been talking about committing the perfect murder. It was some kind of game or something. I didn't take her seriously, of course, we both like a bit of the melodrama. I had no way of knowing they were really *serious* about it all."

"You really are a piece of cake," Ida said.

"Liar!" Fanny shouted. Then she turned to Crouch. "Look at the evidence!"

"She's lying!" Grady said. Crouch held up his hand and asked Sandy to continue. Grady sat down hard on the bench, and ran his hands through his hair.

"It's true that an unfortunate accident happened at Otis and Grace's house. Eldon, Otis's brother, accidentally died in the bathtub. I just got off the phone with Grace who told me the whole thing. I'd called to warn her about these crazy old fools, because I knew she was next on their hit list."

"What reason would we have to shoot Otis?" I challenged the officer to come up with a good reason, but he didn't have to.

Sandy provided the motive.

"This bunch of crazies thought they had their perfect murder. Shoot Otis, bury him with Eldon, and they could chalk it up in their little black book. What could poor Grace say then?

That she'd made a terrible mistake and buried the wrong brother?" Sandy started talking more quickly. "But I was onto them. Otis was my friend, you see. He was a good man. I couldn't go to his funeral, because I had this awful cold. I felt really bad about missing his funeral."

"Maybe if you wore some clothes on your fat butt you wouldn't catch cold, liar," Fanny said.

Sandy waved Fanny away. "So I went out there tonight. You know, to put some flowers on his grave, to pay my last respects. That's when I saw those weirdos digging up the grave with a backhoe. You go check for yourself. Fanny's fingerprints will be all over the gears. I hid behind a tree and just watched. It was horrible. They had Otis, and they just dumped him in the grave, right on top of his brother. Check the wheelbarrow, too. More prints."

Sandy continued. "I just couldn't stand by any longer. I came out from behind the tree and shouted at them, I told them what I knew, and I told them I was going to the police. That was when they started running after me."

"Liar!" Fanny shouted. She slid her eyes over to the cop's gun again.

Ida started wheezing heavily. Then she plopped down beside her husband. Grady found a crumpled magazine and fanned his wife.

Sandy pressed on. "I just ran and ran. When I looked back, they had taken Otis out of the grave, and they had Eldon, too. They put them in a wheelbarrow. I think I spooked them. Check the wheelbarrow. You'll find fingerprints."

I couldn't believe this woman! But, tragically, everything she said would check out. There was no getting around the fact that we'd left fingerprints everywhere, not to mention we'd deposited two dead brothers on the desk. How could we have been so careless? But how could we have anticipated this turn of events?

"I doubled back," Sandy went on. "I hid in the bushes by the road. I was so terrified! They looked for me for a long time, and they acted really worried. They knew I'd be able to tell ya'll what happened, so they hauled out the brothers, put Otis and

Eldon in the back of their van, or whatever it is. I thought I was in the clear, but just then they saw me. I was so tired, but I tried to run again. Unfortunately, I wasn't fast enough."

"They knew they had to get rid of me, so they tied me up. Then they took me over to the Waning Years lounge. They stripped off my clothes, just to humiliate me, locked me in and then set a device to blast out the underground pool. I escaped just in time, though. If you get someone over to the estate, you'll be able to confirm my story. The sports complex was demolished."

It was looking more and more like we wouldn't be able to talk our way out of this. Everything Sandy said could be verified. Then the next thing she said clenched our fate.

"I grabbed some towels on my way out of the sports complex—to use as clothes—and walked back to the cemetery. I knew your boys patrol that area, and I wanted to flag someone down to help me. Some cars drove by, but they didn't stop. When I got to the cemetery fence, I found this."

Sandy reached into her coat pocket and produced a paper bag. I could smell them. Tamales.

"It was left by the side of the road." Sandy walked over and upended the bag on the front desk. A leaky foil package of tamales fell out, followed by some soggy postcards and the heavy clunk of a gun. "Check it for prints. You'll find hers." She pointed at me. "And his." She pointed at Ted. "It's the murder weapon."

The desk sergeant put a pencil through the trigger thingy and lifted it up. He smelled the barrel and reeled back. Those tamales were strong.

"Put that into evidence," our officer said.

"I got a ride back to my house with some policemen. I didn't even take the time to get dressed. I just grabbed my coat and drove over here."

"She's lying, don't you see? Aren't you just a little bit concerned that your missing policemen haven't called in? Where are they?"

"I guess you're talking about officers Haws and Connor?" Sandy asked.

Crouch nodded.

"They went to check on the damage over at the Estates. I don't know why they wouldn't have called by now. You've got yourself some good men there."

Another fact we couldn't dispute, at least about where the cops had gone, and if there had been some trace evidence left in the squad car, it would be explained away—not in our favor.

We were looking more and more culpable by the second.

"We haven't been able to reach them all night. I'll admit we were a little concerned," Crouch said.

"That's certainly understandable, but I assure you they're safe and sound."

A creeping sensation was making its way up my back. Ted liked to call it my radar, or maybe it was intuition, or just a good bogus meter. It was all starting to make sense. How this woman managed to concoct such a story in such a short amount of time shouldn't have surprised me, she was quite practiced at it, but it looked like the cops were buying it hook, line and sinker.

Suddenly, I knew where the Ramirez couple could be found, I knew how their demise would be explained, along with the unfortunate deaths of the police officers, gone to investigate a disturbance at the sports complex.

"Peter's got them at the sports complex! Oh my god, he's going to kill them and blame it on the B&E!"

I thrust my hands at the officer. "Lock us up if you have to. Throw us in the pokey; give me some of those steel bracelets if it will make you feel better, but please send someone over to the Waning Years Sports Complex now! You just might have enough time to keep four innocent people from getting murdered!"

THIRTY-TWO

IT WAS A GOOD THING Fanny had at one time been married to an L.A. detective. She knew the law, and she told the desk sergeant as much. They couldn't hold us because of an accusation; they needed proof. If they weren't going to read us our Miranda's, they would have to let us go.

But, by the same token, they couldn't hold Sandy either.

The police officer was in no hurry. He told the dispatcher to continue attempts at trying to raise Haws and Connor. He must have thought he had all of the important players in his office, and his officers were simply away from their car, wandering around the sports complex.

But he didn't know what Peter could do, and he didn't know what had really happened.

We all screamed at him to get help out to the Estate sports complex. He threatened to lock us up for disturbing the peace and, because he looked serious, we settled down.

"Wait a gosh darn minute," Fanny shouted. She grabbed the officer by the sleeve. He thought she was going for his gun again and the slapfest started anew.

"Good grief. I told ya to check the evidence! You'll find all the proof you need to show we didn't kill Otis. Just check it, and hurry up!" Fanny said.

The officer called for the evidence envelope. The dispatcher raced to the back and retrieved it.

"Hurry up, please hurry," I said.

"Yes, hurry," Ida wheezed.

The officer methodically pulled out one baggie after another. Fanny shook her head each time. "Keep going," she said.

Sandy was getting uneasy.

"That's it. Look in that one," Fanny said.

The officer gently pulled open the bag. Fanny handed him her tweezers. The officer plucked at something, brought it up, and held it in the light. It was small, but I knew exactly what he'd found.

"Now, check her nails. If you don't find a match, I'll eat my shorts," Bob said.

The officer looked at Sandy with narrowed eyes. He palmed the broken nail in his hand and walked over to Sandy.

"If you wouldn't mind, I'd like to take a look at your hands," he said.

Sandy smiled sweetly. She seemed relieved! When she held up her hands, I expected Bob to begin a strip tease. It was shorts eatin' time.

Sandy's nails were clear, unpolished, and clipped down to her fingertips. She held up her hands and presented them to all of us. We were doomed.

"Aaargh!" Fanny said.

I rubbed my forehead and leaned against the front desk. I looked over the evidence, knowing that all we had gathered would look worse for us than for Sandy. Then I noticed something odd.

"Officer, may I borrow those tweezers a minute?" My heart was pounding away. Fanny had been very thorough. She'd gathered evidence like a gangbuster, and she was good. But while she had counted on the fingernail to establish Sandy's complicity in the murder, she had missed an important detail.

I lifted a baggie with two bloody slugs resting in a fold at the bottom.

Everyone gathered around. The desk sergeant was back on his perch. He pushed his glasses up on his nose. Crouch looked over my shoulder.

Sandy opened and closed her coat, trying to draw attention back to her. She failed.

Carefully, I tweezed the bullets but they kept slipping out of my grasp.

"Here," Ida said, "dump them on these." She smoothed out some tissues. I looked at Crouch for permission and he nodded.

"Do these look the same to you?" I pointed at the bullets with the pointy end of the tweezers.

"Well, I'll be," the desk sergeant looked more carefully. "These couldn't have been fired from the same gun. We'll get a ballistics test, but you're right, ma'am, two different guns fired these bullets. You say they were taken from Mr. Culpepper?"

"Both from his face," Fanny said.

"You dug those out of his face?" Bob asked.

Sandy looked honestly confused. "What?" She rushed forward, but I was afraid she was going to try and hide this important bit of evidence and grabbed her by the coat tails.

"Not so fast, Missy," I said firmly.

"Well, this does put a kink in things. I'm not sure what it means, just yet, but we'll get this sorted out soon enough." Crouch was scratching his cheek.

I squeezed Ted's arm joyfully. This was getting good.

Sandy looked just as stymied as the rest of us. Her story was falling apart, and there was no way she could explain the two-gun bullet wounds. She had her coat on the floor again but this time it wasn't working. The police officer was closely examining the bullets again.

"Sandy, didn't you say Peter shot Otis?" I was feeling very confident. I had her running scared. "Did he use two different guns?"

"No! He only had the one…I mean, you, you killed Otis. You must have had two different guns, and you each took turns!"

Crouch stared at Sandy.

"Please put your coat on, ma'am," Crouch said, then he hollered for the dispatcher. She raced around to the front of the desk, took one look at the bloody bullets and threw up on the floor again. Crouch couldn't be bothered by that, so he ordered her to find out what was happening at the sports complex. She smiled weakly, nodded and went back to her radio. The desk sergeant ran for a mop.

What we heard come across in static blasts made Sandy pale, made the rest of us cry out in joy, and made the desk sergeant rub his eyes.

The missing officers had been found.

"THEY'VE GOT THE PERP, and they're bringing him in," the dispatcher hollered through a window. "He apparently tried to shove Haws and Connor into a demolished underground pool."

"What about Mr. and Mrs. Ramirez?"

"Wait," Bob said, "they're here."

We all raced toward the doors, but Crouch ordered us to stay put. Mr. and Mrs. Ramirez pushed into the station. They looked dirty and tired, but very much alive. Following them came Peter with his hands in cuffs, escorted by Haws and Connor. Another officer followed the first two.

"I found them all at the sports complex," he explained. "This guy was trying to throw them down into a demolished pool."

"He told us he had a gun," Haws explained.

"The fall would have killed us," Mr. Ramirez said.

"Lucky I got there in time," the third officer said, "and this is his gun." He held out a short branch. "He had it in his pocket."

"How could we know?" Connor looked embarrassed.

Peter's head was down. He wasn't talking.

"Peter, it's time to fess up for the record. You shot Otis didn't you?" I lifted my chin and narrowed my eyes. It's not too difficult to be tough in a police station.

Peter remained silent.

"Would it surprise you if I said Otis was already dead when you pulled the trigger?" I asked. "Remember when you said Otis didn't even flinch when you shot him? That he was just sitting quietly in Sandy's easy chair? Did you think it was funny that it was so easy?"

Peter lifted his head and glared at Sandy. "You shot him first?"

"No! He did it! He shot Otis!" Sandy pointed her finger at Peter. "He did it!"

"He shot Otis, remember? He said it!" She looked at me, still trying to carry the story, but I wasn't going for it.

"Or maybe, he just *thought* he did. Maybe that was your plan all along." I stepped up to get close to Sandy. "Make Peter think he'd killed Otis, and then push him into helping you rough up the wife for Otis's money. Am I close? Was Otis dead in that recliner when Peter took aim?"

I'd thought of something even Fanny hadn't considered.

"Did Peter close his eyes when he pulled the trigger? I'm guessing you kept Otis in the shadows to make it hard for Peter to see he was already dead. Right? I'm pretty sure you'll find another gun somewhere in Sandy's house if you get working on a search warrant."

I was on a roll. I looked at Sandy. No fear. "And once Peter was no longer of any use to you, you would set him up, send him off to jail, and have a great time spending Grace's insurance money after threatening to expose her, too. Am I right?"

"Is that true, Sandy?" Grace asked calmly.

We hadn't heard the door open behind us. Grace must have slipped in, unannounced.

"No, Grace! Remember when Otis disappeared and you came looking for him, and I told you how we could get his money? I was just kidding. It was just a joke. I had no way of knowing Peter would really shoot Otis. It was all his idea!" Sandy's upper lip was glistening with nervous sweat.

So Grace had known, poor thing.

"Otis was no good, that's true," Grace said. She was standing on her own now. "He had girlfriends all over town. He was racking up debts everywhere, and he made me sit on my legs for months. When his brother died in our bathtub, it was a good way to fake his death, but I never really wanted Otis dead. He was my husband." Grace glared at Sandy.

Peter glared at Sandy.

"Slut," Fanny said, pointing her chin in Sandy's direction.

The back of my neck was throbbing. My joints were aching, and I needed to sit.

"Now what are you waiting for?" Fanny pointed at the policeman's handcuffs. "Get 'em locked up for heaven's sake!"

"Don't worry, ma'am, we've still got some details to work through." I could see the fatigue on Crouch's face. All that paperwork.

Crouch lifted his handcuffs and sighed. He walked over to Sandy, ready to give her the shackle treatment, but he stopped when she threw her head back and laughed.

"I don't think so," she said.

The officer looked shocked and a little disappointed. I think he was really looking forward to conducting the frisk and body search.

"You don't have a signed confession, and, remember, there's all of that physical evidence I told you about. Who's gonna know what the truth is, really? I'm certain an attorney will be able to get a conviction for that one on the fingerprints alone." She pointed at me. "And let's not forget, they hauled the bodies over here. Fanny, you of all people know what trace evidence is. I'm sure they'll find all kinds of things to link you all to the murder of our dear Otis. And motive? Well, you're all a bit crazy, aren't you?"

Peter had perked up. He was obviously hoping Sandy could win this argument.

Sandy turned and looked at Grace who was seething. "As for you, so what if Otis was your husband? He was in love with me, remember? Why would I want to kill him? He was ready to leave you and sign me on as his beneficiary. I would have nothing to gain by killing him. The old fart was at least twenty years older than me. I would just have to bide my time until he died on his own. Too bad you can't keep a man in your own bed—I'd call that motive enough."

That did it.

Grace was at least ten feet from Sandy, but I don't think her feet touched the floor once when she launched herself at the wicked blonde. She screamed like a banshee, and knocked Sandy backward onto the bench.

"Cat fight," Bob said, and crossed his arms over his belly.

Grady, who was sitting on the bench with Ida, pulled his wife clear but not before Ida slapped a forearm up and across Sandy's descending mug. A dental bridge with two front teeth plopped out onto the floor. Sandy hollered in rage. Grace grappled and hauled her back by the hair of her head. The beautiful blonde locks came away, revealing a head full of white fuzz. Sandy twisted around and tried to claw at Grace, but her nubby fingers were useless. A long set of false eyelashes fell onto Sandy's cheek, looking like a big spider.

Very unbecoming.

Grace found Grady's discarded magazine and started banging away. The two women fought their way onto the floor. Sandy's coat fell away, and the naked woman lay on her back, completely caught up in the scuffle. Grace flipped Sandy onto her stomach and pinned her arms behind her.

We could have helped, but it was just more fun to watch.

Then I remembered something Fanny had taught me earlier in my other life. I went down on my knees, crawled over to the bench, yanked a phone cord out of the wall and had Sandy hog-tied, wrists to ankles, before too much damage was done. Sandy was spitting through the gap in her teeth.

Fanny, Ida and I gave each other high fives, and nodded approval at Grace. The policemen applauded.

THIRTY-THREE

THE WORD OF the event got around town fast. Within minutes, the precinct was once again full of our biker friends, passing around cups and making coffee, while we all provided details for the police.

The officer got a pile of papers from the desk sergeant and started handing them around. He told us we needed to fill in the blanks and eventually we would get it all sorted out.

"Here, officer, let me help you with that." Fanny gently took the papers. She was being way too generous. She took the pile of forms and tossed them into the air. "You sort it out. We haven't eaten all night, and I'm starved."

Bob agreed. He twirled his finger around his head. "Everyone to the Black Angus! Ted's buying!"

Before we left, I reached into my wallet. I found a business card and left it on the front desk with instructions to leave it for Sandy. "She'll be needing this," I said.

On the card it said *Janet Scott, Attorney at Law.*

IT WAS NEAR CLOSING TIME when we got to the restaurant. We asked the waitresses to push several tables together so we could all be close. I counted sixteen bikers, the Ramirez couple, Grady, Ida, Fanny, Bob, Ted and, of course, me. Ted bought five bottles of champagne, but the bikers said they were Baptists and didn't imbibe. Mr. and Mrs. Ramirez, though, made short work of three bottles even before we gave our menu orders. They ended up giggling under the table, so we left them alone.

"Sandy wasn't looking too good when we left," Bob said.

He looked sad. It couldn't have been fun to have a fantasy stolen away like that.

"I told you she wasn't your type," Fanny said. "A few more smacks with the magazine and Grace would have shown you what those perky pods were really made of. They'd have popped like two water balloons."

"Fanny," I scolded, but the vision was pretty fun to entertain.

"So, who killed Otis?" Cigar Face asked. He passed bread around.

"Otis did." Crouch walked up to our table, and Ted offered him a chair.

"I just came from the morgue. While I was watching the sawbones work over Otis, a couple other officers searched Sandy's home, and here's what happened."

For the first time this evening, quiet ascended over the crew.

"I guess Otis was worried enough about the goons that he bought himself a handgun and kept it at Sandy's house. It was registered and legal, but we checked records. He'd never owned one before. By the looks of things, he was pretty unskilled. He didn't know how to use it. The lab analysis showed powder burns on his face…"

"A close contact gunshot," Fanny explained.

"And there was gunpowder residue on his hands."

"He fired the gun?" Fanny exploded in laughter.

"Yup, he fired the shot into his own forehead, probably checking out his gun. He was dead when the second shot was fired. We know this because…"

"There was no bleeding from the second wound," I said, not giving Fanny a chance to explain—I'd seen some of those detective shows, too.

"Sooo," Bob said, "Otis shot Otis?"

"Suicide," Ted said.

"It looks like it, although it's probably pretty certain that he did it accidentally. But, the coroner ruled it suicide, and that means nobody will get his life insurance money. All that's void in the case of suicide."

"Where did you find his gun?" I said.

"It had fallen under some drapes."

"I don't remember seeing an easy chair by the drapes," I said.

"Sandy told us where to find that. She and Peter hauled it over to the city landfill. We have forensics going over that right now."

"Good job, Officer Crouch," Ted said. "We knew you'd get to the bottom of things."

"Something I've been meaning to ask you, why did you go out to the cemetery in the first place?"

I explained, feeling smart again. "We were going to get Eldon's fingerprints, to prove to you he wasn't Otis." I smiled all around and got approving smiles back from everyone around the table.

Crouch furrowed his brow. "It's standard procedure to get fingerprints on a stiff. They should have been on the autopsy report."

"Nope, wrong officer." I put the smug look on my face. "Check for yourself. Ted?" I motioned for my husband to hand over my purse.

Ted looked a little bit funny when I pulled out the report. I passed it to him and he unfolded it carefully and spread it out over the tablecloth.

"See?" Crouch pointed. "It's right…" Then he stopped at the singed portion of the report. "Well, it should be right here. Looks like it got burned off."

Ted blushed crimson. "Sorry, guys," he said.

"Ted, did you know?" I looked at my husband, who stared off at the wall.

The officer chuckled and put his hand on Ted's shoulder. "Doesn't matter now, does it? By the way. I promise next time to take you more seriously. Just do one thing for me, okay?"

"What's that?" we all asked.

"Next time, leave the bodies. Our dispatcher has lost five pounds already. I don't think she can handle much more."

Mrs. Ramirez popped her head up from under the tablecloth. She smiled drunkenly between Ted's legs. "I can handle one more, I promish."

Her husband must have hauled her under then, because she slid away backward and disappeared. We all laughed, and Ted ordered two more bottles of champagne.

THIRTY-FOUR

EVERYTHING IS BACK to normal. The gang was given a reward from Crime Helpers, and we all agreed it should go toward rebuilding the sports complex. Ted and I are home again, and Trixie is planning ways to get back at me for leaving her at the Poochie Hooch.

Sandy and Peter are facing jail time; Grace will be doing some community service and was ordered to repay the money she obtained by defrauding the disability folks.

Otis found his way back into his grave, and Eldon is resting in peace in Portland, Oregon.

The dispatcher has left the precinct to work as an au pair.

Crouch is attending more autopsies and doing research on crop circles.

Haws and Connor are on leave.

Ted is encouraging me to take my writing more seriously.

I think I'll start a new book today.

But what in the world do I have to write about?